AVOIDING THE SACK

SUNNY HART

❀ Created with Vellum

To all the young athletes who were pushed too hard too early and suffered the abuse that came with that. I hope this story can help provide you as much peace as it gave me by writing it.

Also to the guy whose name I can't even remember now but definitely started with a J. Thanks for one of the weirdest worst first dates I've ever been on. I immortalized it in this book.

AUTHOR'S NOTE

This book was previously published under Maddi Hart. In late 2023, it was republished under Sunny Hart.

I have done my level best to make the sport of football seem realistic in this book. That being said, I'm not a sports person, so please forgive any errors or impracticalities you find when I describe the game. Go sports!

If you find an error in this book, please reach out to me directly via my Facebook page or email me at sunnyhartauthor@gmail.com. I do have an excellent team of beta readers and editors, but mistakes do slip through! I appreciate you letting me know directly!

Trigger warnings: mentions and flashbacks to sexual assault, mentions of attempted suicide (not described in detail). If you have any questions about the triggers, please reach out to me at sunnyhartauthor@gmail.com and I'll be happy to answer any questions!

DESCRIPTION

Meet Lexi, a talented quarterback who has faced many challenges both on and off the field. Despite her success, she can't shake the memories of a traumatic event that occurred years ago, leaving her wary of getting too close to anyone.

But when her best friends and teammates suggest a friends-with-benefits arrangement for their senior year, Lexi starts to see her guys in a new light. As they work together to lead their team to victory, the lines between friendship and something more start to blur. However, with her past still haunting her, Lexi is hesitant to take things further.

Can her guys break through the walls she's built around her heart and convince her that they're worth the risk? Find out in *Avoiding the Sack*, a heartwarming and exhilarating story about the power of friendship, the thrill of competition, and the courage it takes to open yourself up to love. Fans of sports romance and friends-to-lovers tropes won't be able to put this book down!

This is a MMMMMF why-choose HEA, where the female main character won't have to choose between any of the guys and it will end in a happily ever after!

Trigger Warnings: mentions and flashbacks to sexual assault, mentions of attempted suicide (not described in detail).

LEXI

I stared up at the ceiling, mentally counting the number of assignments I still needed to complete this week.

"Do you like that?" A voice I was quickly finding annoying had me looking down.

Some frat guy I had picked up was rubbing my left fold vigorously like he was whisking an egg. Except incorrectly with his fingers and not his wrists. If he was as awful with cooking as he was with foreplay, I should probably make a campus warning sign for him.

God, was it so hard to find someone who knew where the clitoris was these days? I mean, it was 2023. Hadn't we educated all the men by now? Although the second I thought that, I heard the voice of my best friend Inez in my head, "Men ain't shit."

Realizing the frat guy was still waiting for a response, I sat up. He stopped. *Finally.*

"Actually, Chad," I said, getting off the bed and finding my pants discarded on the floor. He hadn't even taken my shirt off before going straight in on rubbing like it was his job. "I'm just not feeling you."

"Well, I could put on some mood music or something. I know it's a bit loud in the house."

I buttoned my jeans and grabbed my jacket. "No, it's not that. I'm just not feeling *you*. Have a good one."

I breezed past him.

"My name's not Chad," he yelled down the stairs after me.

I laughed. I figured it wasn't, but I could not for the life of me remember it. *Besides*, I thought as I exited the frat house and walked down Greek row, *it seemed like Chad was the name of every third guy who lived here.*

I cut through campus, hands in my pockets, thankful I had remembered to grab my jacket before I left that disappointing dick appointment. The last thing I needed was Chad, or whatever his name was, bragging that he fucked the football team's quarterback.

Yep, you read that right.

Standing at 5'10", with long, wavy brown hair, and packed with lean muscles, no one would ever mistake me for a cheerleader, but they were often surprised when I showed up on the field instead. No hate to the cheerleaders at all; I had seen the skills required to do some of their tricks. And my best friend, the head cheerleader, Inez, would kill me if she heard me or anyone badmouthing her girls.

I was going into my senior year at Grandview University. It was a small Division 2 school in the mountains. I had been starting quarterback for two years now, and even though I had no intentions of pursuing it after school, I loved the game.

"Hey, Cap!"

A few people greeted me as I cut across the dining center's courtyard. I waved hello but didn't stop to chat. "Cap" was my nickname around campus, although Inez was trying her hardest to get "Ball Crusher" to catch on instead. Grandview University was small, with a student body population of just under two thousand, which meant everyone knew everyone or of everyone.

Leaving the bustle of the dining center behind, I left the campus grounds and started down a residential street. Mostly upperclassmen lived on this street, renting out the big historic houses. We threw some parties, but not often, which added to the mystique and intrigue surrounding us.

Our house was at the end of the street. The guys had bitched about having to walk the extra distance, but I didn't mind it. Yep, you read that right too. I lived with five guys. They were both the biggest pains in my ass and my best friends.

I had grown up playing football with Jamison Towers and Lewis Baker all through middle school and high school. Jamison was my wide receiver, while Lewis was on the offense line and made sure I didn't get sacked. Well, most of the time...

When Grandview University offered scholarships to the three of us, we jumped on the chance. We had met Asher and Noah Reynolds, the twins, at team training camp the summer before our freshmen year. They played on the defense team, but the two of them clicked with our group like they had been a part of it for years.

I had bumped into Derek Anderson in some classes in freshman year, and the guys had quickly accepted him as one of their own. Derek was pre-med and a certified genius. He wanted to specialize in neurosurgery, so some of his classes overlapped with my psychology ones. He didn't play on the football team, but he was interning with the athletic trainer this year, so we got to spend more time with him.

I was grateful for that, as it was senior year, and after this year, we were all going our own separate ways. Not because we wanted to, but because life wasn't a fairytale. I'd learned that the hard way. No, we wouldn't get to pursue our separate careers and still live in the same city. I mean, the guys talked about trying to make it all work, of course, but I was firmly grounded in reality and determined to make this year full of memories to make up for it.

I pushed open the door to the old historic two-story brick home, rolling my eyes that they had left it unlocked again.

Asher poked his head down the hallway from the kitchen.

"What are you doing back so early? I thought you were getting laid?"

Asher had dark brown hair he kept cut close to his head, unlike his twin Noah, who let his hair grow out long enough to curl around his ears. Both twins had chocolate-brown eyes, stood at an impressive 6'5", and were packed with the muscles necessary to be defense linemen.

"I was until he spent like ten minutes rubbing the left side of my vagina, then asked if it felt good as his only form of foreplay."

I liked sex just as much as the next person. For me, it was a way to take my power back from my past; but good sex was a great stress reliever as well.

Strong arms and the scent of oranges wrapped around me from behind, picking me up so I rested on the top of his feet as he walked us both into the kitchen.

"Lewis, really?" I complained good-naturedly but let him do what he wanted.

Most guys I met were intimidated by my height, but my guys had never made me feel awkward about it. If anything, I often felt tiny next to them. All of them, including Derek, were at least 6'2".

"That sucks," Asher said. "Well, fuck him. Actually, I guess, don't."

I laughed as Lewis released me, and I took a seat at one of the barstools. "I didn't. But what does a girl gotta do to get some decent dick around here? Maybe Inez is right, and I need to actually start dating."

Inez was head-over-heels for her girlfriend of the last two

years, Meena, and now believed that sex was best when you were in love. For me, sex was best when my partner could at least find my clit.

The looks of horror I got from Asher and Lewis, both notorious playboys themselves, had me doubling over.

"You don't want anyone on campus," Derek said, dropping a kiss on my hair as he entered the room, clearly having overheard some of our conversation.

Derek was like the 'mom' of our group, always doing little things for me and the guys that showed he cared. We'd picked up our nerdy soon-to-be doctor during sophomore year. He had inky black hair, and his thick-framed glasses hid gray eyes that sparkled with intelligence.

"Yeah, I'd probably have to go older and maybe date someone off campus," I mused.

Older could mean more mature and maybe someone who actually knew how to get a woman off.

A muscle in Lewis's jaw ticked, and I narrowed my eyes at him. "What?"

He always tried to be ridiculously overprotective of me, and it had led to some rousing fights in high school. At 6'6", and also packed with muscles, he stood like a small mountain between me and the rest of the world. He had finally started growing out his beard when we hit college, and now he looked like a lumberjack. Something I teased him all the time about.

"At least we know who they are if they're on campus. How are we supposed to vet someone from off campus? Besides, what's the rush?"

I rolled my eyes. Although I was perfectly capable of taking care of myself, living with the guys and having been friends with them for so long had them seeing me as a little sister.

"I'm trying to get laid this year," I complained. "Any longer and Inez is going to take my dry spell as me turning into a lesbian."

5

Derek took a sip of water just as I said this and choked. I pounded on his back. My sweet nerdy guy still wasn't used to my vulgarity, even after the last three years.

"Surely, there's a few guys on campus who can make that happen?" he sputtered.

"If there are, I either haven't found them yet or I live with them."

"And what's wrong with us?" Asher spread his arms out and looked offended.

"I live with you guys. You're practically my brothers. Besides, you know I don't sleep with anyone on the team."

Other sports teams were fair game, but I had a strict rule about not sleeping with anyone on the football team. Especially not as team captain. Most of the guys on the team were really cool with a female quarterback. We had a few who were less great about it, but my success on the field kept their grumbling to a minimum. There was no way I would risk what I'd built by sleeping with a teammate.

"Derek's not on the team," Lewis pointed out unhelpfully, raking a hand through his reddish-brown hair.

Derek blushed and avoided eye contact. I rolled my eyes again.

"See the first two points. I live with you guys, and you're practically my brothers. Besides, I would eat Derek alive," I teased playfully.

Derek met my eyes over his glass as he took another sip. "Maybe," he murmured, his gray eyes darkening briefly.

I would be lying if I said my guys weren't hot, and Derek was no different. With his lean body, tousled black hair, and steely gray eyes framed with thick black lashes, he was a nerdy Clark Kent look-alike. He had his own share of fangirls on campus, just like the rest of the guys did. And I'd heard the rumors from the cheerleaders about their skills in the bedroom more times than I'd care to count. But I wouldn't risk our friendships like that ever, and after years of living together, I was confident they didn't see me as anything other than a little sister. I wouldn't want anything to change and lose what we had. These boys had saved me more than they knew, both on the field and off it, as cheesy as that sounded. I wasn't risking that for a quick roll in the hay.

That night, I called Inez after I finished studying.

"What's up? How was the D?"

"Nonstarter." I groaned. "I'm actually switching the age range on my dating profile right now to older men."

"That bad, huh? Sure you don't want to come over to the dark side?"

"You would be the first person I would fuck if that were the case. Meena would have to share you."

"She knows you're my ride-or-die bitch. How did the guys take the older man thing?"

Inez was convinced that my guys had feelings for me and just didn't show it. I didn't see it. While Jamison and Asher were some of the worst manwhores, the other guys had healthy sex lives as well. None of them had long-term relationships, but that just wasn't their style. Although when pressed, they would joke that I was the only one for them, which only fueled Inez's fantasies.

"Like overprotective big brothers." I rolled my eyes.

"Mmmhmm..." Inez drew it out, and I laughed.

"You're not still on that train, are you? Girl, it's going nowhere. You know I don't sleep with guys on the team."

"I know the stupid rule you have, and I still stand by that it's a dumb rule. The hottest guys are on the football team."

"I don't know... Remember that lacrosse player last year who graduated?"

"Yeah, but you can't even remember his name."

"I remember it. Brandon. I remember the good ones. Too bad he graduated and moved home." If he hadn't, I would probably have reached out to him tonight instead of coming home. A girl has needs.

"I still stand by the fact that football players are the hottest. Even as a lesbian, I've heard stories about the men in your house."

A pang of a weird feeling went through me, but I wrote it off as awkwardness. They were practically my brothers, and thinking about their sex lives was just weird. Lord knows, I didn't think about Talen's sex life. My younger brother was still living at home.

"And still team captain, so that's not happening. Anyways, how was your day?"

As we chatted about our days, I started swiping on the dating app Inez and I had set up. After finding five solid yeses, I was feeling better about finding some decent dick this year.

LEWIS

I grunted as I slammed Collins to the ground. My bones jarred with the force of the tackle and Collins's head snapped back.

"All right, Lewis. Get off of me." He groaned good-naturedly. "Ya know, one of these days I'm going to sack her."

I huffed out a laugh as I helped him up. "Not if I can help it."

Finn Collins wasn't a bad guy; he was just doing his best on defense to tackle my girl. *Not my girl, my quarterback,* I mentally corrected myself. The slip was easy to make. Lexie and I had been playing together since middle school, and it was my job to protect her on the field. And off of it, apparently, with her new idea of dating off campus.

She had told us about it this morning as we all jogged to the athletic center for morning practice. She and Inez had come up with the bright idea that she needed to go off campus to find Lexi a decent "dick appointment," as they called them. I was less than thrilled with the idea. A guy on campus was someone we could reach if things went badly. Off campus was a whole different ball game.

"Stop brooding," Lexi chided as she jogged up next to me. "I wouldn't have told you if you were going to get all sulky about it."

"Since when do we keep secrets from each other, Pixie?"

Her eyes narrowed at the use of her nickname, as they always did, and I hid a grin.

"We don't, which is why I told you," Lexi said, not looking at me.

I frowned, having a feeling there was more she wasn't telling me.

"Simmons, Baker," Mac barked at us. "Huddle up!"

Lexi and I turned and jogged towards our head coach.

"I actually need Collins playable for the game this weekend, Baker," Mac said to me.

Our head coach was gruff but a good man under all that bark. He scared the shit out of all the underclassmen when we first started, but we quickly learned his bark was worse than his bite. And he was a brilliant tactician on the field. It was early in the playoff game schedule, but we had won our first-round game two weeks ago, and the team was feeling good about the second-round game this weekend.

I shrugged. "Shouldn't have tried to sack my quarterback then."

Mac rolled his eyes as a few guys on the team laughed. Lexi just shook her head at me, but I was unapologetic. I would always protect her both on and off the field.

"Let's run it again." Mac dismissed us all.

We were playing two small scrimmage games on the field, having divided the team in two. Jamison, Noah, and Asher were on the other team, so Lexi just had me to watch her back on this side. Today was the last practice we would scrimmage like this before the game. We would just run drills or train in the weight room for the rest of the week. Mac didn't want anyone accidentally injured in practice.

Lexi called a start to the play, ball close to her chest as she looked for Ryan, our running back and a general douche. Ryan ran in front of her, and Lexi threw a short, tight pass. Ryan made it only a few steps before Dante tackled him.

"What the hell, Ryan? You're supposed to cut left on that play!" Lexi shouted at him.

"I saw an opportunity, and I took it," Ryan jeered back at her as he got to his feet.

Most of the guys were cool with Lexi being a woman, but Ryan Crawford had been a pain in the ass since we started on the team together.

"An opportunity to get tackled by Dante?"

I cracked a smile. Lexi was always quick on her feet and with her wit.

"At least take me out first," Dante ribbed Ryan, who shoved at him.

"Break it up!" Mac shouted. "Again! And, Crawford, learn your rights from lefts before I bench you."

Even though Mac had been the one to correct him, Ryan sneered at Lexi as we got ready to run the play again. I kept a close eye on the little fucker. He was always causing problems.

Forty-five minutes later, Mac finally deemed us 'adequate' for this weekend. With that round of encouragement, I trailed Lexi towards the locker room.

"Well, that sucked." Noah came up next to us, whining. "We didn't get to play together at all."

"Dude, we don't usually get a chance, anyways." His twin, Asher, came up behind him. "We're on defense."

"But still," Noah whined.

Asher and I rolled our eyes. Noah was like a needy little puppy if you let him be, but Lexi always humored him.

"I'm sorry," she comforted him. "Maybe next scrimmage?"

Noah shook his head. "Not enough. What about breakfast?"

Lexi winced, and my internal radar went off. "I can't. I've got that date."

"Already?" Jamison caught up, throwing an arm around Lexi.

"Says one of the biggest manwhores on campus," Lexi shot back. "And get off me; you're all sweaty."

"I don't sweat, I glow," Jamison claimed, and I groaned. He'd been using that dumbass line since middle school.

"You could ditch him," Asher offered.

Outside of Lexi and Jamison, Asher and I had a special bond. We were both silent protectors and had delivered more than one beatdown together over the last few years.

"I can't ditch him. I told you; I'm trying to find decent dick this year."

"Don't understand why you can't find it on campus," I grumbled as we entered the locker room.

Lexi rolled her eyes at me but didn't respond as she split off for the women's locker room.

"Dude, you've got to lay off," Asher commented as we headed into the men's locker room.

"Don't tell me you agree with her going on dates with random guys."

Asher and Noah had approached Jamison, Derek, and me a few months into our friendship and had confessed feelings for Lexi. I understood. Jamison and I had been in love with her since high school but had never made any moves because neither of us was willing to back down and lose her. But nerdy Derek had shocked all of us when he brought up sharing her. I had almost pummeled his face, enraged that he had viewed Lexi as a toy to be passed around, before he had explained what polyamory was. His parents were polyamorous, with a steady third in their relationship, and he had some experience on the topic.

We had headed to Asher and Noah's dorm after some party while Lexi was off campus, where we got a little drunk and talked about it. The following conversation with all of them had to be one of the strangest I had ever experienced, but we ultimately decided not to pursue Lexi. If it happened naturally, it would happen naturally, but over the years, Lexi had never given any indication that she saw us as more than friends, so we hadn't broached the topic with her. But the feelings never went away.

Asher lifted his hands. "You know I don't. But if we push her too hard, she's just going to stop telling us stuff."

"Lexi tells me everything," I said, but even as I said it, I thought of that moment earlier in practice. Maybe I didn't know all of my Pixie's secrets like I thought.

LEXI

*D*espite my guys' concern, I was actually capable of
taking care of myself on a date.

"Jeremy, right?" I greeted a guy who looked like the profile
picture of the man I had been texting this morning. He was
definitely shorter than 6'2". I was 5'10" and could see the top of
his head, but I kept a smile on my face.

"Yes. Lexi, I'm assuming?"

I nodded as he extended a hand to shake. According to his
profile, Jeremy was 27 and was working at a local construction
and engineering company.

"Thanks for meeting me here." I gestured towards Chocolate
Chasings, the local hot chocolate and coffee shop that sat right
at the edge of campus. The location was convenient for my class
in a few hours and Meena, Inez's girlfriend, had the morning
shift and had agreed to watch out for me in case I needed an
out. *See, Lewis, I could take care of myself.*

I pushed thoughts of one of my overprotective best friends
out of my mind as Jeremy held the door open for me. Point in
his favor. Maybe that chivalry would carry over into the
bedroom. While I was really looking for a bed partner, I

wasn't completely relationship adverse. It was nice to be held by someone, but I came with baggage, and that baggage made me a little broken, so relationships didn't always work out for me.

"Do you come here often?" he asked, stepping up to the counter.

"A bit," I said evasively. Dating 101, as I had learned, was to be vague about where you hung out. I hadn't fallen victim to a stalker yet, and Inez swore it was from all of her true crime podcast tips.

"Hey, what can I get you?" Meena bounced up to the counter and smiled broadly at me. She didn't out us as knowing each other, but the twinkle in her eye was easy to read.

"I'll just get a coffee, black," Jeremy said. "And whatever she wants."

Meena and I stared at each other wide-eyed for a second before we schooled our expressions. Black coffee? At a place known for its hot chocolate?

"Any cream and sugar with that?" Meena asked, scrawling his order on a to-go cup instead of a mug.

She clearly didn't think we would be here long, and I was starting to doubt if I would be as well. What kind of person drank black coffee? The guys didn't drink it super sweet, but they at least put some milk and sugar in. Asher drank the sugary drinks like me, and Derek was a tea drinker.

"No, just black," he said. What kind of psychopath drank just black coffee?

Instead of commenting on his black coffee order, I instead focused on the other part of his earlier sentence. "I can actually get my own. Thanks, though."

"Are you sure? I can get it," Jeremy offered.

"No, I got it," I said firmly.

Meena rang him up quickly and then turned to me. "What can I get you?"

"Can I get a mocha with caramel, please?" I asked her for my regular order.

"Got it." Meena scribbled my order across the to-go cup and tapped on the register.

I tapped my student ID on the screen. Mac wanted to make sure the players ate enough, so we were all required to be on a meal plan on campus. Luckily, it was included in my scholarship and came with some campus bucks that the shop accepted as well.

Jeremy continued to stand awkwardly at the counter, and I scanned the shop.

"Let's grab that table." I pointed at a small corner table near the front of the shop.

Jeremy nodded and followed me over to the table. I dropped my bag on the floor next to the seat with its back to the wall and settled into the chair.

"Military?" Jeremy asked.

I raised my eyebrows. "I'm sorry, what?"

"I was just wondering if you were military," he said. "Sitting with your back to the wall; it's something they teach us."

"Oh, no." I laughed nervously. "Just aware of my surroundings." If I had been more aware as a teenager, maybe I wouldn't have been caught so off guard by ghosts of the past. "You were in the military, though?"

"I was."

I bit the inside of my bottom lip and waited for him to elaborate. When he didn't, I asked more questions. "How long were you in? Did you enjoy it?"

"Four years, and no, I didn't enjoy it."

"That's fair." I shrugged. "It's not for everyone, from what I hear."

"Yeah, wasn't my calling. My mom said she could have told me that, but I didn't listen. It paid for my education, though."

"Oh, yeah? What did you get your degree in?"

"Mechanical engineering."

"Oh, nice," I said, impressed. So, he was smart. That was good. "Is that what you do now?"

"Kind of. I don't know. I don't enjoy it either. I think corporate life isn't for me."

Was there anything this guy liked? So far not. But maybe we could rally here. "What's your dream job, then?"

He shrugged. "I don't know. Maybe a teacher. My mom stayed with me last week, and she was looking at jobs for me."

I barely kept my eyebrows from rising. That was the second time he'd mentioned his mom. Which wouldn't be weird if his eyes didn't light up when he talked about her. He really liked his mom.

The second strange thing—or maybe the fifth strange thing at this point—was that he still hadn't asked me a single question in return. From my psychology classes, I knew that polite social expectations dictated that he should be mirroring my questions back to me so the conversation could bounce back and forth, but he seemed to just be content drinking the black coffee Meena had poured for him. Maybe he was just shy, though.

Meena set my drink down in front of me, and I smiled up at her. "Thanks."

"So…" I took a sip of the amazingness that was in this cup as I wracked my brain for another question that was acceptable at a first meeting. "Any pets?" I asked awkwardly.

He shook his head. "I wanted to get a dog, but my mom wants me to get a cat. So she's coming here this weekend, and we're going to look at cats."

I took another sip of my drink, so I didn't let the "what the fuck" slip from my lips. He clearly had a… special relationship with his mother. I looked at the clock up on the wall. Damnit. Only fifteen minutes had passed. I already knew that this guy and I would not be going on a second date. Or sleeping together. Even if he was amazing in bed, I had a feeling his mom would be the third person in that arrangement. But I also didn't want to be rude, and fifteen minutes was still too early to beg off. I could send Inez an SOS message, but then she would want endless details, and I just wanted this over with. I took another sip as I tried to think of questions.

Trying a new tactic, I let the silence lengthen between us. It was a psychology trick. People usually hated silence in conversations. Four seconds was roughly the time when people started to get antsy and try to break the silence. But as the seconds ticked by, Jeremy gave no indication that the silence bothered him. Maybe he really was a psychopath. First black coffee and then the increased silence. Logically, I knew that wasn't what made someone a psychopath, but still... I could be having breakfast at the dining hall with the guys right now. At least Noah, because he and I didn't have morning classes. I shook off thoughts of breakfast and focused back on the conversation. Oh, I could ask him if he was from here. That should kill some time.

"So are you from here?" I asked.

"No, I'm from Brenton."

Brenton was about an hour away from Grandview. Clearly, that was the right question to ask. He rambled on a bit about the town, about how his mother was still living there, and about how he wanted to go back there because he didn't like being so far from home.

"And I hate driving," he announced. "Road trips are overrated."

Yep, nope. I could not keep sitting here. Road trips were sacred parts of our summers. We would have a few weeks off training each summer. The first week, the guys and I would spend with our respective families, but then we would all load into Asher and Noah's SUV and road trip somewhere new. We would just drive in a random direction until we found something interesting and stopped there. We'd had some great adventures over the last few years for sure, and I was already sad thinking about how it would all end after this year when we all went our separate directions.

I looked at the clock again. Forty minutes. Was dating always this bad? It wasn't like I hadn't dated before. I had avoided it in high school, but I had been dealing with... things already, so it didn't seem worth it. When I entered college, though, I had been determined to reclaim my body again and shake off the ghosts of my past, so I'd entered the dating scene. Or the hookup scene, at least.

My first few encounters weren't great but weren't terrible. Much better than my first sexual experience, at least, and by sophomore year, I felt like I had reclaimed my body and no longer flinched at casual, unexpected touches. The guys had helped with that, too, since they were a touchy-feely bunch.

And with the sex came the dating experience, as not everyone was comfortable hopping into bed right away. So I've been on more than a few dates, but this one... this had, by far, been the worst. This guy couldn't even ask me a question back; he was so focused on his mom. In fact, he hadn't even realized he had lost my interest, as he was deep into a story about his mom and her rotary club.

Meena kept looking over at me and snickering at her phone from behind the counter as she served other customers. I had no doubt Inez was getting a play-by-play of this entire disaster.

"You know what?" I said, interrupting Jeremy. "I just realized I have a paper due for my next class and I haven't finished it."

"Oh no!" Jeremy seemed genuinely concerned. "Did you want to work on it here? I can keep you company."

I held in my grimace. I definitely did not want to do that, even if the paper wasn't imaginary. "No, I focus best in the library. Sorry to cut the coffee short."

"It's fine," he said. "I'll let you go." He waited as I gathered my stuff. I had hoped he would just head out, but he seemed determined to be a gentleman.

He held the door for me again, and I turned awkwardly to him once we were outside.

"Well, I've got to go that way." I jerked my thumb in the direction of campus. "It was nice meeting you." I hoped that would dissuade him from following me.

Jeremy nodded. "Hey, look, I know this was an early morning coffee date, but how about a kiss?"

This time, my eyebrows did shoot up. What part of any of this date made him think that it went well enough for a kiss? Clearly, this guy was even worse at reading a room than I had thought. My brain was still struggling to come up with an answer, so I just said, "No, sorry." Then spun on my heel and walked away. I didn't look back to see if he followed me; I just kept speed walking away.

Operation "get Lexi laid" was off to a terrible start. Hopefully, the next guy would be better. While I walked, I pulled out my phone and texted Noah. Seemed like I would have time to get breakfast with him after all.

LEXI

"Wait, he said what about his mom?" Jamison sputtered out his drink at the kitchen table as the others roared in laughter. His dark brown eyes went wide at my words.

I rolled my eyes. It was Wednesday, which meant family dinner night, a tradition we had instituted in sophomore year when our class schedules started pulling us all in different directions. I saw Derek in classes the most, as he was a neuroscience major and some of our psychology classes overlapped, but the others I didn't see often outside of practice.

Usually, we made time to cook one of our favorite meals, but today had been a bit crazy, so we'd gotten takeout from our favorite Chinese place. Now I was about halfway through my story, and takeout boxes littered the large eight-person table Lewis had insisted on when we'd gotten this house.

Jamison looked very offended on my behalf, but the others all chuckled.

"I know, I know," I said, waving my fork in front of me. "I wasn't fifteen minutes into the date and knew it wasn't going anywhere. But I couldn't just leave, so I had to keep asking questions."

"Why couldn't you have just left?" Jamison interrupted. He had never enjoyed when I had been on dates before. Lewis wasn't the only one who was overprotective, but Jeremy seemed to really have gotten under his skin for some reason.

"Because it would have been rude, and I wasn't finished my drink."

The guys all groaned, except for Asher. We looked at each other and rolled our eyes. Only Asher understood my love for sugary drinks. He also loved them.

"So, anyway," I said, stabbing a piece of broccoli with my fork. "I asked him if he was from around here, and he said he was from Brenton and that he's thinking of moving back home there—"

"To be with his mom, for sure," Noah interrupted.

I laughed. "Oh, definitely, but then the most blasphemous thing came out of his mouth during his long monologue about how much he loved his mother."

"He drinks his coffee black because his mom does," Derek guessed.

"He thinks female quarterbacks are a myth," Noah countered.

"He thinks aliens don't exist." That one was from Jamison, but there were tight lines around his eyes.

I frowned briefly at him, trying to figure out what he was so upset about. I was the one with the awful date.

"If I could finish," I said, arching my eyebrow at the hooligans I lived with.

"Proceed." Asher waved his hand in front of him like he was a king giving me permission to speak, and I rolled my eyes at him.

"No, he said…" I lowered my voice to a stage whisper. "That he hates driving and road trips are overrated."

Noah did not disappoint with his theatrical gasp, and Lewis busted out laughing. "Yep, that was an immediate no, I'm guessing."

"Well, obviously. If the sex was good, I could have gotten over the black coffee thing, but with his mommy issues, it was going to be a no; then his view on road trips just cinched the deal," I said, reaching for more fried rice. "But he didn't think so."

"What do you mean?" Asher frowned at me.

"When we were leaving and were outside the coffee shop, he was like, 'I know it was an early morning coffee date, but how about a kiss?'" I parroted how he sounded, and this time, I did not hold in my shudder of revulsion.

"What the fuck?" Various exclamations echoed around the table. Even Derek's quiet voice chimed in.

"What did you do?" Derek asked, concern in his gray eyes.

"I said, 'sorry no,' and hightailed it out of there." I laughed. "Then I texted Noah to go get breakfast."

"Did he try to follow you?" Jamison asked, his dark brown eyes narrowed on my face.

I shrugged. "Don't know. I didn't look back."

"Has he tried to text you since?" Asher asked.

I shook my head, and just then, my phone dinged. "Well, speak of the devil," I said, unlocking my phone. I scanned Jeremy's message quickly. He wanted to see me again. I typed out a quick reply and sent it.

"What did he want?" Lewis asked, glaring at my phone like it personally offended him.

"He wanted to see me again. I told him no," I said, scooping another bite of fried rice into my mouth. I wasn't really still hungry, but the food was just so *good*.

"Good for you. You deserve better," Derek said softly. I smiled at my gentle-souled friend.

"Got any more dates planned?" Asher asked.

I shrugged. "I have a few people I'm talking to, but I don't know. How hard is it to find good sex these days?"

"With someone who isn't going to murder you afterwards," Noah said off-handedly, looking down at his plate as he sopped up some sauce with one of the egg rolls. We all just stared at him, and he looked up. "What?" he said defensively. "I listen to those true crime podcasts, too."

I laughed and rolled my eyes.

"If you're looking for good sex with someone who's not going to murder you afterwards, then we're offering," Jamison said out of the blue.

I froze, and silence fell over the table. I looked up at him, convinced he was joking, but the expression on his face was dead serious. He couldn't be serious, right?

I let out a forced laugh. "Um, no. I can't do that. We're friends... practically family. Having sex with one of you would be just weird. Plus, there's the team to think of."

"No, it would be with all of us," Jamison corrected.

What? What was he saying? All of them?

He continued, "I mean, it makes sense. You know us. We know you. You trust us. Besides, with us, we wouldn't be worried about being murdered by a guy because you didn't live up to his idea of his mother. And we're all busy, but there are five of us, so someone will be around at all times."

"So this is a pity offering?" I said, ignoring everything else he said.

This was a terrible idea. Why was he even offering it? Surely, they all weren't on board with the plan. A quick glance around the table showed the guys all looking at me expectantly. Not a single one was disagreeing with Jamison. What the fuck? While the larger part of my brain was freaking out, there was a small voice that whispered that it wasn't such a bad idea.

"It's not a pity offering." Jamison leaned forward in his chair, dark brown eyes intent on me. "Don't overthink it. It would be a

24

purely physical relationship. No one else would have to know. And it would be totally safe."

I looked around the table again. None of them denied or rebutted Jamison's words at all. My brain was spinning, and my head felt like it was floating above the table looking down on the scene.

"You're serious about this. All of you?" I needed confirmation.

The guys all nodded, some more hesitantly than others, and I just blinked. Never in a million years did I think the guys thought of me like that. Well, that wasn't true. Jamison and Noah were outrageous flirts, and I had seen their looks when I dressed up for a party, but since I had firmly put them in the best friend category, I had thought they had done the same to me. But I had never outright asked them. Maybe because I was scared of what the answer was.

No, I was actually scared of losing what we had. The guys had gotten me through so many important times in my life. Their friendship was my consistent anchor throughout all the ups and downs. I'd never dreamed of risking it like this. But apparently, they had been thinking about it.

My brain just spun, and it felt like the air was sucked out of the room. I pushed back from the table. "I need to think. I can do the dishes later."

Derek stood up next to me, and I tensed, thinking he wanted to talk about this now, but I should have known better. He took the plate out of my hands.

"Go think," he gently encouraged. "We've got the dishes."

No one said another word as I escaped up the stairs.

ASHER

"*A* purely physical relationship?" I snarled at Jamison. "Way to make her feel cheap."

What the fuck? I loved the dude like a brother, but that was possibly the worst way he could have delivered that.

"I know, I know." Jamison ran his hands through his hair, gripping the sides of it as he looked at the stairs Lexi disappeared up. "I just froze. She looked so panicked at the idea of it being more that I just blurted it out."

"It wasn't the best way to say it," Derek agreed, ever the peacemaker. "But it's out there now, so how do we want to deal with it?"

"Well, she'll say no, right?" Lewis said, looking around the table.

"What if she says yes, though?" I countered. "If she says no, then we go back to business as usual. But what if she says yes?"

Everyone fell silent as they thought about my words. We had been in love with Lexi since meeting her. Jamison and Lewis had been in love with her since high school but had never admitted it until Noah and I had told them one night that we wanted to make a move. We were drunk, but I remember that evening clearly.

Lexi had been home visiting her parents, and we had all decided to go out and get drunk at this party. Derek had just started hanging out with us more, and we had been talking on the way to the party about our plans to get a house next year and host our own parties. We had some shots at the party and were trying to get in the party mood, but without Lexi, it felt weird to be hanging out there.

Girls had kept coming onto all of us, something that we usually welcomed, but that night, with her absence, it felt different. So we grabbed a bottle of whiskey and headed back to the dorm Noah and I were sharing. As the night progressed, and we got progressively drunker, Lexi came up in conversation.

"I just... I just really fucking like her," my drunk brother blurted.

Even drunk, I knew exactly what he was talking about and sat up straight, keeping a wary eye on Lewis. The big lineman and I had become quick friends, but I knew he held a secret torch for Lexi, and my dumbass brother had just blurted it all out.

"I think Asher and I are going to ask her out," Noah continued, and Lewis's eyes snapped to mine.

"She's not a toy to be passed around," he growled, standing up.

I stood up, too, so we were chest to chest. Even if my twin was a dumbass sometimes, I wasn't going to let him be punched.

"She's not a toy," I said firmly. *"She's an amazing woman, and we want to date her."*

Lewis's eyes widened, and his gaze darted around the room.

Noah, trying to make it better, waved his glass at Jamison and Lewis. "I know you've got the protective older brother thing going, but she gets to make the decision."

"I am not her brother," Lewis snarled. *"And you can't ask her out, because I loved her first." His eyes widened again, like he hadn't expected the declaration to come out of his mouth. His fists tightened at his side.*

"Actually," Jamison drawled. "I saw her first, and I even told you dibs in the parking lot of that middle school club team practice. If memory serves, you punched me in the stomach."

"So you love her, too?" Noah asked.

Jamison took a swig of whiskey. "Of course I love her, too. I'm not blind. She's gorgeous and funny and an amazing player. And skittish as fuck about intimacy."

It was my turn to stare at Jamison. That was surprisingly insightful for the cocky manwhore.

"If we are doing confessions," Derek said quietly. "Then I also really like her. I don't have the history with her that you all do, but I was going to ask her out as well."

Lewis whirled away from the group and shoved his hands through his hair. "She's not a toy to be passed around," he repeated, then turned back around. "We can't all date her."

Jamison raised his glass. "Let the best man win."

"Why does she have to choose?"

We all turned to stare at the quiet nerd. Derek shrugged. "It's called polyamory when one person dates multiple people. My parents are polyamorous. It takes a ton of communication and love, but it's one of the most beautiful relationships I've witnessed."

I exchanged a wide-eyed glance with Noah. I would never dream that quiet Derek grew up in that kind of family. I mean, Noah and I had two moms, but I had never met anyone who had polyamorous parents.

"There's no way Lexi would go for that," Lewis said.

I thought quickly. Most people looked at me and assumed I was a dumb jock, but I was actually pretty smart, as well and good at reading people. It was why I'd decided on a criminology major. I thought about Lexi's interactions with us and how she responded to each of us. She always seemed to split her time equally between all of us, even with the history that Jamison and Lewis shared with her. What Jamison said about her being skittish around intimacy was *correct. She did shy away from intimacy with partners; instead, she was almost as much of a player as Jamison. Could this actually work?*

"She's not ready yet," I said. "But we could wait until she is. And in the meantime, if one of us can't date her, we all can't date her."

"Dude, how would that even work?" Lewis looked at me like I was crazy.

"We need boundaries. And rules of communication," Derek said. "We can figure it out as we go, though. Relationships develop naturally, and that's what we're doing here."

"You're all really serious." Lewis looked at all of us.

I thought about it briefly and realized I was. I really was. There was a sense of rightness that settled in my bones about it.

"Yes." I grinned at him. "You all are my brothers. And I think, together, we could make her really happy. Besides, do you really think you could be happy watching Lexi seriously date some other guy who wasn't one of us? We would take care of her, treat her right."

Even though we were only sophomores, I was already thinking about the future. I didn't want to lose these guys or Lexi, and this relationship might be the glue that held us all together after college. It was perfect. If we all agreed. I looked back at Lewis, who was staring with unfocused eyes at the wall, lost in his head. Finally, after what felt like an eternity, he turned back to us.

"We don't rush her," he said gruffly. "We let her come to us at her own pace."

"Agreed."

And we had all agreed not to rush her. Until Jamison blurted it out today. And now Lexi was up there freaking out and probably talking to Inez, and I didn't know if that conversation was going to weigh in our favor or not. But maybe, in some ways, it was a blessing that Jamison had spilled the beans.

Lexi had not given much indication that she saw us as more than friends. Every so often, her blue eyes would darken when she looked at us, or there would be a little light flirting. Those scraps of attention were what kept us going on this dream. But maybe now she needed the push. It was senior year, and we wanted her in our lives forever. Maybe it was time to stop being so careful around her.

"We need to talk about boundaries again," Derek said. "It's been ages since we first brought up this conversation, but now the cat is out of the bag." He looked pointedly at Jamison, and I smirked.

Lexi might think he was still the quiet, shy nerd we met in freshman year, but Derek had really grown into his own over the last few years. He was like quiet steel, especially when it came to Lexi.

"We need to talk about it again."

"No talking with each other about our time with her," I started us off. "And no encroaching on each other's time. She leads the pace."

"Obviously," Lewis said, taking a break from glaring at Jamison.

"Even though Dumbass over here said only a physical relationship." I jerked my thumb at Jamison but softened my words with a grin at him. "I think we should still date her and make sure she knows she's the only one for us."

"No more sleeping around." Derek looked at Noah and Jamison specifically on that one. "She's the only one for us."

"I haven't slept with anyone in the last year." Jamison's quiet admission shocked us. He had a reputation on campus of being a manwhore—albeit a gentlemanly one—but never tied down. He looked up from the table to see us all looking at him. He shrugged. "Couldn't do it anymore. Didn't want anyone else."

Now that I understood. Everyone paled next to Lexi.

Satisfied we had a good game plan for moving forward, we finished cleaning up dinner. It was Noah and Derek's turn to do the dishes, so I headed up to take a shower.

I slowed as I passed by Lexi's door, and I could hear muffled voices on the other side. I smiled as I recognized Inez's voice, but I couldn't make out the words, so I moved on. I wondered if Lexi was freaking out or actually considering it. Even though she might be thinking it would be a purely physical relationship, we would treasure her forever if she let us.

LEXI

"*He* e said WHAT!?" Inez screeched down the phone.

I winced and moved it away from my ear. I wasn't trying to blow out an eardrum; I was just trying to get advice from my best friend.

"Tell me everything," she demanded.

"I'm trying to," I shot back. "You're the one trying to deafen me."

"Oh, please," Inez said. "You've heard me be louder."

"I have, and that's not an experience I'm trying to repeat."

I quickly finished the story about Jamison making this weird friends-with-benefits offer and saying it would purely be a physical relationship.

Once I finished, Inez asked, "So what are you thinking?"

This was why I loved her. Instead of jumping in on what I should do or think, she always checked in with me about what I was thinking.

"Honestly, I'm still stuck on what the fuck?" I said. And that was true. My brain hadn't stopped spinning in a circle, replaying the last hour in my mind over and over again.

"That's fair," Inez said. "I know this is coming as a shock to you."

There was something about how she phrased the statement that made me pause. "For me?" I asked.

Inez sighed, and I could hear rustling on the other end of the phone. "I'm going to FaceTime you. One sec."

I frowned even as I pulled the phone away from my ear to accept the video call. Inez only FaceTimed me when she was going to say something she wanted to see my reaction for. Usually, whatever she said provided me with some much needed clarity about the situation, but I didn't know what could provide clarity here. Or what was even the question. I wasn't going to take Jamison up on his offer. Was I?

Inez's face filled my screen. She was sitting at her desk, her messy bed in the frame behind her.

"Okay," she said, sitting up straight. "I hate to break it to you, but the guys haven't exactly been subtle about their feelings for you. At least, not in my opinion."

I furrowed my brow. "What do you mean? We've always been just friends."

Even as I said the words, I could taste the bitter lie on my tongue. I had seen some signs over the years. The light flirting, the comfortable touches. So many people used to assume or still did that I was dating one of the guys, but I had never wanted to risk the friendship I had with any of them. Much less all of them.

I liked the safety and security our friendships provided. I didn't want any of that to blow up, much less affect us on the field. Especially not with this being our senior year. The entire team was counting on us to win the championship this year. The guys loved the game and had been talking about the championship constantly. I couldn't risk that for a quick roll in the sheets, right?

Inez arched her eyebrow at me in her classic are-you-shit-

33

ting-me-right-now look. But she kept her voice patient as she asked, "Well, how do you feel about them? Do you see yourself with them like that?"

I hesitated. If I were honest, I'd always thought the guys were hot, but I had spent so many years putting them firmly in the just-friends category in my head that I didn't know what I felt. I had a denial on the tip of my tongue when Inez spoke up again.

"Bitch, don't you dare lie to me," Inez said. "I've let you get away with not admitting your feelings for them for years, thinking you would come to your own conclusions naturally, but clearly, that was a mistake. You *like* them."

I sighed and threw myself backwards on the bed. "Of course I like them. They're my best friends."

"No, you *like* like them," she corrected me.

"What are we, in middle school?" I shot back.

"Stop deflecting before I come over there and sit on you till you answer honestly."

I sighed as I stared up at the ceiling. She would absolutely follow through on the threat.

"I don't think I've ever let myself see them that way," I confessed softly. "So I don't know if I like them like that."

"That's fair," Inez said. "But I've seen how you interact with them and, more importantly, how they interact with you. The feelings are there, even if you won't name them."

I ignored what she had just said. I was not ready to touch that statement yet. "I've always said I wouldn't sleep with anyone on the football team. I had to do that to get the guys to respect me."

"This wouldn't be just anyone, though," Inez pointed out. "And you wouldn't have to tell anyone at the start if you wanted to see how it went. Also, it's senior year, and the season is almost over. What's your next obstacle?"

"We have the championships coming up. We can't afford to be distracted."

Inez hummed. I knew I wasn't going to be able to convince her how important winning this championship was to me. Everything was going to change after this year. Winning the championship together was going to give us one more memory to hold on to. And it would be the culmination of my football career. I didn't plan on pursuing it after college. I wasn't NFL material, nor did I want to be. But winning this championship was going to help to heal a fundamental part of me that had been broken in high school. I needed this win for more reasons than I could count.

"Then make that a boundary of the relationship. That nothing affects the game." Inez shrugged casually. "In fact, boundaries and rules are only going to make this experience better. Clear expectations from each of you on what to expect."

When she saw me hesitating, she continued. "Look, if you want to keep going on dates with momma's boys and not be able to have anything but lackluster sex this year, we can be done with this conversation. But Jamison isn't wrong, even if his delivery was off. You all know each other and trust each other. You already communicate well; this is just an additional level of communication. We can brainstorm different boundaries that will allow you to keep your unhealthy obsession with football but still allow you to have orgasmic sex regularly."

"Orgasmic?" I arched my eyebrow at her through the screen.

"Oh, please. I've heard the rumors about your guys." Inez rolled her eyes at me.

"They're not mine," I corrected automatically. The same correction I had given countless times over the last few years.

"Not yet," Inez said. "But they will be if you let them. So what will it be?"

LEXI

I was still mulling over Inez's question the next morning. Seeing that I didn't have an answer, we had moved on to talking about the different boundaries or rules I could put into place. There was a part of me that was shocked I was seriously considering this, but there was another part of me that was slowly gaining a louder voice.

Could I eat my cake and have it too? Could I have my best friends and great sex? Could we make this work? Could these be more memories we could hold on to after college? The thought of us laughing around the table ten years from now about senior year when we were all married and had kids made my stomach sour a little bit, but maybe, for this year, I could live the fantasy. I could eat my cake and have it too.

I took a sip of my mocha as I crossed the grounds towards the athletic center. We had to be in the weight room for a few hours starting at 10 a.m., and it would be the first time I had seen them since last night. I had slipped out of the house early this morning to the library to avoid seeing any of my guys. *The guys.* Not my guys.

As I walked through campus, I ran through my pros and

cons list in my head. Inez always teased me about doing that, but it was the only way I could sort my chaotic brain some days. The pros: I did trust them, and the ease and familiarity we had with each other was going to lend itself to a healthy physical relationship. But could I keep it just physical and not let it affect the game? That was the question.

That small voice inside me whispered that this could be more trouble than it was worth. But Inez had brought up a good point last night. Regardless of whether we started the friends-with-benefits agreement or not, we did need to have a conversation about it. I couldn't stick my head in the sand and pretend that they hadn't made the offer. Ignoring it would still lead to tension on the team, so we needed to resolve it quickly before the game this weekend.

I just still wasn't sure how to start the conversation. Like *hey, guys, getting fucked by all of you sounds really good. Let's do it?* I knew more about them all than I had ever known about a sexual partner before. Could we make this transition from friends to friends-with-benefits and then back again after senior year without destroying our friendships?

I finished the last of my chocolate goodness just as the anxiety crept back in. I tossed my cup in the trash can just inside the door and headed to the locker room to change. I was a few minutes late by design, not wanting to have run into any of the guys before I had all my thoughts straight. Anxiety was making me her bitch today. I knew a conversation with the guys would make me feel better, but anxiety was in my head, whispering about all the ways this could go wrong.

Tugging my sports shirt down, I walked out of the locker room and into the weight room. The room was loud and chaotic, as always, and smelled like old sweat. A stench they never seemed to get out, no matter how many times they bleached everything.

The team was all milling around on various equipment,

chatting loudly as we waited for the trainer to walk in. My guys were all sitting in a tight circle, apparently deep in conversation, but when I walked through the door, their gazes snapped to me. The weight of them felt like a caress up and down my body, and I fought not to shiver as I walked in their direction. I kept my steps even as I headed to them. We had always hung out together, so it would look weird if I didn't join them this morning.

Fuck. That was another thing we would have to talk about. If the rest of the team found out I was sleeping with them, it would ruin my credibility as quarterback and leave a stain on my record here at Grandview. Not to mention, it could affect our playing in the next few games leading up to the championship.

Jamison opened his mouth as I approached, but Lyle, our fitness trainer, walked into the room at that moment, Derek on his heels. Apparently, the gang was all here today. Derek didn't always join us for training, but he seemed to be making an effort to do so more and more lately.

"All right, let's get started," Lyle said, quickly separating us into groups.

Lewis ended up in my group, and Lyle sent us to the bench press stations. The guys looked like they were going to protest the assignments for just a moment, and I mentally willed them not to. Asher clapped Jamison on the shoulder and tugged him towards the squat rack. I shot him a grateful look and mouthed *Later*. He nodded and flashed me an easy grin.

Lewis and I took one of the benches on the end, and I racked up my weight first. He looked like he was going to say something, and I shook my head.

"We can talk later tonight," I said quickly.

This was not a conversation we should have in front of the entire team. Especially when I didn't have all the answers yet.

Unluckily for us, Ryan Crawford and Finn Collins took the bench next to us. I didn't have anything against Finn—he was actually a decent guy. But Ryan had been determined since freshman year to be the loudest voice on the team against my being quarterback. If I were any less confident in my playing, I would have taken it personally, but I knew I was good. Football was practically my life, after all. Mac had caught him badmouthing me once after a game and had laid into him. Ryan had lowered his voice quite a bit after that. He still tried to influence the freshmen as they came in, but once they saw me play, they usually got over it.

Unfortunately, he was a good running back when he actually followed the damn plays, and Mac kept him on the team. Ryan could also be a huge gossip, however, and I wasn't going to lie and say he hadn't crossed my mind as a potential problem with this friends-with-benefits situation. He already made shots about my relationship with the guys, so it wouldn't be out of the norm.

"Looking rough, Simmons," Ryan started in. "Did you get bent over last night?"

I rolled my eyes at his lewd innuendo. He was predictable, if nothing else.

"Sure did. Have you called your mom and asked how she's walking this morning?"

The guys in my group laughed and heckled Ryan, and I smiled and shook my head. Guys had been predictable since middle school. A well-done "your mom" joke usually got them off my back.

Lyle came by, and we all quickly got down to business. I fell into an easy routine with my breath and pumped out the reps in three sets. Lewis and I worked together to add more weight to the bar when it was his turn, then I spotted him.

We worked steadily through the rest of the drills, spending time on the squat racks, doing a core circuit, and running on the treadmill. During one of our breaks, Asher caught me by the water station.

I cut him off before he could say anything. "We can all talk later tonight."

"Okay," he said slowly. "I was just going to ask if you were okay."

"I am." I kept my answer short. I didn't know who was listening. "Can you tell the rest of them we'll talk later?"

Asher studied me a beat longer before nodding his head. "I will."

Asher had adopted Lewis's role of my protector, but where Lewis would growl and grumble, Asher was more of a watcher. I was never quite sure what he saw when he looked at me like that.

Lyle barked at us to get back to our stations, and I hurried over to the treadmill. I watched as Asher whispered to Jamison and the others what I had said. The tension visibly bled out of their shoulders. Regardless of how the conversation went tonight, it was needed either way. And who knew? They might think the rules and boundaries I was leaning towards were too much and we would just laugh it off and go on about our lives.

Even as I had the thought, I knew it was more than something we could laugh off. This felt pivotal, like our friendships were hanging in the balance. And the weight of it suddenly threatened to choke me. I didn't want to lose them, but I knew that wasn't a guarantee. Life was a cruel teacher, and I had already been taught some of its lessons. It remained to be seen if tonight's conversation would be another such lesson.

When Lyle called an end to training, I powered off the treadmill and headed for the training room. I grabbed a towel from the trainer's area and flashed Derek a quick grin as he taped up one of the freshman's knees. Mac walked through the door next to me, and I tried to fight down the instinctive tenseness in my muscles from the proximity of a coach that I hadn't been able to shake since high school.

"Ah, Simmons," he said, stopping near me. I never knew if he could sense my wariness around him, but he always kept a healthy dose of space between us that I appreciated. "How do you think the team is going into the game this weekend?"

I used the question as an excuse to break eye contact and scan the room. Everyone was in top performance, and I felt more confident in this team than I had last year going into the championship.

I nodded. "Really good, actually. Provided no one does anything stupid before the game, we should be in excellent shape this weekend. Also provided the team takes Western seriously."

Mac nodded. Western University hadn't been a major force in football for a while, but they had an up-and-coming quarter-back who was doing well, and they had made it to the playoffs. Our team had been joking last week that it would be an easy game, but pride goes before a fall, as the saying went. Yeah, so I was cynical. Sue me.

"Gather 'round," Mac barked out, and the guys hustled over. This close, everyone stunk. I was so looking forward to a shower.

"Listen up," Mac said. "Good training today. Lyle says most of you are adequate, at least. Remember, no dumbass decisions for the next few days. If I get a call from the town jail again, Fitzpatrick, I will leave you in there to rot and call your mother to come get you out."

We all laughed at the lanky Fitzpatrick, who shrugged sheepishly. Last year, he had gone out and gotten drunk before a regular season game and had been arrested for public urination. Mac had been furious when he had found out. Fitzpatrick was never living that one down.

"Also," Mac said, cutting through the laughter and jibes at

Fitzpatrick. "I know some of you think Western will be a breeze this weekend."

"Well, it is Western," Collins said with a smirk.

"Do not underestimate them," Mac said, as if Collins hadn't spoken. "I know I've got a team of idiots most days, but do not underestimate them. I've known Jim for over thirty years. He's a wily old fucker of a coach, and his new star isn't a slouch either. That's why we're running play drills tomorrow until I'm satisfied."

A collective groan went up from the team, and Mac rolled his eyes. "You get a rest day the day after. Although if you're smart, you'll go on a run or something to keep your muscles loose. Then it's game time. Now get to class." He dismissed us in his gruff, abrupt way, then turned on his heel.

I headed with the rush of bodies into the hall and split off for my locker room. I flipped the lock behind me and headed for the showers. I didn't have class for another hour, so I stayed under the spray until voices faded in the hall and the building was mostly empty. I plaited my wet hair into a braid and flipped it over my shoulder as I grabbed my backpack and duffle bag. I would need to wash my gym clothes tonight, so I would carry the bag to class. I only had one class today, a two-hour long psychology seminar with Derek, who I imagined had gone on already. He liked to get there early and settle in.

To my surprise, when I pushed open the doors to the athletic center, Derek was sitting on the bench, waiting for me. He jumped up as I approached and waved his phone at me.

"Asher said we were talking later?"

I nodded, grateful that Asher had already shared that with him.

"Do you need to talk about anything now?" Derek offered. "Happy to listen."

"I know." I smiled at him. "I'm good, though."

Derek studied me a second longer. It always felt like he

could see straight into my soul with those gray eyes. "Okay," he said softly. He turned towards our class building and began walking. "How many students do we think are going to fall asleep during Professor Bryant's lecture today?"

I laughed. Our old professor had one of the driest voices I'd ever heard from a professor and was almost completely blind. He never used slides, just sat at the front and talked for two hours straight. More than one student had taken a nap during his class. But this seminar was required to graduate, and Derek and I had decided to take it together and suffer through it.

"At least three," I said as he held the door for me.

"I'll take that bet," Derek said, following me up the auditorium steps to our usual seats about halfway up. We exchanged cursory greetings with the classmates next to us before Professor Bryant called the class to order.

Not ten minutes into the lecture and I knew I was going to have to get the notes from Derek. My mind kept drifting to the conversation we needed to have tonight. Trying to combat my anxiety, I started daydreaming about what it might be like. Visions of great sex and cuddling on the couch and dirty inside jokes flashed through my mind.

There was a part of me that craved that connection with someone. I never believed I could have it, but what if, for a brief time, I could pretend? It would be just until the end of senior year, anyway, as we were all going different directions after college. And if we could work it out that it didn't affect our playing or the championship run, then it could be perfect.

Rustling bags around us brought me back to the present. The class was packing up. I glanced at the clock and raised my eyebrows. Professor Bryant was dismissing us a half hour early.

Derek huffed out a small laugh. "I'll send you the notes," he promised.

"You're the best." I laughed as I packed up my untouched notebook.

"Are you headed home?" Derek asked.

I sighed and bit my lip. The guys all had class for another two hours, and I did not want to sit at home waiting for them. "I think I might grab lunch and then hit the library."

"Sounds good." He nodded. "Do you want company after my class?"

I hesitated. All this self-doubt was throwing me off. I was used to being confident in all areas of my life. Confidence was excellent for hiding my broken pieces.

"It's okay if you want space." Derek smiled. He truly was the best. They all were.

"If you don't mind?" I said, hating the thread of doubt in my tone.

If it were any other day, I would have taken him up on his offer; but I felt the need for a little space before the conversation we'd be having later. Even if I was leaning towards saying yes, I felt a little raw right now and needed the time to get my barriers back in place. The only way this would work was if we didn't add any feelings to the mix. That might be the only way I could survive losing them after senior year.

"Not at all. Whatever you need." He squeezed my arm gently, then headed to class.

I stared at his retreating back. Would all of them echo his sentiments? Whatever I needed? Even as I thought about the question, a little voice whispered in my head. *You know they would. And that's what scares you.*

LEXI

I'd been sitting on the couch in the living room, mindlessly clicking through the channels for over an hour, looking for something that would hold my attention until the guys got home.

A gentle hand touched my shoulder, and I jolted.

"Sorry," Derek said sheepishly. "I called your name, but you were a million miles away."

I gave him a quick smile, although I could feel how fake it felt on my face. "It's okay." I looked past him to see that the rest of the guys had gathered in the kitchen, standing there awkwardly with their hands shoved in their pockets. Noah was twiddling a pencil in his fingers.

"Did you want to talk now or wait?" Derek studied my face, as if he could read all my secrets. Thankfully, he couldn't; although it felt like every year we were friends, he could read me more and more.

"Might as well get it over with." I bit my lip, then gave him a quick grin that felt a little more real.

The guys' faces fell, but they masked or schooled their

expressions. I realized they expected me to say no, and they were... disappointed? I bit my lip, gathering my thoughts, as they all took seats on the large sectional around me. I hadn't really thought about it much in the last few hours, putting off the decision until I absolutely had to make it. But their disappointment was causing my brain to spin. They wanted the friends-with-benefits offer. Surely it wasn't just for sex? They could get sex elsewhere. Maybe, like me, they were tired of it being with strangers.

I let my mind wander for a moment, imagining what it could be like, and my body heated unexpectedly. I shifted in my seat and sat up straight. My guys—because they were my guys—stared back at me with guarded expressions. They expected me to say no, and if they didn't agree with my boundaries, I still might; but I trusted them. Trusted our friendship. We could make this work.

"If we're going to do this," I began, drawing on my psychology classes to keep my voice strong and steady. "There need to be rules."

Slow smiles spread across their faces as cautious hope bloomed, and Derek nodded. "Whatever you need."

I quickly continued before I lost my nerve. "The biggest rule is nothing can affect the team. If it looks like even one of us is off in the games or in practice, we call it off. We're too close to the championship to risk it."

The championship had to take priority here. It was our last shot and would give us one more memory to tie us together after we all went our separate ways.

Lewis nodded. "That's fine," he said gruffly.

I studied him for a second. I had been surprised when he hadn't dismissed Jamison's offer immediately last night. Lewis had always been my gruff protector. I had expected him to immediately balk at sharing me, but he hadn't.

"No fighting either," I said. "I don't want to risk our friendships."

Asher raised his hand at that one. "I don't think that's a fair one. We've fought before in our friendships, and we'll fight in the future. That's a natural part of relationships."

Derek nodded. "Fighting is a natural part of the communication process. But that being said, what if we amended it to communication is key? Clear communication is an important part in any relationship but especially in polyamory."

Especially in what? I had known that Derek's family life was unusual, but I hadn't known there was a term for it. Or maybe I hadn't wanted to learn. I felt bad now, and he turned his smile on me as if he knew what I was thinking.

"That's fine," I said slowly. We had fought in the past, but it was usually over small stuff, nothing major. I hesitated over the next rule but knew it was going to be important. "Kind of in line with the first rule, I think we should keep feelings out of it. A purely physical relationship, like you said," I said to Jamison.

His jaw tightened, and I caught Asher frowning at him from the corner of my eye.

"Define purely physical," Jamison bit out.

I furrowed my brow. Isn't that what he wanted? "I mean purely physical. I know there's just one of me and five of you, so if we wanted to see other people outside of this, that would be okay."

I eyed them closely as I spoke. Inez had said this one would prove to me if they really had serious feelings for me. I told her it was ridiculous. This arrangement couldn't work if we caught feelings. Feelings meant jealousy and anger, and that would rip our friendships and our team apart. Besides, the guys deserved someone who could give them their all in a relationship, and I couldn't. I was too broken to give them my everything, but I could give them a physical relationship. And besides, this relationship already had an expiration date.

Their expressions tightened as they processed my words. "Do you think you will be looking for sex outside of us?" Noah asked finally. "Because I can assure you, we can keep you satisfied." He wiggled his eyebrows dramatically at me, and I rolled my eyebrows as I huffed out a laugh.

"Look, I'm aware you all have a reputation as being..." I paused and pretended to think of the word, tapping my finger against my chin. The words *amazing* or *orgasmic* probably applied here, but I couldn't resist fucking with them a little. "Adequate at sex..." I finished.

Lewis's eyebrows shot up. Then he smirked at me. "Just adequate, Pixie?"

Jamison sat up straight, offended, and opened his mouth to speak, but then seemed to think of something and sank back into the couch.

"What is it?" I asked, arching my eyebrows at him.

He shrugged. "Just looking forward to proving you wrong."

I rolled my eyes but couldn't ignore the flash of heat that filled me. "Whatever. Do you all agree with the rule?"

"Yes." Asher's firm word cut off what anyone else was going to say, but none of them refuted his statement. I didn't know if I quite believed them, but time would tell.

"Is that it?" Derek asked.

I shook my head. "I would also like to keep this a secret outside this household." I held up my hand to cut off any protests. "I already get enough shit for living with you all. And everyone knows my 'no football team' rule. I don't want to risk it."

"We can agree to that, too. Just us." Asher nodded, his hazel eyes flaming but his tone steady.

"That's it then." I spread my hands wide. "Really, the most important rule is the first one. This cannot affect the team at all."

"Then we agree with your terms," Asher said.

I felt like my eyebrows were going to be permanently plastered to the top of my head at this rate. "Just like that? No discussion, nothing?"

I had half expected some pushback on at least one of the rules, but they all seemed to be in agreement based on the head nods around the room.

Derek quirked his lips at me. "We talked a bit last night. We're all on the same page."

They had talked about this last night? About me? I didn't know how I felt about that, but I guess I had gone straight upstairs and called Inez, so that was fair.

The silence dragged on for a few moments, and I didn't know what to say or do. Would our 'physical relationship' start tonight? What happened now?

I jolted slightly when Noah sat straight up. "You know what we need now?"

Jamison stared at him with furrowed eyebrows as he tilted his head. "What?"

"Chocolate chip pancakes!"

Despite the crazy day, my lips spread into a grin that matched Noah's. Time to go to Jimbo's.

* * *

WE HAD BEEN to Jimbo's countless times before, but for some reason, piling into our usual big corner booth felt different this time. I was intimately aware of Lewis and Noah on either side of me.

Jamison snapped open a menu from across the table. "So, are we thinking omelets? What do you want, Lex?"

"Pancakes," Noah whined. "You want pancakes, right?"

Isn't that a loaded question? I thought as I opened my own menu to hide my red cheeks. There were so many options.

"Why choose?" Asher said, causing me to peek over my

menu at him. His eyes were dancing, although his face was serious. "Let's get a little bit of everything and just share."

Oh boy. Why did I have a feeling this 'purely physical' relationship was going to tear me apart by the time it was over?

ASHER

*O*ur girl was on fire today.

Drill after drill, pass after pass, Lexi was on her game in a way I had never seen before. Our drill had just ended, and I was by the water cooler with Derek as we watched Lexi execute another perfectly spiraled pass to Jamison's chest. He caught it, turned, and ran fifteen yards, then dropped back to a walk.

"She's on fire today," I commented to Derek, impressed, as I watched Jamison pitch the ball back to Lexi.

"Hmm..."

His tone suggested that he didn't share my sentiments, so I turned to him, brow furrowed. "What are you seeing that I'm not?" I asked quietly, turning back to watch her on the field and trying to see what he was seeing.

"She's got this tension around her eyes I don't like," Derek murmured. "She keeps rubbing her temples, and her movements are jerky, which means her muscles are too tight."

I did a quick scan to make sure no one else was around before I answered. Last thing Lexi needed was rumors flying.

We would shout to the world that she was ours and we were hers, but she still needed time.

I shuffled a little closer to him and spoke as quietly as I could. "Do you think it's because of last night?"

"She seemed at ease with everything last night," Derek said. "After Jimbo's, I mean. Did you see her this morning at all?"

I shook my head. Derek had an early morning Thursday class. I didn't have classes until this afternoon, but Lexi hadn't come out of her room this morning until it was time to go to practice, claiming she had homework to finish.

Derek hummed again, and worry twisted my gut. As much as I wanted her to be ours, I didn't want her to be stressed about it. If she would just lean on us a little more and talk to us, we could help with whatever was bothering her. I didn't like seeing her stressed.

"Noah and I will take her to lunch after practice," I murmured to Derek. "See if we can get her to relax and tell us what's wrong."

Derek nodded. "That'll be good."

We both watched as Mac walked up to Lexi and Jamison. Whatever he said to Lexi had her muscles relaxing and a shy smile spreading across her face. She always seemed to have that reaction to compliments. Like a shy pleasure she didn't like anyone seeing. Jamison and Lexi broke away from Mac and ran another play. The ball floated from Lexi's hands to Jamison's chest, and Mac gave a sharp nod.

"Gather 'round!" he barked.

I left Derek at the water station and jogged with the rest of the team towards Mac and the other assistant coaches.

"Well, that wasn't terrible," Mac said in his usual way. That was high praise coming from him. "If y'all play half as good as you drilled today, you should be able to take Western this week-end. But!" He shook a finger at our group. "That doesn't mean you should skate through by the seat of your pants, either. Got it?"

"Yes, Mac," we chorused, and he nodded.

"Dismissed. Hit the showers. Don't forget to eat today."

I caught Noah's eyes and jerked my head towards Lexi imperceptibly. My usually good-natured twin's eyes were solemn. He had also caught Lexi's mood today.

We dashed through the showers quickly. I ran a quick towel through my hair, something I might regret later in the chilly fall air, but I wanted to make sure Lexi didn't get away.

Noah beat me out of the locker room, and I exited it to find his arm around Lexi's shoulders, while he playfully tugged on her braid. I had never been jealous of my twin. Hell, we had even shared a girl or two before. But I would gladly take his place right now with Lexi pressed up against me.

"Are we doing the dining hall or Ramsey's?" I asked as I walked up to them.

Lexi arched an eyebrow at me. "Oh, we're going to lunch?"

I smirked at her, enjoying the way her eyes darkened briefly. "Of course. Didn't Noah tell you you're being kidnapped?"

"Hey," Noah protested. "Don't you know that there's less of a scene if the kidnappee knows her kidnappers and follows them willingly?"

Lexi and I stared at Noah, and his eyes widened. "What did I say?"

Lexi laughed, and I smiled at the sound. She had a husky laugh that almost sounded raspy. Like she didn't laugh a lot. Which wasn't true. She laughed with us, but the rest of the campus got the cool, confident quarterback all the time. It's a side of her only we got to see, and it made me possessive as hell over her laughter.

"Let's do Ramsey's," Lexi suggested. "You heard Mac. Can't forget to eat today."

Ramsey's was a dining center near the athletic complex that

catered primarily to the athletes. Full, balanced portions of hot and cold items, as well as an extensive smoothie bar. It had been our favorite when we lived on campus.

"How were drills on your side today?" Lexi asked us as we made the short ten-minute walk to the dining center. We had been on separate drills, as Noah and I played on the defense team.

"They were good," I answered. "Team seems solid."

I meant that. We had a solid run at the championships this year. I wasn't as into football as Lexi and Jamison were, but I still loved the game, and the thought of holding that championship trophy got my blood pumping.

"Good," Lexi said. "If Crawford can get his head out of his ass, I'll feel a lot better about this weekend."

Ryan Crawford seemed to have had it out for Lexi ever since she joined the team. I think he was expecting to be the rookie hotshot, but Lexi quickly overshadowed any rookie that year. When she was awarded Rookie of the Year by the coaching staff, his dislike for her seemed to cement into a chip on his shoulder he carried around to this day.

"He won't jeopardize the game," Noah said. "He loves it too much."

Lexi just hummed. "I hope he remembers that this weekend." Her expression was solemn, and I was determined to get that smile back on her face.

"No more football talk," I announced as I held the door for Noah and Lexi. "At least for the rest of lunch," I teased her. "Surely you can give it a break for that long."

She rolled her eyes at me, but a small smile played on her lips. "I don't talk about it that much."

"Only 24/7," Noah retorted, and we were rewarded with her husky laugh.

Once inside, we separated, each heading to a different food station after swiping our student IDs at the register. I got my hot bar items first, so I found a table against the wall of windows. In addition to great food, Ramsey's offered a great view of the mountains that surrounded Grandview University. It was a sight I would never grow tired of.

Lexi and Noah joined me after a few minutes, both of their trays heaped with food. For the first few minutes, all we did was shovel food into our mouths. Practice always took a lot out of us, and I worked up an appetite every time. Once the initial hunger was sated, our eating slowed.

Lexi wiped the corner of her mouth with a napkin. "How's your family? How's Ainsley?"

Over the years, we had all spent various breaks crashing at different houses. Lexi had bonded with Ainsley, our younger sister and a competitive gymnast, the last spring break we had spent at our family's cabin on the lake.

My muscles tensed, and Noah and I exchanged a look. It wasn't from Lexi's question. We still weren't over what had happened with Ainsley this month.

"What is it?" Lexi asked, her face pinched as she nibbled on her bottom lip. "Is Ainsley okay?"

"She is," I assured her. "It's nothing like that. We're just still a little…" I struggled to find the words.

"Pissed," Noah said.

Lexi's eyebrows shot up. "Why?"

"Ainsley moved gyms last month."

"She's no longer at Hilland's?" Lexi asked.

"No," I said, gritting my teeth. Even after a month, the familiar anger—ignited when my parents first told us the news —still rose in me. "The Hilland's head coach was arrested on sexual assault charges."

Across from me, Lexi's face went pale, and her fork clattered to her plate. "What? Did Ainsley…"

"No," Noah said, anger etched across his face. "Not Ainsley. But her best friend, Skylar."

"Oh no," Lexi breathed, shock and horror coloring her voice.

Her lips pressed together, and her leg started bouncing under the table. She moved her hands under the table, and I just knew she was pinching the skin on the back of her hand. It was one of her anxious habits, which showed just how much the news about Ainsley rocked her. I knew that she and Ainsley still texted occasionally, but my heart warmed at how much she cared about my sister.

"Yeah, it fucking sucks," Noah said heatedly. "Wish I could have been there and gotten my hands on that sick bastard."

If I hadn't been watching her closely, I would have missed the slight widening of her eyes at Noah's reaction. Almost as if she were shocked at the force of his response.

"He's in prison?" she confirmed softly.

"He is," I said. "I hope he rots there. I know my mom had some of her old friends on the force spread the reason why he's there, so hopefully the sick fuck gets what he deserves, even if he only got a ten-year sentence."

I worried about her reaction when my words came out more forcefully than I intended, but a flash of longing crossed over her face before she smiled. "Ainsley's lucky to have you," she said softly. "How is she doing?"

"She's doing okay. Our parents have her in therapy. She was the one Skylar first told, and she convinced her to report him."

Lexi's knee bounced hard and hit the table, making it jerk. She murmured an apology and tucked a strand of hair behind her ear, eyes darting around the dining room.

I frowned. Something about her reaction seemed too intense for just hearing the news about Ainsley's coach. But she had already been having a stressful morning, so maybe this news just pushed her over the edge. Noah seemed to recognize it, too.

"Hey," he said, reaching across the table and squeezing her shoulder. "Ainsley's going to be fine. Skylar, too. They've got good support networks, so it'll be okay."

Lexi gave him a quick, clearly fake smile and picked up her fork again. "You're right. Sorry, I was just worried about her."

"Don't be sorry for that, Lex," I said. "I'm sure she wouldn't mind hearing from you."

Lexi nodded. "I'll text her after we're done eating."

Conversation died down as we finished our food. Well, Noah and I finished eating; Lexi just pushed her food around on her plate. Noah took our trays to the conveyor belt once our plates were bare, and I walked with Lexi to the entrance of the hall.

"Are you okay?" I asked, keeping my voice pitched low as we waited for Noah.

"I'm fine," Lexi said.

"I don't just mean about the Ainsley stuff. I mean about earlier. You seemed... tense at practice, and I just wanted to make sure you didn't feel pressured..." I let my words die when a group of baseball players jostled by.

"Asher, I'm fine," she said, her blue eyes meeting mine, then darting away.

Noah interrupted us then, throwing his arms dramatically around Lexi and spinning her around. "Lexi, my heart, my joy, I nearly didn't recover from being separated from you."

A few students around us chuckled. Noah's antics were well known throughout the small campus. Lexi smacked him in the stomach once he put her down.

"Hey! What did we say about the spinning? And if you can't survive that, how are you going to survive going to class?"

Noah lifted the back of his hand to his forehead. "Don't speak of that travesty. I don't know how I'll survive it."

While my twin had always had the flair for the dramatics, I knew that statement was rooted in fact. We were all so serious about Lexi, and the only one who didn't know it was her.

Lexi rolled her eyes, but her attention kept darting around the room, and she bounced slightly on her feet. Almost unnoticeable, but I saw it. Our girl was still worried about something.

"You okay?" I asked again. "Noah didn't crush you, right?"

Lexi shook her head, giving Noah a teasing look. "No, but I definitely need another shower after that."

"Hey, I'm clean!" Noah protested.

"You're something." I rolled my eyes. "All right then. We'll see you after class?"

"My professor canceled today," Lexi said. "I think I'm just going to head back to the house and get some studying done." Her foot tapped, and I frowned, but she was already backing away.

I stared after her as she quickly walked away. She had claimed she just needed a shower, but she looked about ready to crawl out of her skin. Was it because of the news about Ainsley, about our friends-with-benefits arrangements, or was there something else going on with our girl that we didn't know about?

LEXI

The shower washed the tears away, the only visible evidence of my inner turmoil.

The hot water streamed over my tight muscles. Any normal day and the warmth would ease the tightness in my shoulders. Today, though, they remained rock solid under the almost punishing heat.

Most days, I thought I was healed. I had shoved everything deep down into a very sturdy box.

Most days, I lied to myself.

Most days, I didn't think about it. Didn't allow myself to. I kept those memories buried deep inside me, locked in that sturdy box, pushed far out of my mind. Every so often, though, the lid on that box cracked. And Noah and Asher had broken the seal earlier.

Not because of them. No, none of my guys knew what had happened to me back in high school. It was a shameful thing that didn't fit in the image of the strong female quarterback I had worked so hard to craft. Partly so I wouldn't feel broken. I couldn't be broken if I had taken our high school team to state, right? Couldn't be broken if I won Rookie of the Year as a freshman and Player of the Year for the last two years. Couldn't be broken if I was poised to take my team to championships, winning the title for the first time in Grandview University's history.

No. I couldn't be broken.

With those words repeating like a mantra in my mind, I took deep, shuddering breaths, letting the water wash away every stain from my soul. *If only it worked like that.* But still I took deep breaths until the air didn't hitch when I inhaled. Until my exhales were even and steady. Until the drops of water circling the drain took all the itchy, anxious tremors from my shoulders. Until I no longer felt like crawling out of my skin.

When the water started running cool, I lifted a hand to turn it off, proud that my hand didn't shake. I grabbed my towel off the hook, using an end of it to wipe off the mirror to make sure no evidence of my breakdown showed on my face. I looked a little flushed, but the steam that fogged the room could explain that. My blue eyes were slightly dull, but practice had been difficult. All things I could explain away easily. I was used to doing that, explaining away any physical signs of my trauma.

I glanced at the corner of the counter where I usually placed my clothes. The gleaming white countertop glistened at me.

"Fuck," I mumbled. I had been so out of it when I returned home that I hadn't grabbed clothes, too focused on washing away the brokenness that threatened to creep out from inside me.

I dried my hair quickly and wrapped the towel around my body. It wasn't a big deal, just a reminder of my mental breakdown. When we had moved into the house, the guys had insisted that I take the master bedroom with the attached bathroom, and I hadn't protested too much. I didn't mind sharing a bathroom, and my guys were relatively neat, but having my own space had been great. Especially after today, when I needed to break down in private after our conversation over our lunch date. *Nope, not a date.* It was just time spent between friends. Friends who were fucking. Well, not fucking yet. But still not a date.

I pushed the door open to my bedroom, still lost in my thoughts about how it was not a date and wondering if it was a date. Movement on my bed had me jumping and clutching my towel.

"Jamison, what the fuck?" I said, taking a dramatic breath. "You scared the shit out of me."

It was not unusual to find one of the guys in my room. As much as they tried, personal space was not a big thing for them. It usually didn't bother me much, but I shifted as I felt his eyes trace the exposed skin.

Jamison laughed from his position lying on my bed. He looked better than he had any right to be. "Jumpy much, Lex?"

I rolled my eyes at him. "Lot on my mind. Long practice."

Jamison hummed and waggled his eyebrows. "I thought your mind would be on something else long," he said as he grabbed something at his side and waved my bright blue vibrator in my direction. "Is this how you've been getting by after dates with momma's boys?"

I rolled my eyes at him before plucking the vibrator out of his hand and tossing it back in my bedside drawer. "Don't insult BOB. He does a fantastic job when a girl has needs."

Truthfully, I didn't use him often, as I usually had regular sex, but he'd been getting a bit of a workout the last few months. Besides, who better to know what I needed than me?

Jamison rolled so he was sitting on the side of my bed, inches away from where I was standing. A flush crept up my cheeks, betraying my body's reaction to his proximity. It wasn't that I hadn't thought all of my guys were hot; it was just that I had never allowed myself to think of them in that way.

Maybe I was still keyed up from earlier, because there was

nothing I wanted more in this moment than to push him back and have my way with him.

Jamison's eyes darkened, and he reached out and pulled me in closer. The towel gaped dangerously as he pulled me in between his legs.

"Care to try the real thing?"

There was a challenge in his eyes. He was taunting me. Did I dare reach out and take what he was offering?

I already knew I would. Jamison had always challenged me. Always pushed me. To be better, to live life more fully, to take risks both on and off the field. And now, he was laying down a challenge here, in my bedroom? I was more than ready to pick up what he was laying down.

Smirking, I dropped the towel and placed one knee on the bed and then the other, practically climbing into his lap.

"Impress me, Towers."

Jamison froze slightly, but there was no mistaking the heat in his eyes. He recovered quickly and swept his gaze down my body. It felt like a physical caress. Then his hands rose to settle on my hips.

"I can assure you, I'm more than capable of completing the play."

I laughed. "Did you just make a football pun?"

Some of the earlier tension drained away. Jamison could always do that, wind me up and relax me at the same time.

He grinned. "Oh, I've got more where that one came from."

Faster than I could react, he stood up, cradling me in his arms, then turned around, pressing me back into the bed. There was something decadent about a fully clothed guy pressed up against my naked body.

I arched up against him, and he couldn't hide the small grunt when I rubbed against him. A smile played at the corner of my lips, and his eyes narrowed at me.

"None of that now. I've been waiting a long time for this. I'm going to take my time."

I furrowed my brows. What did he mean, he'd been waiting a long time for this? Before I could assess his words more, his lips covered mine and all rational thought fled. Man, could he kiss.

Light and teasing, he coaxed my lips open before tangling our tongues together. His hands ran up and down my sides, teasing but never quite touching where I wanted him to. It wasn't until a low groan of frustration bubbled out of me that he broke the kiss and chuckled.

"Patience, Lex. We both know a good assist makes the touchdown."

I groaned again at his terrible pun, but it quickly turned into a gasp as he pressed a suckling kiss beneath my jaw. It was a sensitive spot for me that usually took guys a while to find. He didn't linger there long, though, pressing wet kisses down the column of my throat and between my breasts.

Finally, he cupped one of my breasts with a calloused hand. The roughness of his palm against the sensitive skin had my nipple puckering, and he groaned, lowering his head.

"Absolutely perfect," he breathed before lashing my nipple with his tongue.

Sparks of sensation lit up all over my body.

Unbidden, a flush spread across my chest. I knew what my body looked like. Ripped with the muscles necessary to be an excellent quarterback, it was far from an ideal woman's body. There was no softness anywhere, instead hard muscles layered over each other, creating the perfect athlete's body but maybe not the perfect woman's body. Some of my bed partners had commented on it—some favorably, some not—but no one had said anything about it with the reverence Jamison had in his tone.

Jamison moved from one breast to the other, alternating his attention until I was writhing on the bed.

"Enough," I finally panted.

He looked up and raised an eyebrow, a grin teasing his lips. "You want me to stop?"

I knew if I said yes, he would have immediately stopped, but I didn't want him to. I wanted him to move lower.

"No. But I could use that mouth somewhere else," I said, wiggling my eyebrows at him.

A wicked grin flashed across his face. "Oh? Are you talking about here?" He lowered his mouth to my ribcage, mouthing kisses across my skin.

"You're getting closer," I said, ignoring the goosebumps that puckered every inch of skin his mouth covered.

He scooted down the bed, wrapping his arms around my hips. Then he tugged me until I was splayed out across my bed with him on his knees in front of me. My breath hitched as I took him in. I tried to play it cool, but he gave me a devilish look, as if he knew how much he affected me. Cocky bastard

"How about here?" He pressed a kiss to my lower stomach.

"So close, just a bit lower."

My words cut off with a gasp as he finally lowered his head and gave a long lick right over my clit. Fuck, of course he was one of the guys who could find it right away. He traced circles over it with his tongue, drawing them tighter and tighter. My hips bucked, but he laid his forearm across them, pinning me down so I could only take what he gave me.

He abandoned my clit to drag his tongue down and thrust it into me. I let out a throaty moan, and he lifted his head. "Mmmm… I like that sound."

"Then keep doing that," I ordered playfully.

"Yes, ma'am," he teased, then dropped his head again.

Every stroke of his talented tongue drove me closer and closer to the edge. Pleasure coiled tightly in my center, ready to erupt. He backed off. I growled.

"N—"

He pushed two fingers inside of me, and I moaned. The stretch burned but quickly melted into searing warmth.

Using his mouth and his fingers now, he resumed his efforts at driving me off the edge. His fingers twisted inside of me, seeking that spot that had my hips rocketing off the bed. He focused his efforts there, driving me higher and higher as I gasped for air. Right as I teetered on the brink again, he withdrew. I popped up on my elbows, giving him a glare.

He laughed. "Patience, Lex. Your previous partners must have been lacking."

"Couldn't have been lacking if they made me come," I shot back.

"If they didn't worship you like this, then they were definitely lacking."

Worship? I mean, they had gone down on me, and I had returned the favor; but worship was a bit too far. It included a level of intimacy I had never shared with past partners. I wasn't about to tell Jamison that, though.

"I don't know. I'm beginning to think you're not up for the task," I challenged. I was not the only person who responded to a dare.

Sure enough, a devilish look flashed in Jamison's eyes, and he lowered his head. This time, he didn't stop. He worked me over with his tongue and fingers until I was thrashing on the bed. My hips arched into him, even as I tugged his hair to get more and get away from the overwhelming sensations.

He gripped my hip with one hand and, with the other, curled his fingers inside of me, brushing against my G-spot. He sucked my clit into his mouth and lightly grazed his teeth over it. The pinch of pain and pleasure sent me soaring over the cliff, and my whole body shook as my orgasm rocked through me. *Fuuuu-uccckkk!* He was too good at that. It had been ages since someone else made me come that hard.

He pushed me through it, tongue laving over my clit until I

whimpered. Grinning, he pressed wet kisses across my skin until he reached my jaw, giving that same sensitive spot a suckling kiss before he pushed off me.

"Let me go get a condom."

"Bottom drawer," I said breathlessly, throwing one arm in the direction of the nightstand.

A look I couldn't identify flashed across his face, but he reached over me to grab one out of the box. Taking it from him, I tore it open with my teeth and arched my eyebrow at him.

"Are you forgetting something?"

He looked at me, brow furrowed.

I tugged on his shirt. "You're still clothed."

I laughed as he pushed off the bed and practically tore his clothes off. "Are you laughing at me, Lex?" He grinned. "That's not very nice, especially after I gave you an earth-shattering orgasm."

"Earth-shattering?" I arched an eyebrow. "That's a high estimation of your abilities."

"What can I say? My coaches have always had me in the starting lineup."

I wrapped my hand around his dick, giving it a firm stroke with my hand to shut him up. His grin turned into a gasp, and he braced himself on his arms. A fine tremble shook his muscles as I explored. As far as dicks went, he had a good one, objectively speaking. It was long with a slight curve that I knew was going to feel amazing. Suddenly not interested in teasing him anymore, I quickly rolled the condom on.

"All right, player, show me your game."

His lips quirked up at the challenge, and he notched the tip of his dick at my entrance. A small shudder racked through me as he began pushing into me. My walls were still over-sensitized from my previous orgasm, and I groaned at the stretch.

"That's why worshiping is required," Jamison said breathlessly.

"Shut up." I couldn't seem to come up with a better comeback; then he pushed all the way into me. I moaned.

"Insults are a flag on the play," he joked, and I groaned at the awful pun.

I opened my mouth, a retort on my lips, when he shifted his hips, dragging out of me and slamming back into me with a force that had me gasping. He began a series of slow, steady thrusts that had me rocking up on the bed.

"Fuck," I breathed as he hit the exact right spot.

"Isn't that what we're doing?" Jamison joked breathlessly.

I tightened my muscles around him, and it was his turn to swear.

I laughed breathlessly, but his next thrust had me groaning again. How did he hit every button for me with this being our first time? It was like he had spent years exploring every sensitive spot that had me gasping for more. Fuck, was this how it was going to be with all of them?

All conscious thought fled from my mind as, on his next thrust, Jamison ground his hips against mine, trapping my clit in between our bodies. Stars flashed across my vision, and I came with a shout, body shaking as I rode the line of too much sensation. It was almost painful.

With a groan and a whisper of my name on his lips, he buried his face in my neck and came. The extra warmth sent me into another mini-orgasm, and I clenched down on him. He groaned out another laugh.

"You've got to stop doing that, or I'm going to be ready to go again."

"And that's a bad thing, how?" I asked, peeking at the clock on my nightstand. "We have another few hours before everyone gets home."

"I like the way you think." Jamison rolled his hips, and I gasped out a laugh. There were definitely some perks to this whole friends-with-benefits thing.

LEXI

I was in an excellent mood. Good sex did that to you. And I felt great, despite being slightly sore this morning.

Even though we were two miles into our run, I was barely breathing heavily, and my arms pumped at my sides in a steady rhythm. Next to me, Lewis's footfalls echoed in pace with my own as we made a loop around campus. The rest of the guys had gone running earlier, but Lewis and I shared an early morning sociology class, so we usually ran after it on the days before game day.

I took a deep breath as we jogged around the library. Grandview was a gorgeous campus. The charming brick buildings had been a big draw when we had toured campuses during our junior year in high school. Nestled in the mountains, the brick only accentuated the classic style of the campus and stood out against the green grass and the brilliant carpets of snow that would come later this winter. Several of the buildings still had traditional fireplaces, and smoke pumped from the chimneys. The crisp fall air had a bitter edge as it went into my lungs, but it felt great on my heated skin.

Yep, the campus was beautiful, but the full-ride athletic scholarships that Grandview had offered Lewis, Jamison, and me had sealed the deal.

Beside me, Lewis let out a soft grunt as the terrain changed and we began running up one of the several hills on campus. Lewis had always been a steadying presence to Jamison's and my antics. Like a quiet anchor in the relentless storm that was life. He could have as much tact as a bull in a china shop, though.

"Are you really okay with this friends-with-benefits thing?" he asked as the terrain leveled out and we could breathe a little easier again.

A smile played on my lips. Case in point.

I was silent for a moment. I was okay with it. I mean, I was still worried it would affect our playing or our friendships, but it seemed like it might work. And the sex had been amazing. I felt so relaxed this morning. But this was going to be the true test: everyone else's reaction to knowing I slept with one of them. The guys had assured me they were okay with it, but saying it and believing it were two different things. But there was no point in beating around the bush. Lewis valued honesty and straight shooting, and I did as well.

"Well, I had sex with Jamison last night. So yes, I'm okay with it."

Lewis tripped.

Startled, I paused and looked over at him. He recovered quickly and ran past me. Brow furrowed, I quickened my pace to catch up. When I matched his pace again, I glanced over. His jaw was tight, and he looked... pissed?

"What's that face for? Are you angry?"

He jerked his head from side to side. "No."

I bumped his arm with my shoulder. "You're doing a stellar job of convincing me. I thought we didn't lie to each other."

Lewis gave me a look like he knew I also kept secrets, and I dipped my head in acknowledgement but waited for him to answer me.

"I'm not angry. I was just taken off guard. I didn't expect you to have already slept with him."

"Careful there," I said, anger rising in me. "That sounds an awful lot like slut-shaming. And you were the one who asked me the question first."

"That's not... I didn't mean it like that. You know that. I just... I'm just processing, but it's fine."

"Well, what are you processing?" I asked, anger lacing my tone. I knew he hadn't meant it to slut-shame, but my hackles were up. If the other guys on the team slept around, they were players, but if I did it, I was a slut. The double standard always drove me mad.

"There's nothing to process. I'm not mad. I just need time to digest."

"Time to digest that I slept with Jamison? I thought that was the agreement? That I sleep with all of you."

"Pixie, I don't want to argue with you about this."

"We're not arguing. We're talking about it. If we can't talk about it, I'll call this whole thing off. We talk about everything."

"Everything?" He glanced at me out of the corner of his eye. "Then how are you actually feeling about all of this? Because you were playing differently yesterday."

My lips thinned, and I shrugged. He wasn't wrong, but some days I hated how Lewis could read me so well. "I don't know. The sex was great, but I don't want this to affect our friendships or the team."

"It won't," he said.

I gave him a look like, *what's all this, then?*

He rolled his eyes. "It won't. We did talk about it after Jamison blurted it out. Everyone's relationships will go at a different pace and will stay private."

"They're not relationships," I reminded him. "They're just physical."

He gave me a look I couldn't quite decipher. "Yes... physical relationships." His face softened. "I am really fine with it, though. Promise I'll tell you if that changes."

Something in me warmed at his words. My biggest fear in all of this was losing them.

"So not just adequate sex, then?" He smirked.

I rolled my eyes. "Fine, it wasn't just adequate. But don't you dare tell Jamison I said that. I'll never hear the end of it."

"I won't," he said. He smiled, but his eyes were still tight. "I'll race you home." He took off running.

I took off after him, but my heart wasn't in it. My mind was wandering and overthinking Lewis's words. Could this really work, or should I call it off before it got any messier and ruined our chance at the championships?

*　*　*

THE NEXT DAY, my worries seemed to hold more weight to them. This was the second-round game of the playoffs and would determine who made it into the quarterfinals. It was supposed to be an easy win over Western, but from the moment we hit the field, we struggled.

Jamison and I managed some great plays, but then he uncharacteristically dropped the ball on one play, and Crawford just couldn't seem to get it together.

The worst part? It didn't seem like the guys on the team cared. There was joking on the bench and in the locker room at halftime, despite my efforts to rally them to focus. I mean, sure, we were ahead by ten points, but still, this wasn't something to take lightly. Mac kept barking at everyone, but nothing he said seemed to work. Their heads just weren't in it, and I was worried that I was distracting four of them with this new relationship.

I was standing on the sidelines next to Derek, watching our defense out on the field.

"You're practically growling," he pointed out, and he wasn't wrong.

"I don't understand. We played better at practice than we are tonight."

"I think you might be just a little hard on yourself," he suggested gently.

I wrinkled my nose at him, and he laughed. Derek had always been a bit lanky, but somewhere in the last three years, that lankiness had turned into lean muscle. He wouldn't ever be as built as the twins or Lewis, but he had clearly been working out. His thick-rimmed glasses reminded me of Superman's disguise, but they complimented his gray eyes and strong jaw. He was like a nerdy dream.

He cleared his throat, and my cheeks burned. I couldn't believe I'd been caught staring. This was exactly what I was worried about, getting distracted from the game over one of them.

I looked back out onto the field. "They aren't taking this seriously. They're distracted. We can't afford to mess this up." If we lost this game, we would be out of the running for the championships.

"They won't. It'll be fine. We're up by ten points. What else is going on in your head?"

Usually Derek was an excellent listener, always willing to lend an ear, but now I hesitated to unload on him. He was part of the reason why I was so tense, so I just stayed silent.

As we watched, the other team scored, then made the extra point. As the offense team prepared to take the field, I noticed Derek talking quietly to a few of the other players, checking in with them while the receiving team took the field. He was always doing that, and the guys appreciated it. Maybe he could talk some sense into them when Mac and I couldn't.

Snapping my helmet into place, I jogged out onto the field on the thirty-yard line. It wasn't a great starting point, as Western's team had been fired up from their touchdown and blocked our receiving team from getting very far. The crowd roared, and a rush of adrenaline flooded through my veins. It didn't matter how many times we took the field at a home game, the crowd was always there to cheer us on. I joined the huddle with everyone else.

"All right, let's start with play 37," I said.

Play 37 meant I would hand the ball off to Crawford to run through a hole the offense line would create for him. Next to me, Crawford nodded, his helmet bobbing, and I broke up the huddle.

"Ready, set!" I yelled.

Springer, our center, snapped the ball back into my hands. I pivoted and handed it off to Crawford, who barely made it one yard before one of Western's players tackled him. I groaned under my breath but held it together as the ref blew the whistle and we huddled back up. It was only the second down. It was fine.

The next play we tried was another rushing play. This time Jennings made it two yards before Western's defense took him out. What the fuck was going on? Western's defense usually wasn't that good. A quick glance to the sidelines told me Mac was fuming. We needed to get this together.

Third down and the play I called was an easy passing play to Jamison. Except it took him a half second longer to get to position, and with Western's defense putting pressure on my pocket, forcing me to get rid of the ball, one of the Western players batted my shaky pass out of the air. Jamison dove for it at the same time as the Western player, and I was relieved when he popped up with it in his hands. An interception at the thirty-five-yard line could have cost us the game.

"You okay?" I asked him when he joined the huddle.

"I'm fine," he said shortly. I knew he would be pissed at himself for missing the position marker. I was pissed at myself for the shaky pass, but I was also frustrated with the team. We were better than this.

"Look, it's fourth down," I barked at everyone in the huddle. "We have got to get our heads in the game here."

I knew Mac would want us to go with a safe play, but looking around the group, I wasn't so sure. Despite that shaky pass, Jamison and I were usually very in sync with each other. The great sex aside the other day, nothing else had changed. I needed to rely on that synchronicity right now.

"Let's run play 23 now," I said.

That was the play where I pretended to throw the ball to Crawford but would actually throw it to Jamison deep behind their defense line. It was a bit of a risky play but one that Jamison and I had practiced a thousand times before. His dark brown eyes met mine, and he nodded. I refused to let myself get distracted when they lingered.

I shoved everything aside as I continued, "Let's focus now. A few good plays, and we'll be kicking their ass back to Western."

"Let's do this!" Calloway, one of the offense linemen, cheered. He was like this big, adorable teddy bear who could crush you with his bare hands, but his cheerful mood helped keep some of the rowdier guys focused.

We broke into our positions, and I counted down to the play. The ref blew the whistle and the center snapped the ball into my hands. Crawford darted forward, running down the line about five yards from me, while Jamison sprinted down the field. Grunts and the slamming of bodies echoed from in front of me as my offense line, including Lewis, gave me precious seconds to find Jamison just as he cut away from the defender guarding him.

I tossed a perfect spiral right into his arms, and he darted down the field. He only made it about five yards before he was tackled. I winced as he hit the turf, but he popped back up quickly. Injuries were a part of the game, but I always held my breath when one of us went down.

Even though he only made it five yards, the pass had been at least twenty yards, and the crowd was on their feet as we drove the ball past the fifty-yard line. A few plays later, and Crawford dove through the defense line to get the ball into the end zone. It had been dicey, but we had done it!

When I jogged off the field, Derek was waiting. "See." He smiled. "Nothing to worry about."

"You can't tell me that went well. Or is even how we normally play," I shot back at him.

We had made way too many mistakes, and from Mac's set jaw, he had noticed as well. His jaw only got tighter as he watched Western score again, bringing the score back into a three-point range with only two minutes left on the clock.

"Go out there and score, but more importantly, do not screw around. You were on fire this week at practice, but clearly something has happened," he barked at us before we took the field again.

I shifted on my feet and tried not to look at Jamison and Lewis. Something *had* happened since practice, and that was, I slept with one of my best friends and fellow teammates. Was that why we were struggling so much? Logically, I knew it wasn't. There were always other factors at play. But there was a small voice inside of me that was whispering, *See, I knew this would be a bad idea.* I shoved that voice aside as Mac continued.

"Just get out there and hold on to the ball and run out the clock. Don't go for the risky plays here. I'm looking at you, Simmons."

I winced internally as I gave Mac a nod. He definitely hadn't approved of my decision to throw that Hail Mary pass to Jamison earlier, but, hey, we had scored.

The guys seemed to realize this was serious now. Even Crawford didn't have a quip, so we took the field. I called out our first play, a rushing play that gained us a few yards. The second play, I snapped out a short pass to Crawford, who thankfully caught it this time and was able to score a first down before being tackled. We steadily crawled across the field as the clock ran out. When the refs called the game, we were still thirty yards from the end zone, but we'd kept the ball in our possession.

The crowd went wild. For them, a win was a win. Around me, the guys celebrated. I went through the motions, but my heart wasn't in it. That was too close. We had made too many mistakes. Silly, juvenile mistakes that we were past making. I knew it wasn't all my fault. Or even my guys' fault, either. Lewis, Jamison, Noah, and Asher had played a good game. But we had still been making more mistakes than normal.

Once the fanfare died down, and Mac chewed us out in the locker room, we were dismissed to the showers.

"Come on, Simmons," Calloway called as I exited the locker room, "We're headed down to Pinscer Street to celebrate."

Pinscer Street was the name of the local bar scene. I usually went out with the team after we won a game to celebrate, but tonight, my heart just wasn't in it.

"I'm going to pass tonight," I said as the other guys, including Noah and Asher, gathered around. "We've got that game against Missou next week, and I don't want to throw off my sleep schedule. We're in the quarterfinals now. Time to get serious."

Calloway and the others groaned but headed out towards the parking lot. My guys stayed behind, gathered around me.

"Are you sure about not going out tonight?" Jamison asked.

"We even convinced Derek to go." Bars weren't really Derek's scene, but he often joined us after games.

"I'm sure." I gave a half-hearted smile. "I think I'm just going to head home. You guys should go out, though."

They gave each other dubious looks, and I knew I hadn't been convincing at all. All I wanted to do was go home and lie in bed and run through the game in my head. I usually did that, but this time I wanted to make sure that our friends-with-benefits arrangement wasn't messing with my head. I had enjoyed sex with Jamison; but no sex—amazing or orgasmic—was worth costing us the championships.

"If you're not going to go, then I'd rather go home with you," Derek said, pushing his glasses farther up on his nose.

"No, you should go," I protested lightly. "Don't change your plans because of me."

"Lexi girl," Noah said, throwing his arm over my shoulder. "When are you going to realize that we would change every plan for you?"

It wasn't the first time Noah or one of the other guys had said something like that to me, but it was the first time I believed they might actually be serious. Part of me preened at the feeling of being important to them, but the dark voice inside me whispered that I was going to cut them with my broken edges. And they were too perfect to be with a broken girl like me.

LEXI

"*A*lexa Simmons, are you avoiding me?"

I shielded my eyes against the bright sunlight. The glaring sun was trying its best to chase away the chill of the fall air, but it was failing. I pulled my coat closer around me as I searched for Inez amongst the crowd of students.

She was standing by the low brick wall that separated the psychology building from the large grassy courtyard that sprawled between the different department buildings. Arms folded, tapping the toe of a heeled boot, Inez was dressed to perfection, like she usually was. Despite the chill, she wore a gray miniskirt that fell midway down her toned thighs and a black sweater that hung artfully off one olive-skinned shoulder. She was drop-dead gorgeous, as one expected a cheerleader to be, but she was also wicked strong, and I knew her exercise regimen could rival my own.

Inez had forcefully adopted me my first week of school. The guys and I had been sitting with Noah and Asher and a few others on the team at Ramsey's when Inez had marched her way over and hip checked Jamison until he scooted down the bench. She had plopped her tray down and announced that there was too much testosterone at the table and that she was here to save me from it. I had humored her at first, but our friendship had blossomed quickly. She was the person who had first introduced me to Chocolate Chasing, our favorite coffee shop, and she had been a solid rock for me over the last three years.

"How am I avoiding you if we were texting last night?" I rolled my eyes at her as I walked over.

"You skipped out on our lunch date?" she said indignantly.

I sighed and threw my arm over her shoulder, guiding her towards Chocolate Chasings. Meena and Inez had started dating our sophomore year, but Inez had always said I was her ride-or-die bitch, and we had a standing lunch date on Friday afternoons that I totally skipped out on this week with a weak excuse. Inez had apparently been willing to give me the weekend, but I was answering for it now.

"I was busy. I told you that," I muttered.

"Busy being overwhelmed and wallowing after the game, I know. That's why I graciously gave you the weekend."

"Thank you, my kind goddess," I teased her. "Whatever would I do without your generosity?"

Inez sniffed. "Don't you forget it."

"I would never." I held the door open for her.

The sweet smell of chocolate mixed with the tangy aroma of coffee as we stepped into Chocolate Chasings. Meena wasn't working today, but Carson and Maya called greetings from behind the counter.

We ordered our drinks and found our usual table in the corner.

Inez barely let me sit down. "So have you had sex with all of them yet?"

"No. Jesus!" I said. "It's only been like three days?"

"So you haven't had any sex?"

I take a sip of my hot chocolate and avoid her eyes. "I didn't say that."

"You better spill now," Inez threatened. "Or I'll dump your hot chocolate in the trash."

"First, have you considered a career in the FBI, Ms. Interrogator? Second, you know better than to threaten my hot chocolate." I cradled the cup close to my chest. "My precious," I hissed at her.

"Fine. But start talking!"

"Fine. It was Jamison."

"Okay, and? Details, woman! Is he as good as I hear from the girls on the team?"

Something panged in my gut at the thought of him with someone else, but I shoved that feeling away. I wanted to lie to her, but I knew better. Inez could sniff out a lie better than anyone I know.

"Better," I reluctantly admitted.

"Yes, girl," Inez crowed.

"Geez, keep your voice down. I don't need everyone hearing. We agreed this was going to be a secret."

"Did they agree, or did you tell them that it was going to be a secret," Inez pushed.

I shot her a glare. "You know why we are keeping it a secret. I get enough crap as it is. The team has to come first. We can't compromise that. Who knows what the school would say if they found out?"

I didn't voice it, but the threat was clear. If the administration found out, they might force Mac to bench me from the team. I shoved down the churning in my gut at even the thought of it. I had been threatened with the bench before, and I had kept quiet. Football was everything to me. It was what gave me focus and a reason to live after some of my darkest days. If it were taken away from me, I'm not sure I would survive it.

"You've given your whole career here to the football team and carrying Grandview to the best record they've ever had. If they're dumb enough to jeopardize that over a bit of sex, then they don't deserve the championship."

I could see what Inez was saying, but my love for football was the one thing she never truly understood about me. Probably because I had never given her the full story of how the game had saved me. But I had never given anyone that story. I would take that story to the grave.

"I'm not risking it. Besides, after our performance at the game this weekend, I'm rethinking if the sex is really worth it."

"You hush your mouth." Inez sat up straight in her seat. "You're not seriously thinking of calling this off? It's barely even started."

I groaned and rubbed a hand over my face. "I know, but I don't know. I didn't think it was going to be this complicated."

"What about it is complicated?" Inez asked.

I opened my mouth to answer her and shut it. Was it really complicated? I mean, the basis was simple. Whenever I wanted sex, I just went to one of them. That sounded like a one-sided agreement, but the guys had agreed to it, so they got something out of it too. Right? Well, they just got me, so maybe that wasn't much of a deal.

"It feels one-sided," I finally admitted to Inez. "Like I get them, but they only get me? They even agreed that I could date outside of the group, but they said they were only sleeping with me. Like in what world would any guy agree to that?"

"Those boys would do anything for you," Inez said. "The only one who can't see that is you."

I rolled my eyes. "Come on, be serious."

"I am serious. But since you don't believe me, I'll play along. They get you. Sex is always better when there is love between the two partners."

"Woah." I sat back in my seat, eyes wide. "No one said anything about love." I loved the guys like friends, but that was it. There was no way they loved me as any more than a sister. Well... not a sister, but a best friend.

She rolled her eyes. "I swear you're like a teenage boy. Fine. Not love, then. How about familiarity, trust, affection? Call it whatever you want, but was the sex better with Jamison than it was with Brandon?"

I hesitated, and she pinned me with her dark brown eyes. I huffed. "Fine, yes, it was better."

"See, my point is proven."

"And what was that point exactly?" I was rewarded with a long-suffering sigh, and I took a sip of my hot chocolate to hide my grin.

"That sex is better when there is familiarity or trust or love between the partners, and you have all of that with your guys. They've told you they're okay with it. So just enjoy the sex until you don't enjoy it anymore. But I don't think that'll happen."

"But what if it does?" I whisper, feeling strangely vulnerable.

Losing football would be nothing compared to losing the guys. I mean, I knew I was going to lose them at the end of senior year, but that was just to life and different circumstances, not because of something I did. What if this all blew up in our faces?

Inez's face softened. "You won't."

I shot her a look that said *how do you know* in our secret look language.

She smiled. "Do you trust me?"

"Yes."

"Then trust me when I tell you that you won't lose the guys over this. Just relax and enjoy it. You all are best friends. You have rock-solid friendships. Focus on enjoying this little extra layer added on top." She tapped her finger against her chin. "Well, maybe it's not a little layer. It might be a big, long layer." She waggled her eyebrows at me, and we both burst into giggles.

"You're too much," I told her.

"But I'm always right," she shot back.

We'd see. But she was right about one thing. The guys and I were already best friends. We had that foundation. Surely adding this friends-with-benefits situationship wouldn't rock that friendship. Right?

LEWIS

I let out a breath at the sight in front of me. The guys and I had been worried about Pixie for the past few days. She was such a perfectionist, and we knew the performance from the game on Saturday night had been killing her. That was one of the reasons we'd skipped going out with the team afterwards. Well, that and going down to Pinscer Street to bar hop lost its appeal without her.

God, we were all screwed.

Completely and totally in love with a woman who thought herself incapable of being loved.

I leaned my hip against the wall and folded my arms, watching the scene in front of me and letting the tension bleed out of my muscles. Pixie and Derek were cooking one of our favorite one-pot pasta meals. Noah and Jamison sat at the bar stools across the island from them, slathering way too much garlic butter on thick loaves of french bread Derek had picked up from the store. Although their focus was less on the task in front of them and more on the captivating woman swaying in front of the stove as she stirred the pot. Instead of the familiar muscle tension, her shoulders were relaxed, and she laughed at something Derek said. Whatever had happened today to make her so relaxed, I didn't know, but I was grateful for it.

"She talked to Inez yesterday," Asher murmured from behind me.

I looked over my shoulder and arched an eyebrow at him.

"Inez told me. Not what she said," he said quickly. "Just that she talked to her."

I smirked. Inez was straight-up dynamite and fiercely protective of Lexi. There was no chance in hell she was going to spill what they talked about.

"Good," I grunted, turning back to the kitchen.

"Are you two going to lurk in the shadows or pitch in to help?" my Pixie called from the kitchen.

"Maybe they like the shadows," Noah teased. "They've succumbed to the dark side."

"I'll show you the dark side." Asher lunged at Noah playfully. Noah squeaked and threw his hands up, flinging butter onto Asher's face.

"All right," Derek chided, reaching across the island and sliding the bread and butter towards him. "Let's not add any casualties to this dinner. Jamison, are you done?"

Jamison nodded and slid his load closer to Derek. With quick, surgical efficiency, Derek wrapped both loaves in foil. He placed both hands on Lexi's hips and moved her over so he could slide the bread into the oven. Lexi's hair was thrown up in a messy bun on her head, and he moved a strand behind her ear after he closed the oven door. A faint dusting of red grazed her cheeks, and Derek smiled softly before turning away from her. She watched him go until she saw me watching her. Lexi stuck her tongue out at me, and I laughed.

"Careful there. I might take that as a challenge," I teased.

"Take what as a challenge?" Noah popped his head up from where he and Asher were wrestling on the floor.

"Nothing," Lexi said primly.

"Aww, come on, Lexi. Sharing is caring." Jamison smirked at her.

She rolled her eyes and turned back to stirring the sauce.

Jamison lost his smirk when she turned back around, and it was replaced with a soft look. One I recognized all too well. God, we were such fools for her. Even though I had a brief moment of wanting to pummel him when I first learned he had slept with Lexi, it was replaced with a quiet jealousy that he got to share that with her, and I didn't. We had all been moving slowly with Lexi after our conversation last week, letting her make the first move. But Jamison had always been a pusher. I had no doubt that he pushed, but I also knew he would never do anything to hurt her. And that was why I hadn't pummeled him. Or any of them. We all placed Lexi first. And that was why this was going to work.

"Come on." I clapped a hand on Jamison's shoulder. "Let's set the table."

Asher and Noah abandoned their wrestling on the floor to help us. I was glad I had insisted that we buy this large eight-person table when we had moved into this house. I was a nurturer at heart. Yeah, I was tough on the field, but I enjoyed taking care of people, specifically my Pixie and the guys. A sense of pride filled me when I took care of people.

The timer beeped, and Asher and Noah headed into the kitchen. Derek pulled the bread out of the oven and carried it to the table. Asher snaked a hand around Lexi's waist and pulled her away from the stove, ignoring her protests. She rolled her eyes as he picked up the pot she was stirring on the stove and carried it to the table.

"I can carry it, you know," Lexi complained.

"We know you can." Noah came up next to her, holding the salad bowl in his hands. He leaned over and smacked a kiss on her cheek. "But why would we let you?"

Lexi's cheeks heated again, and I hid a smirk. She was

adorable when she blushed. Adorable wasn't a word most people would use to describe Lexi. She was lean and muscular, with a harsh jawline and high cheekbones. But when she blushed, it softened all her features, and she became adorable.

It wasn't clear if his words or his stolen kiss had left Lexi speechless, but she took a seat at the table without any more protesting. Asher stole her plate and scooped a healthy amount of pasta onto her plate before passing it to Noah, who dumped salad onto it and then passed it to Derek, who placed two slices of bread on it before passing it to me. I set it back in front of her, and she shook her head with a small smile on her face.

"Another thing you won't let me do?"

"Another thing we want to do for you," I corrected softly. It wasn't like we didn't take care of each other, but with this new agreement in place, we were slowly easing Lexi into the idea of what it would be like to be ours.

To avoid answering me, she stuffed a bite of pasta in her mouth, letting out a soft hum of approval. Next to her, Asher shifted at her soft sound of pleasure. My own dick hardened as she took a bite out of the bread and let out a groan.

"Hey, let up on the sex noises," Jamison teased from across the table. "Some of us are trying to eat over here."

Lexi flipped him off, and I huffed out a laugh.

For a few minutes, the only sounds were the clinking of forks against plates as we shoveled food into our mouths. This one-pot pasta dish was a favorite of ours. It was a pound of ground turkey, a block of soft cheese, a jar of tomato sauce, and a family-sized packet of tortellini pasta with Italian seasoning. It was the perfect meal when paired with the garlic bread and salad.

Mac didn't micromanage our meals like some coaches did, but he did make us sit down with a nutritionist twice a semester to go over meal plans and different tips and tricks to make sure we were fueling our bodies the way our sport demanded.

"How's accounting going?" Lexi asked Noah.

Noah, Jamison, and Asher were all business majors. I was pursuing criminal justice, and Lexi and Derek were the smarty-pants of the group.

Noah groaned dramatically, and we all laughed. "Why are numbers so confusing?"

"Dude, if those numbers are confusing, you're doing it wrong," Jamison teased. "It's all balance sheets and P&L statements."

"Then I'm definitely doing it wrong, because it's all Russian to me," Noah complained.

"You have Professor Brown, right? I think I have my notes from him from a few semesters ago if you want," Jamison offered.

"Dude, you would be a lifesaver. I got a 70 on the last test. I need to ace the next one."

"We can do group study nights," Lexi offered. "Here at the house. We could invite a few guys on the team like we used to."

I exchanged a look with Asher. He and I had shut down group study night with the team when Crawford kept running his mouth about Lexi.

"Maybe," Asher offered. "Or we could keep it with just us for now?"

"So, like a normal evening," Lexi said, a teasing glint in her eyes.

"You can't blame us for wanting more time with you, Pixie," I said. "Especially with this being our senior year."

Lexi frowned, and her blue eyes lost their sparkle. "Don't remind me," she muttered while taking another bite.

"You can't get rid of us that easily," Derek said softly.

I swear this man had a radar system solely tuned to Lexi's emotions, but I appreciated it. Pixie needed more people in her corner. Lexi thought Derek was all quiet and shy. Quiet, maybe, but I'd also seen him verbally eviscerate anyone who dared to make fun of Lexi behind her back. No, not quiet and shy... Quiet and deadly was more like it.

"Exactly, Lexi-girl," Noah said. "You're stuck with us for life."

A flash of what looked like longing flew over Lexi's face before she grinned. "It's a nice dream, guys, but we all have to get on with life after school. College is a four-year vacation from real life."

"I don't know if I would call it a vacation," Noah grumbled.

"You and Derek are going back for another four years of it, anyways," Asher pointed out. "So just get into schools close to each other, and the rest of us will find jobs somewhere in the middle."

"Sure, I'll get right on that," Lexi said sarcastically.

I caught Asher's eye and shook my head slightly. Lexi might be unaware that was the plan, but I knew we were all making moves to ensure it was. But we didn't want to spook Lexi before she realized she was the center of our world. I knew Derek had applied to med schools close to where Lexi had applied for graduate school. He was so smart, he could probably get in anywhere, but we had decided our junior year that we were going to stay together.

"All your applications are submitted, right?" Jamison asked Lexi.

"Yep. Last one was a few weeks ago to Manchester. They've got a PsyD program that sounds pretty promising. Can you pass the bread?"

While Asher was getting her another piece of bread, I looked at Derek, arching an eyebrow at him. Had he applied to that one?

He nodded with a small smile. And I rolled my eyes at his amusement. I was a worrier, sue me. Was it so wrong to want my family to all stay together? Even though I had taken a bit longer to warm up to the idea of sharing Lexi, these guys were my family, and talking through it with Derek and learning more about how his family worked helped ease my concerns. Now I got to have the best of both worlds: the men I called brothers and the woman I loved. Now to just get her on the same page.

"Oooo! We should do a movie night!" Noah said excitedly. "It's been ages since we've done one of those."

"A movie night would be fun," Derek said. "I've got a few articles to annotate, but I can do that during the movie."

"Are you sure?" Lexi said, "I know your semester is insane."

"I'm sure." Derek smiled warmly at her.

Jamison pushed back from the table. "I'll get started on cleanup. You sit there and look pretty," he directed at Lexi.

"You're an idiot." She shook her head at him.

"But I'm your idiot," he called over his shoulder.

She rolled her eyes, but there was a small smile playing on her lips. I grinned. She might grumble, but I had an inkling that her feelings were just as strong for us as ours were for her. We just had to show her it was safe to show them.

"I'll help him." I rose to my feet. "You go pick out a movie when you're done."

Lexi opened her mouth to protest, but Noah rose from his seat, cutting her off. "Come on, come on, come on," he chanted like a five-year-old boy.

Lexi shook her head at him, but there was a grin on her face.

"Okay, okay," she said, stuffing the last bite of bread in her mouth and rising from her seat. There was a small smudge of sauce at the corner of her mouth.

"Hold on," I said softly. I lifted my hand and wiped off the small smudge of sauce at the corner of her mouth.

That adorable blush was back instantly, and she shyly lifted her eyes to mine.

"All good," I smiled.

"Thanks," she murmured.

"Any time, Pixie. Now go pick a movie before Noah puts on *The Notebook* again."

"Hey!" Noah protested from behind me. "That was Asher's pick last time."

Lexi sidestepped me, eyes averted, although the blush still danced on her cheeks. I gathered the serving dishes up from the table and moved into the kitchen. Jamison and I worked together quickly to scoop the leftovers into our meal prep containers and rinse off the dishes. We worked seamlessly together, and we finished quickly.

Jamison and I had actually been friends before meeting Lexi. He could be a little shit, but he was one of the best guys I knew. Which is why the flash of jealousy I felt when Lexi admitted they'd slept together had surprised me at first. But after I had a second to think about it, I was fine with it.

Jamison and I finished up in the kitchen, and I trailed him into the living room. He pulled Lexi down between him and Noah, and I caught Lexi watching me carefully. I had clearly spooked her a little with my reaction, and I wanted to kick myself over it. I gave her a small smile and inclined my head towards the TV, where the movie was playing. She narrowed her eyes at me before relaxing back into the couch, and I chuckled softly. Noah threw his arm around her on the back of the couch, and Jamison placed a hand on her leg.

This was going to work. The guys and I had talked after this weekend about making sure we stayed focused during the games, then spread that word to the other guys on the team. It wasn't that I didn't care about winning the championships. It would be a great way to go out for our senior season. But what I cared about more was winning my Pixie's heart.

LEXI

hoosh

The ball sliced through the air. It spiraled perfectly, just like an arrow, and landed in Jamison's arms. He dodged a Missou player, his feet practically dancing across the turf. Then he spun around and sprinted for the end zone.

I held my breath as I waited for him to cross over the end zone.

Ten yards.

Five yards.

One yard.

TOUCHDOWN!

I whooped and hollered along with the guys and high-fived Finn.

"Great throw, Cap!" Finn cheered.

"Jamison is the one who made the play," I said, giving Jamison a thumbs up as we jogged back towards the sideline. We were three quarters into our quarterfinal match against Missou College, and Jamison had just scored us another touchdown, putting us twenty-one points ahead of the other team.

We had run onto the field at the start of the game like we

were on fire. The change in the team from last week's game to this week's game was incredible. Everyone was buckled down and seriously focused, and it showed.

"Simmons, Towers, nice job," Mac barked as we ran past. "Get some water."

"Thanks, Mac," I said, heading to the water cooler.

I waved at Inez down at the end zone, and she shook her pompom at me. We needed to catch up soon. All we had been able to do for the last few days was text. Strong arms picked me up from behind and swung me around.

"That pass was a thing of beauty!" Jamison said excitedly.

"So was that sprint towards the end zone!"

"Stop being modest, Lex. We're up by three touchdowns. Have your moment."

"You know I won't do that till the clock runs out," I rolled my eyes and reminded him.

"I know. You need to lighten up, though. We're on fire today."

"He's right," Lewis said, handing me my water bottle. He didn't move until I lifted the bottle to take a drink, and I tried not to groan at his mother-hen tendencies.

We found a spot on the bench, returning the fist bumps and high fives as the special team came off the field after making the kick for the extra point. Jamison swatted Noah on the ass as the defense team took the field.

One of our support staff came by handing out towels, and I took one, yanking my helmet off and wiping the sweat off my forehead. Missou was about three hours south of Grandview, and the temperature difference was noticeable even in the fall.

"How are you all feeling?" Derek asked as he walked up. "Drinking enough water?" he asked, looking at me.

I pinched my lips together. "Yes, Dad."

Geez, a girl goes light-headed one time at a game and never hears the end of it. A few years ago, I had been so focused on the events on the field that I had forgotten to drink water and had nearly passed out. Now Lewis followed me around like a shadow with my water bottle during our breaks, and Derek had joined in his overprotective tendencies when he joined the athletic training team this year.

Derek's eyes darkened at the dad reference, but I refused to let the heat in his gaze affect me. Or, at least, that was what I told myself. Did someone have a daddy kink?

Nope, I was not going there. Well, I wasn't going to go there during a game. I had been clear with the guys that we had to focus on football. I couldn't break my own rules.

Booing from Missou's stands caught my attention. I looked at the field to see Asher with the ball, running towards our end zone. I leapt to my feet, along with the rest of our team, cheering him on. Unfortunately, two of Missou's players took him down only a few yards into his run, but it didn't matter. We had gotten the ball!

I pulled my helmet back on and jogged over to Mac before our offense took the field.

"Gather 'round!" Mac barked. "All right, don't take this lead for granted. Go out there and play like we've practiced. No funny shit. Play it safe but play hard. Simmons, call the plays as you see them."

"Got it, Mac," I said, "Let's go, boys."

"Let's get it!" Jamison bounced next to me.

We jogged out onto the field. Our marching band played us on from the stands and the small crowd of Grandview Rams's fans that traveled with us did their best to drown out Missou's booing crowd. I didn't take the boos personally. No team liked to lose on their home field.

Springer snapped the ball into my hands. I pivoted on my foot and slid the ball into Johnson's waiting arms. Johnson was a rookie who was starting to make a name for himself. He darted through a hole in Missou's defense, running about fifteen yards before he was tackled.

He popped up and jogged back towards us. A Missou player shoulder-checked him sharply, and he whirled around, a snarl on his face under his helmet.

"Johnson!" My voice was sharp and cut through the haze of anger surrounding him.

He swung back to face me, and I shook my head at him. Last thing we needed was a fight on the field.

The same Missou player who shoulder-checked him held his hands out and jeered, "How does it feel to be led around by your dicks by a little girl?"

It wasn't an unfamiliar insult, and it washed over me without getting under my skin. Over the years, I had heard all sorts of insults from boys who were unable to take getting beaten by a girl. It bothered me in middle school, but I'd grown a thicker skin in high school. Now the insults were amusing at best.

That didn't mean that everyone else on my team felt the same way.

I felt Jamison and Lewis stiffen beside me. I put a hand up so they wouldn't engage just as Johnson opened his mouth. "How does it feel to get your ass kicked by a girl?"

I let out a surprised laugh that had the Missou player's eyes narrowing on me. I smirked at him. "Let's play ball, boys," I drawled. "Unless you want to keep gossiping like little old ladies?"

"Forty-three, back on your side," the ref barked at the Missou player. I didn't like the look on Forty-three's face as he jogged away, but I focused on the guys around me.

"All right, Johnson, let it go. Let's show them what we've got instead."

Johnson grinned crookedly at me. "Aye, aye, captain!"

I called our next play, a short passing play to Crawford. Springer snapped the ball into my hands. I scanned the players in front of me, trying to find Crawford. He was trying to get clear of his Missou defenseman, but the player was all over him. Okay, time for plan B. I kept my feet moving as I pivoted towards Jamison. Damn it, he was being covered by two Missou players.

In front of me, Lewis and the others were trying to keep the pocket around me intact, but the longer the play went on, the more of a chance I would get sacked. I scanned the field one more time but didn't see anyone open, and I had no path forward for a rushing play. Fuck.

Doing the smart thing, I decided to take a knee. We would lose the yards, but it was only first down, and we were up by three touchdowns. The second my knee touched the field, the referee blew the whistle, signaling the end of the play.

Lewis shouted my name just as a flash of white shot towards me. A hard body crashed into mine. I twisted my body, trying to take the impact on my back and not my throwing shoulder. My upper back smacked the ground with a thud, stealing the breath from my lungs, and my head snapped back. The impact with the ground rattled my teeth, and I nearly dropped the football. I tightened my arms around it. I needed to keep hold of it. What the fuck just happened? The play was over. Who just tackled me?

I blinked a few times and groaned.

Worried dark brown eyes in a gold helmet appeared above me. "Lexi, Lexi, Lexi?" Was that Jamison's voice?

Finally, my lungs allowed me to breathe again, and I took a quick gasping breath. And then another one. I tried to sit up, but Jamison pushed on my shoulders, keeping me down.

"Stay down, Alexa," Derek barked as he fell to his knees next to me. Lyle, our head athletic trainer, kneeled on my other side. Where had that stern voice come from? Surely not out of our nerdy Derek?

"I'm fine," I said. Shock at the sternness in Derek's voice kept me from trying to push against his hand on my shoulder.

"What year is it, Simmons?" Lyle barked at me.

"2023," I answered. I hadn't hit my head that hard. The helmet had done its job.

"Where are you?" he barked next.

"On the field, trying to win a football game," I snarked. The guys above me let out strained chuckles. I still wasn't sure who'd hit me or what had happened.

"I don't need your sass," Lyle grumbled good-naturedly. "Mac will have my head if I let you up before you've satisfactorily answered my questions. Any dizziness?"

"No, I'm fine." I didn't feel any dizziness lying down. "There was no opening, so I took a knee. Who hit me?"

"A dead man walking if Lewis gets his way," Johnson grumbled.

My eyes widened. Lewis could not get thrown out of the game for fighting.

"It's fine. Noah and Asher got him," Derek said. His soft voice was such a contrast from his stern command to me just a few seconds ago that it was giving me more whiplash than that hit had.

"Can I get up now?" I asked Lyle. "We've got a game to finish."

"You can get up, but you're not finishing the game," Mac barked as he moved players aside to get to where Lyle and Derek were kneeling next to me. "Rory's going in for you. You need to be evaluated."

Rory Jenner was my backup quarterback. He was a sophomore this year, but he was talented.

"I'm fine. I've taken a hit before," I reminded everyone. It was unexpected, but that was football. Part of the game was getting tackled.

"There are only a few weeks till the championship. Not

risking my best quarterback on a game we already have in the bag. And I'm sure the boys won't let you down and let Missou get away with this, will they?"

"No, Mac!" the team chorused, and I fought not to groan.

"Fine, help me up." I held out a hand to Derek.

Lyle grabbed my other arm and both of them helped me to my feet. I ignored the cheers of the crowd as I found my feet. I ached a bit, but it was nothing I couldn't shake off. It seemed that most of the team had come off the sidelines while I was lying there.

"I'll sit out on one condition." I held up a hand when Mac raised his eyebrows. I faced the team. "Play a clean game. Don't let this affect your playing."

"That was a dirty hit Forty-three made," Collins argued. "You were down. The whistle was blown."

"That's for the refs to decide and deal out the consequences," I said. "I'll only sit out if you play a clean game. Like we've practiced. Run the socks off them. Keep your hits hard but clean. We're too close to the championships to fuck this up. The biggest fuck-you we could give Missou is to win by another three touchdowns. Let's set a record of how bad we beat them, not by getting even but by playing the game."

By the end of my short speech, the guys were reluctantly nodding.

Collins clapped Rory on the shoulder. "You heard Cap! Let's score another three touchdowns."

"Get out there," Mac barked, waving his clipboard down the field where the new line of play was. From the looks of it, Missou had earned themselves a 15-yard penalty with that stunt.

Mac stopped in front of me. "You okay, kid?" He scanned me up and down.

"I'm fine. You know, I could really stay in the game." I tried my luck, giving him a sweet smile.

"Nice try." Mac rolled his eyes. "Let's get you off the field. With that little speech there, I wouldn't be surprised if they scored another three touchdowns for you. And you need to be evaluated."

"I really do feel fine. I *have* been hit before." I said, walking towards the sidelines.

My hips twinged a bit, but with the movement, they slowly eased up. Lying there for as long as I had probably hadn't helped the soreness. I was definitely going to need to go for a run tomorrow to keep my muscles loose.

"And I don't need you to be hit again before the championship game. Rory needs some mileage anyway. Let him have this."

I nodded, biting my lip. I could see his point, but I felt *fine*.

Still, Derek and Lyle shadowed my every step until I made it to the sidelines. Noah and Asher were standing there waiting for me, arms crossed over their chests and worried looks on their faces.

"I'm fine," I said.

"I'll be the judge of that," Lyle reminded me. "Up on the table."

I followed him to the training table, taking my helmet off as I did. Noah took it out of my hands before I could set it down. He flashed me a strained grin when I looked at him. Derek helped me up onto the table even though I could have done it, and I frowned. I really did feel fine, but maybe the hit was worse than I realized?

That thought helped settle some of my stubbornness. It wasn't that I didn't take my health seriously, but I really didn't hurt anywhere worse than normal. My back and helmet had taken most of the impact, but maybe it had looked worse from the sidelines.

Lyle quickly and methodically manipulated my joints, starting at my ankles and working his way up to my shoulders, elbows, and wrists. He barked rapid-fire questions at me, and with every answer, my guys around me relaxed more.

"See, I'm really fine," I told them.

"It was a dirty hit, Lex," Asher argued.

"It was, but I was able to twist onto my back in time, and he got penalized for it," I reminded them.

"You're still likely not going back in the game, but I'll tell Mac you're fine. I want you in an ice bath after the game and then follow it up with a hot bath tonight. Let's try to prevent those muscles from tightening up."

"I'll make sure she follows those directions," Derek said, and Lyle nodded.

"Good, I'll brief Mac." Lyle walked away.

"Are you okay?" Noah asked.

"I'm fine." My voice came out sharper than I intended, and I winced. "Sorry. But I'm fine. I could keep playing. Mac is just being overly cautious."

"But he's not." Asher said, meeting my eyes with a stern expression. "You didn't see the hit. That Missou player accelerated towards you after the ref's whistle was blown. It was intentional."

"And I get that." I tried to keep my voice calm but frustration leaked through. He wasn't the first player to be pissed that I was a girl and a good player. And he wasn't the first to try a dirty hit to get me out of the game. "He's not the first player I've faced who's gotten pissy and tackled me. I'm not fragile."

"We know you're not." Noah tried to play peacemaker. "We just worry."

"I worry about you, and you don't see me getting all over-protective every time one of you takes a hit, do you?" I point out.

The three of them exchanged looks, and I rolled my eyes.

"Okay, I'm going to go watch the game," I said, hopping to

my feet and leaving the three of them standing there at the training table.

I could understand the concern, but the overprotectiveness was too much. This was football. It was a contact sport. I took that risk, like every other player on the team, when I took the field. I didn't need them babying me because we were fucking.

NOAH

I have always been the funny twin. Where Asher was serious, I was the jokester. Asher protected people, and I made them laugh. I never minded that role. I enjoyed making people laugh, and I especially enjoyed making our Lexi girl laugh. But I was also more observant than others gave me credit for. Most people looked at me and saw this big, dumb jock, but that only helped me observe people. People tended to let their guard out around me, and I soaked in information about others like a sponge.

It was how I knew that Lexi would be up to something this morning.

After we had bussed home from the game and arrived at the house, Derek immediately had Lewis and Asher lug in the two stock tanks we used for ice baths. Lexi hadn't protested much, at that which told me she was hurting more than she let on. We watched a movie to decompress and chatted about the game as we rotated in and out of the ice bath.

After her ice bath, Derek had checked over Lexi again on the portable training table he had brought home and had manipulated her joints in a similar way that Lyle had at the game. His face was a mask of calmness, but I could see the tension in his jaw. Seeing her take that dirty hit like that had us all on edge. We had watched that Missou player charge at Lexi helplessly from the sidelines. When she'd taken a knee, and he hadn't stopped coming... I would hear that impact for the rest of my life.

Lexi must have also seen the tightness in his jaw as she just sat there and let him do his thing. When he finally cleared her, I swear the entire room let out a breath. I didn't think any of them noticed, though, that Lexi tensed up when Derek told her to just rest the next day. Our girl's mind spun too fast for her to rest. Especially not after a game like that. She would be up all night, thinking about what she could have done differently, and the only way she would be able to outrun her thoughts would be to literally go for a run. Which is why she wasn't going alone.

"Wake up." I shook Asher's shoulder.

The sun was streaming in through the attic windows. When we'd gotten the house, Asher and I had volunteered to share the attic space. We had grown up sharing a room for most of our lives. It was natural for us, and the attic space was large enough to fit two queen beds and our dressers, so it worked perfectly for us.

"Why are you waking me up before 10 a.m.?" Asher groaned.

"Because our girl is about to sneak out of the house to go for a run when Derek leaves to go to study group in a half hour, and we're going with her."

Asher sat up. "But Derek told her to rest today."

I arched an eyebrow at him. "And when has Lexi ever rested when she was supposed to?"

He groaned and scrubbed a hand over his face. "Right. So, running."

"Distracting," I corrected him. "She's going running for the distraction."

"And you want to distract her in a different way?" Asher had always been able to read my mind.

"If she's interested, yes. But until then, let's go get our girl out of her head by joining her for a run."

We dressed quickly. We would only have a short window from when Derek left to when Lexi attempted her escape. Lewis and Jamison were both at work at the rec center, so the house was empty otherwise.

We padded down the stairs on socked feet, holding our running shoes as we passed by Lexi's door. I can hear movement inside, and I grinned at Asher with an I-told-you-so look. He rolled his eyes at me, then stopped by the kitchen and tossed me a banana.

"Thanks, bro," I said, eating it quickly and tossing the peel in the trash. "Let's surprise her on the porch."

We were lacing up our shoes on the porch when the front door creaked open softly. I grinned as I watched Lexi back out of the door softly. She swung the door closed slowly, wincing when it creaked. My grin grew wider. I was right.

"Whatcha doing, Lexi girl?"

She startled and spun to face me. "Jesus, Noah, you gave me a fucking heart attack."

I grin at her irritated expression. "Whatcha doing, Lexi girl?" I ask again.

"I'm going for a run. What are you doing?" Her shoulders slumped and her eyes flickered with resignation as she took in our running clothes.

"Well, we woke up on this beautiful morning and felt like going for a run to enjoy the dawn of winter." I spread my arms and gestured to the fine layer of frost coating the grass even as the sun shone, trying to scare it away.

"Mmhmm," Lexi wasn't buying my story for a minute but I knew she wouldn't. Our girl was too smart for that. " Well, let's go, then."

She took off down the porch, and I muttered a curse under my breath. I was not a cardio guy naturally. Sure, I ran when required for training and practice, but I much preferred getting my cardio in a different way. Nevertheless, I chased after Lexi, with my twin falling into pace next to me. The things we did for love.

We caught up to Lexi quickly. Although her pace was steady, there was a bit of stiffness to her muscles. I didn't know if she took the hot shower Derek instructed her to, but if she had and she was still stiff, maybe the run would do her some good. Her mouth was set in a tight line, and she still had traces of irritation in her face. Her eyes were on the sidewalk in front of her feet as they beat into the pavement in a steady rhythm. The run would help relax her muscles, but I could help relax her brain.

"How are you feeling after being the only quarterback to be sacked ever?" I question, a teasing smirk on my face.

She shot me an exasperated look but couldn't hide the twitch of her lips.

"What? It's a serious question," I said, playing it up. "I mean, you *are* the first quarterback to ever be sacked."

Over Lexi's head, Asher was shooting me a be-careful look, but I was emboldened by the small smile playing over her lips.

"I'm not the only quarterback to be sacked ever," she grumbled.

"Oh!" I said, feigning surprise. "I thought you were by how intensely you keep eyeing the sidewalk." This time I was rewarded with a soft laugh and an eye roll that had the tension lines around her eyes easing.

"It's fine. I'm not upset about that."

That was a lie, but my plan to get her out of her head was working, so I kept going. I loved Lexi's strategic brain. It was a great asset on the field, but sometimes it worked against her, keeping her caught in an endless loop of 'what-ifs.' She might not view me as a protector, like Lewis or Asher, or her challenger, like Jamison, or her quiet healer, like Derek, but I could bring her lightness when she threatened to fall into darkness.

"Of course you're not, little miss perfectionist. What's with the early morning run, then?" I said, my breathing getting slightly labored. God, I really hated running. Eyebrows rising, I shot Asher a look over Lexi's head. If it was a distraction Lexi was after, we could provide one.

"I just needed the cardio workout." A more perfect opportunity could not have fallen into my lap.

"If it was a cardio workout you're after, we can provide one of those for you."

If she shot me down, we wouldn't care. We only wanted what was best for her. I actually expected her to shoot us down. She was still a little gun shy about the whole friends-with-benefits thing. So nothing shocked me more than when she dropped into a walk and eyed us.

"You know what?" she said slowly. "I think sex is exactly the cardio I need."

I was not proud of my stumble, but her laughter rang through the air. She started walking towards the house. I looked at Asher, and the shock in his eyes mirrored mine. We both let out a slow grin. The opportunity to have sex with the girl we were both helplessly in love with? Sign me up!

"Are you coming?" she called over her shoulder.

"Not yet," Asher quipped back as he took off in a run, blowing by her. "Last one there orgasms last."

Lexi took off after him.

"Shit!" I took off after them. I was not about to be last. The idea of edging Lexi between Asher and me gave me a new burst of speed.

I caught up with Lexi easily, and when Asher looked back at me, I silently communicated my plan. Laughter danced in his eyes, and he dipped his head in a slight nod. We hit our street, then our place was only a few houses away. Asher was a little bit in front of Lexi when he turned and grabbed her by the waist. She squealed as he wrapped his arms around her, preventing her from blowing past him and allowing me to sprint for the porch.

"Asher," she complained, although the laughter spilling out of her made it hard to take her complaints seriously. "This is cheating."

"There are no rules, Lexi girl," I called as I made it onto the porch.

Asher turned and kept her in front of him as he backed towards the porch, getting his foot on it before Lexi did and making Lexi the loser of the race. We would make sure she won later.

When he released her, she darted for the door, and I scooped her up, throwing her over my shoulder. "Ah, ah, Lexi girl," I chided. "You wouldn't be trying to cheat now, would you?"

"I thought there were no rules," she snarked.

"There are no rules, but there is a majority consensus," Asher said as he stepped by me to get the door.

"And you're outnumbered," I told her.

It was so faint that I almost didn't feel the shiver that danced through her body. My grin widened. Someone liked the idea of being outnumbered. We joked all the way up the steps and Lexi gripped my forearms when I finally let her down, complaining about the blood rush.

"Shower?" Asher asked.

"Why? We're just going to get all sweaty." Lexi's words had me groaning at the visual.

Christ, I had to get myself together before I went off like a teenager. I let go of her forearms as Asher closed in on her.

"You've got a dirty mouth," Asher said softly, pulling her to him with one hand on her hip. She inhaled softly as he bent his head towards hers. "Let's give it something to do."

He closed his mouth over hers before she could make a witty

comeback, and I held in a groan at the sight. She arched her back, falling into him and letting him take control of the kiss. She wasn't passive for long, yanking his shirt out of his shorts and shoving her hands under the material to roam over his chest.

Asher broke the kiss, allowing her to yank the shirt over his head, then returned the favor. I nearly groaned when her tanned skin came into view. Asher's hands pressed against her back, urging her closer to him as he claimed her mouth again.

Even though she was taller than most girls at 5'10", Asher made her look tiny as his large hands spanned her back. He ran them up and down her back. She shuddered.

"So sensitive," he teased softly, kissing down her jaw.

Lexi gasped and dipped her hands into his shorts, and then Asher was gasping.

"So sensitive," she teased as she stroked his cock beneath the material. Asher's eyes met mine, and I smirked at the plea for help in them. While I was entertained watching Lexi make my usually steady twin lose focus, I was tired of watching.

I stepped up behind her, lightly resting my hands on her hips. She jumped, and I dipped my lips towards her ear. "This okay, Lexi-girl?" I asked. I needed to know that she was okay with both of us at the same time.

Lexi nodded. Relief and anticipation tingled beneath my skin. I stepped in closer, running my hands up her arms and down her shoulders, enjoying the way goosebumps broke out on her skin. Lexi threw her head back, letting it rest on my shoulder as Asher moved lower.

"Girls love a twin sandwich," Asher murmured, tracing his lips across her collarbone.

With Lexi's head on my shoulder, I didn't miss the clench of Lexi's jaw at Asher's words. While I wanted to kick my twin for reminding Lexi of the girls before her, that flash of jealousy gave me confidence. Confidence that this meant something more to her than a quick roll in the hay.

"Do you really want to talk about other girls right now?" Lexi's snarky question had me burying a grin in her shoulder.

Asher looked up. Before my twin could dig a deeper hole for both of us, I mouthed a kiss over her shoulder and spoke up. "No, I would rather you help us get you out of this contraption." I tugged on the strap of the tight sports bra she still wore.

Lexi smirked. "I thought you all were experts at this. Haven't you ever gotten a girl out of a sports bra before?"

"That's not a bra. That's a torture device," I murmured, my mouth still on her skin.

I was quickly becoming addicted to the taste of her. The slight salt on her skin flavored the richer scent of peaches and strawberries that I knew was her shampoo. I nuzzled a spot behind her ear that had her shuddering.

"Come on, Lexi-girl, free the boobies."

Her husky laugh had my cock standing at attention, and I forced myself to back a step up when she raised her elbows, whipping off the offending piece of clothing with a grace that must be witchcraft.

With gentle hands on her hips, I turn her around. I traced my fingers up from the hem of her pants. Dancing patterns across her stomach, I moved my hand up her sternum to cup the side of her throat. Keeping an eye on her facial reactions, I only saw openness and heat in her gaze. I used my thumb under her chin to tilt her head back and then did what I'd dreamed of doing for years. I kissed her.

I meant for it to be a soft kiss, to not scare her off, but the second my lips touched hers and she opened her mouth for me, I was lost. I groaned and let my other hand cup her hip, pulling her closer to me. Now I understand why Asher was losing his mind. The heat of her mouth seared me, and when she let out a breathy moan when my thumb stroked her throat, I was a goner. I was already head-over-heels for this girl. One kiss would never be enough.

She let out a gasp, and I pulled back slightly to see Asher's palms cupping her breasts, rubbing his thumbs over her nipples. He pinched one lightly, rolling it, and she let out a shudder that had me cursing under my breath. She was so damn responsive.

"Let's take this to bed, shall we?" Asher said, scooping Lexi up in his arms.

She let out a little squeal when he tossed her. She flew through the air and landed with a little "oof" on my mattress. She laughed when he pounced on her and pressed noisy kisses up her stomach. That laughter cut off into a husky groan when he moved up to cover one of her nipples with his mouth. Her back arched off the bed, and my cock throbbed at the sight. Giving it a squeeze at the base, I focused back on Lexi.

I yanked on her leggings, pulling her underwear down at the same time, then tossed them over my shoulder. A neat triangle of brown curls practically pointed the way to the prettiest pink pussy I had ever seen. We hadn't even really started touching her and already I could see the wetness between her legs. Just how wet I could make her?

I spread her legs and yanked her down on the bed, then kneeled on the floor. Now I had the perfect angle to feast. I pressed soft kisses to both hips, biting at the sensitive skin where her leg met her hip. She gasped at the bite of pain but went liquid in my grasp. I grinned. Our girl liked a bite of pain with her pleasure.

Taking my time and enjoying the way she started shifting restlessly, I trailed my lips up her inner thigh on first one leg, then the other. When she bucked her hips in my grasp, I finally gave in, pressing my lips to her clit and sucking hard. She let out a cry of pleasure and arched up into my mouth. I groaned at the taste of her and immediately dove in with my tongue, drinking in as much of her taste as I could.

Asher pressed a hand against her stomach, keeping her in place and forcing her to take whatever I gave her. I swirled her clit with my tongue.

"Noah," she moaned. "More."

One of her hands ran through my hair, gripping softly as she tried to guide me to where she needed me most. The other hand buried itself in Asher's hair as he played with her nipples. Her moans and cries of pleasure were the most beautiful soundtrack as we worked together to drive her closer and closer to the edge. I felt her muscles start trembling, a clear sign that she was close, and I pulled back, leaving her hanging.

"Noah, what the fuck?" she said breathlessly, lifting her head from the mattress. "I was so close."

I grinned at her. "You lost the race."

Her eyebrows furrowed and it was clear she had no idea what I was talking about. A sense of masculine pride filled me that we were able to make her lose her head like that.

"Loser orgasms lasts," Asher murmured in her ear, finding a sensitive place under her jaw and kissing it softly as she shuddered. His lips drifted beneath her jaw, and he pressed light kisses against her throat.

She shuddered between us even as she gasped out breathlessly, "I will murder you if you don't make me come."

Her words lacked heat and I smiled. "I don't know... Rules are rules. Asher, what do you think?"

"I mean, bets are sacred in this household... but I have been wondering what she looks like when she comes."

The flash of heat in Lexi's eyes as he talked about her like she wasn't even there caught my attention.

"I bet she's gorgeous when she comes," I said, keeping my eyes locked on hers.

A blush darkened her cheeks, but fire flared in her eyes. Before she could shoot back with another sassy comeback, I sealed my mouth to her entrance again. The keening cry she let out had me harder than granite. I had always enjoyed giving a woman pleasure, but watching Lexi writhe above me was a whole different kind of high. I cupped her ass, lifting her closer to me, and she bucked in my grip.

"For someone so demanding, you sure are moving a lot," Asher murmured.

I knew what was coming when he ran his hand down her leg, catching the back of her knee with his palm. When he pulled it up to her chest to give me more room, Lexi fucking *gushed*. Oh, she loved that.

Determined to torment her, I pulled back again.

"Fuck you, Noah!"

I laughed. "Patience, Lexi-girl. We won't leave you hanging, but we do have to work you up to take both of us at the same time." As I said the words, I pressed my thumb lightly against her ass, testing her reaction.

She locked eyes with me, tensing up at first but relaxing just moments later with heat in her eyes. Our girl wasn't a stranger to ass play. Interesting. It was my turn to be jealous.

"Have you ever had someone in your ass before?" I murmured, trying not to let the jealousy color my tone.

She shook her head, and sharp relief spiked through me.

"Just toys," she murmured, her cheeks red.

I groaned. That visual should not be as hot as it was. I nuzzled her inner thigh. "We'll take care of you."

"I know." Her quiet words had Asher and me exchanging a heated glance. Her trust in us was like an aphrodisiac.

I lowered my head to her entrance again. This time, I slipped first one finger, then two, inside her hot channel. I nearly came in my pants at the feeling of her wet heat enveloping my fingers. When I fluttered my thumb over her ass again, she tensed lightly, then relaxed. I kept my thumb pressed against her ass. I just teased the pressure as I swiveled my fingers around, searching for her G-spot.

Asher swallowed her sharp cry of pleasure when I found it. Instead of backing off when I felt her channel clamp around my fingers, I continued to drive them into her. Her entire body tensed and then tremored as she flew over the edge. I kept my fingers moving as I sucked on her clit, eliciting a new cry of pleasure as I finger-fucked her through her orgasm.

As she came down, Asher rolled over and rustled through the bedside table, then tossed the small bottle of lube down by me. I coated my fingers and then drizzled some over her ass. She groaned as my thumb pushed inside her tight channel.

"Oh, fuck," she moaned, hips bucking as if she weren't sure she wanted to push into my touch or pull away from it.

"You okay?" Asher asked her.

"Yes," Lexi panted. "But if you stop, I might actually murder you."

"Threats will get you everywhere." I chuckled as I pressed a second finger into her.

She gasped, fingers gripping Asher's forearms as she threw her head back.

Asher ran his free hand down her stomach and over her patch of curls to draw tight circles around her clit.

"Yesss," Lexi hissed as her muscles started shaking again.

He pressed down on her clit, drawing a second orgasm out of her as I pressed a third finger inside her ass, letting out a groan as that tight ring of muscles gave way and allowed me entrance.

"Do you want us both inside of you?" Asher asked, his lips tracing her ear as he kept his eyes on where my fingers disappeared into her ass.

I twisted my fingers, and she let out a keening cry.

She nodded.

"I need your words," Asher said.

I slid my fingers out of her, and Asher paused his movements as we waited for her answer. Consent was important to

113

us. Being with two guys at once was overwhelming, and even though she had given consent before, it was different when we were both inside her.

"Yes," Lexi panted. "Absolutely yes."

"Is she ready?" Asher asked me.

I slid two lubed fingers back into her ass. She arched her back, groaning. I smirked. "Yes, she's ready."

Asher shuffled up on the bed until he was leaning against the headboard. "Come here, darling."

Groaning, Lexi turned over. I couldn't resist slapping her ass slightly. She threw me a dirty look over her shoulder, but a grin curled at the edges of her mouth.

"Payback's a bitch," she warned.

I laughed. "Looking forward to it, Lexi girl."

Asher rolled on a condom, then tossed one to me. He snapped his hands out and caught Lexi's hips, tugging and helping her settle over his lap.

"Oh fuck," Lexi groaned, sinking down on Asher's dick.

He groaned, jaw locked tight and muscles straining. I knew he probably wanted to drive into her, but he let her take it at her own pace. When she bottomed out, they both groaned. She rose and sank down onto him again. I watched her ride him for a few minutes, like a live porn show and I had to grab the base of my cock to stave off my impending orgasm. I had dreamed about this moment for years but nothing could compare to the real thing. Her movements became jerky as she sank deeper, and I knew she was close to an orgasm as her body trembled and her moans got louder..

Asher groaned and slipped a hand between them. His fingers found her clit and began to dance.

"Asher," she cried, curling forward and placing her hands on his shoulders as she tried to jerk away.

I pushed against her back with my chest, keeping her in place for my twin. I lubed my cock quickly and then sank a finger into her ass again. She clamped down on my finger, and from Asher's curse, she must have clamped down on him as well. Her body shook with another orgasm.

I slowly stretched her ass as she panted, muscles still trembling. "Fuck, you're both going to kill me."

"But what a way to go," Asher gritted out.

She laughed breathlessly. Her laughter died off as I notched the head of my cock at her ass.

"Ready for me, Lexi girl?"

"Yes," she moaned, pushing back onto my cock.

We both groaned when the head of my cock pushed through the tight ring of muscles. Asher guided her shoulders down, so she was leaning on his chest, stilling her movements as I pushed farther inside her.

Once I was fully seated inside of her, I let out a shaky breath. "You feel so good, Lexi girl. I'm not sure if I'm going to last."

She arched her back, and I sank deeper. "I think I've more than got that cardio workout you promised, so do your worst."

"Oh, darling, you might have wished you hadn't said that," Asher said, driving his hips up into her as I pulled back.

She cursed as we started moving, alternating our thrusts so she was always full of one of us. A litany of grunts and moans filled the air as we found pleasure in each other's bodies. I knew she had already orgasmed, but I was determined to draw one more out of her before I finished. Asher buried his face in her shoulder as he shuddered and came. I wrapped an arm around her stomach and lifted her up onto her knees. I cupped her breast in one hand and pinched her nipple as I drove into her.

"Harder," she gasped, and I groaned.

Asher slipped out of her, but he moved his hand to her clit, sending her over into another orgasm. When she clamped down on me, I let go. The force of my own orgasm slammed into me like a freight train as she screamed in pleasure. Asher caught both of us and guided us down to the bed.

She shuddered as I slipped out of her; her body still shaking with orgasm. Asher got up and threw his condom into the trash. I didn't know how he was capable of movement right now, but he grabbed the blanket off his bed and threw it over us as he crawled back on Lexi's other side.

It was silent except for our heavy breathing as we came down from the highs of pleasure. I couldn't help but trace circles on Lexi's hip as she leaned her forehead into Asher's chest.

"Well, that beats running any day," I joked breathlessly.

Laughter filled the room as I closed my eyes and grinned. That was better than I'd ever dreamed.

DEREK

I was really only half listening to Professor Bryant's lecture. I should be paying more attention. Med school applications were in, but they still looked at your final year GPA. But I was utterly distracted by the woman next to me. I eyed her out of the corner of my gaze, trying not to alert her to how much of a stalker I was being.

Lexi was chewing on the end of her pen as her leg bounced under the table next to me. The vibrations were jostling my bag, which was at my feet, but it wasn't bothering me. She was intently listening to the lecture I was supposed to be focusing on, but my attention kept straying back to her. She was anxious about something, if her bouncing leg was any indication. I hoped it wasn't about yesterday.

Despite my instructions to rest, I knew she wouldn't, and honestly, she probably hadn't needed to. I was just being over-protective, but I couldn't help it. Watching her get hit during the game had been a shock to my system. She had been sacked before but never a dirty sack like that, so I was being overly cautious. I knew that. But I wouldn't change it.

When I'd gotten home, Noah had been waiting for me in the

kitchen. Lexi had been passed out in their bed, sleeping, for three hours cuddled next to Asher, and Noah was freaking out that it was because of them. I had expected a spark of jealousy to push its way up when he said they'd had sex, but it hadn't. Just a deep gratitude they were able to be there for her and get her out of her head when I couldn't. That was the point of polyamory, that we each filled different roles in each other's lives. One role didn't matter more or less; they were just different.

It probably also helped that my parents were polyamorous, and I had been exposed to it all my life. It wasn't easy. It required more communication than a monogamous relationship did, in my opinion. But the aspect of it I loved the most was this idea of compersion. Compersion is the opposite of jealousy. It's the joy of seeing the ones you love be happy, and that's what I felt when Noah told me what happened.

I had reassured him she was fine and likely just tired and to let her sleep. Football games always made Lexi anxious, even if she might not admit it. The perfectionist in her drove her hard, and even though the sack wasn't her fault, she still would have taken it personally. I was grateful that Asher and Noah were able to get her out of her head. She needed that. She spent so much time inside it.

Don't get me wrong, I loved Lexi; we all did. But having these psychology classes also made me more self-aware and aware of those around me. When I first met Lexi back in sophomore year, I had seen a player committed to the game with a fierce intensity. I had thought she had just loved the game, but after a few years of being friends, I had an inkling it was something more.

Our professors always cautioned us to not self-diagnose or diagnose those around us, but her anxiety and intensity about football raised some red flags for me the more I got to know her. She never talked about her high school football years.

Always blew past them as if they never happened. Jamison and Lewis never said anything or gave any other indication that something had happened, but maybe they didn't know. It was hard to believe they wouldn't know, but maybe whatever happened was so traumatic that she didn't share it. She had other signs of trauma, too. She was so jumpy freshman year with touch, especially unexpected touch.

I wished she would open up about it to me. I mean, we talked and had deep conversations frequently, but it always felt like she was holding part of herself back. And I wanted all of her. We all did. We were in this for the long haul. We just needed to convince Lexi.

The sound of shuffling around me broke me out of my thoughts. Shit, now I was the one who needed notes. Lexi laughed next to me and patted my shoulder. Even the little bit of contact had awareness shooting through my body.

"I'll send you the notes," she said, stuffing her laptop into her bag and slinging it over her shoulder.

"You're a lifesaver." I grinned at her. "Let me take you to lunch to repay you?"

I wanted to take her to lunch and see if she would open up to me about everything. I knew she had probably talked to Inez, but we usually bounced things off each other. That was one of my favorite parts of our friendship, our long conversations about everything from the mysteries of the universe to our struggles with school and life. This was slightly different, as it was more personal, but maybe I could get her to open up about it. She needed to talk to someone before she exploded.

Lexi hesitated at my offer for lunch. I glanced around, but all our classmates had already packed up and left. I still lowered my voice, anyway. I would shout it from the rooftops that we were together, but that would send her running.

"It's just lunch. I'm not going to jump your bones in the middle of the cafeteria. We both need to eat."

A faint dusting of red colored her cheekbones. She rolled her eyes but nodded. "Fine, let's get lunch."

A few minutes later, we were loading up on food at Grandview's main food hall. I grabbed a burrito, while Lexi loaded up on chicken, rice, and veggies. We found a table against the wall and threw our book bags into the empty seats so no one would be tempted to sit next to us.

"So what are you thinking about for Professor Baxter's final paper?" I asked.

We had a three-page final paper due in a few weeks about our career aspirations after college. Lexi was interested in social work, but there were different paths she could take with it.

Lexi shrugged. "I'm not sure. I'm actually thinking about sports psychology."

My eyebrows shot straight up. Sports psychology? As an athlete and a psychology major, most people thought that would be Lexi's path, but she'd always been weirdly opposed to it. What changed?

"I thought you weren't going to pursue that," I said carefully.

Lexi shrugged again. "I'm just keeping my options open." Lexi always had a plan. Several, actually, at any given time. Sports psychology had never been one of them.

"Do you want to flesh out our ideas together?" I probed gently. I wanted her to open up, but I didn't want to bulldoze her into doing it.

"Not right now." Lexi flashed me a tentative smile.

The hesitation on her face and turmoil in her eyes had my heart breaking a bit for her. Whatever she was wrestling with was big, but if she didn't want to talk about it, I wouldn't push.

"I'll be here whenever you're ready," I said, bumping my leg against hers under the table. Instead of moving it away, she kept her leg against mine, and my pulse jumped.

"How are applications for med school going?" she asked.

I took another bite of burrito before answering her, willing my body to calm down. It was just a press of our legs together. We had done it many times before sitting on the couch at home together.

"They're going," I said. "Honestly, they're out of my hands now. Just hoping I'll get into a few, so I've got options."

"Of course you'll get into a few. I wouldn't be surprised if you got into all of them. You're a genius," Lexi said, waving her fork at me.

I laughed at her confidence in me. "A lot of people who apply to med school are geniuses."

"Yes, but not everyone who applies cares like you do. I read over your personal statement, remember?"

It was my turn to shrug. I knew my odds were good. Maybe better than others. I just wanted to get into as many med schools as possible to give us all options of cities to live in after graduation. But that was a future problem. And one out of my hands.

"How are you feeling about the game this weekend?" I asked, changing the subject. I wanted to know, but more importantly, I wanted to feel out if that's what was causing Lexi so much stress lately.

Her eyes brightened as her passion for the game shown through them. She loved football, almost more than anyone I knew. Not in the way that she kept track of the stats of different players and teams, but in that she loved the game and constantly was driving herself to be better.

"Yes, I think we're ready. Everyone trained so well together this morning. It really feels like we've kicked it up another gear even compared to the end of last season."

"That's great! I heard Lyle talking this morning that Mac was going to be bringing on a new assistant coach next year because Reeder was leaving?"

"Yeah, Mac told us after practice." Lexi nodded. "Reeder

apparently got an offer to be a head coach at a new program, so the team's stoked for him but also disappointed."

"Makes sense. Lyle said something about interviews next week?"

"Yeah. Mac wants to make sure the new person vibes with the team when we're on a championship run."

"I'm sure he used the word 'vibes,'" I said, chuckling at the thought of gruff Mac using a term like that.

Lexi cracked up. "He probably doesn't even know what it means."

"Definitely not. I wonder who he's going to bring in."

"He didn't give us names or anything. Said he didn't want us to be biased. But the college football coaching pool is small, so it'll likely be someone we know," Lexi said, scooping the last bit of her food into her mouth and chewing thoughtfully as she likely ran through a list of names in her head.

"I guess it won't matter much to us, though," I said. "We'll be long gone by the time he starts."

Lexi frowned, dropping her fork to her plate. "Yeah, I guess a lot of things are changing next year that we don't have control of."

I didn't think we were still talking about football. I took a chance and reached across the table, squeezing her hand. "Yeah, things will change, but you're stuck with us forever."

She smiled at me, but her eyes said she didn't quite believe me. Was that what she was stressing about? Did she think she would lose us after graduation?

I didn't get a chance to ask her as she pushed back from the table and grabbed her tray. I followed her movements, and soon we were heading out into the chilly fall air. I placed a hand at her back as I held the door open for her. A group of rowdy students were trying to come in at the same time as we were coming out, and one of them knocked into her, sending her stumbling back into me. I grabbed her hips to right her and caught the faintest hint of a blush on her cheeks. I hid a smile at my effect on her as the student called out an apology and ushered her out into the cold.

"I freaking hate this weather," she grumbled and tugged her coat tighter around her.

"Shouldn't have picked a school in the mountains, then," I teased softly.

If she hadn't insisted on no one knowing, I would have wrapped my arm around her and tugged her close, but I settled for our knuckles brushing together as we headed towards the house.

I half expected her to pull away and put some distance between us, but like our legs under the table, she kept our knuckles brushing as we hit our street.

We called out greetings into the house but silence echoed back. Looked like we had the house to ourselves. I pulled my bag off from over my shoulder and headed towards the kitchen. I had a paper to get a head start on and figured Lexi would join me in the kitchen.

"Derek?" Her soft voice halted me in my tracks.

I turned back around. She was still standing in the hallway in her coat, backpack still on her shoulders. She was gripping the straps of her backpack so tightly I could see the whites of her knuckles. She looked nervous about something.

"Yes?"

"Do you remember earlier at lunch, when you said..." She paused and took a breath, looking at me with those blue eyes that speared right through me. "Earlier at lunch, when you said you weren't going to jump my bones... What if I wanted to jump yours?"

LEXI

*Y*ou're stuck with us forever.

Derek's words from earlier rang through my head. I wanted so badly to believe them, but I knew they were empty platitudes. My parents had warned me in high school that Jamison, Lewis, and I were unlikely to be able to play together in college. Then when we were, they told me to treat it like a gift. Then we met Asher and Noah and Derek, and while they talked about staying together after college, I knew that was a fairytale. Derek would go off to med school. Jamison, Asher, and Noah would get jobs in different businesses. Lewis would likely become a coach or maybe go into law enforcement.

Everything would change. So what was wrong with seizing the opportunity and making memories today? Ones that would keep me warm when I was in a different city from my best friends.

It took me a moment to realize that Derek hadn't answered me yet. He was just staring at me, standing in the foyer, with a strange expression on his face that I couldn't decipher.

"That is, if you want to," I stammered, my earlier confidence gone for some reason. I tried to relax my grip on the straps of my backpack, but my fingers didn't seem to want to work for some reason.

His lips quirked in an amused expression, like I said something funny, and it only made me more uncertain.

Feeling off kilter, I raised my eyebrows at him. Was he going to say anything or not?

He carefully placed his briefcase bag on our hallway table and moved until he was standing in front of me. I loved that I was smaller than all of them. At 5'10", I was about as tall as most guys my age but not mine. I tilted my head back to meet his gray eyes. One of his hands came up to cup my cheek, and I fought the urge to melt into it.

"I'd like that very much," he said quietly, his eyes peering into mine. "Are you sure?"

I nodded, and his thumb brushed my cheekbone. "Words. I need your words, Alexa."

I couldn't help the small shiver at the sound of my full name from his lips. His voice had dropped an octave, almost purring the syllables. He smirked at my reaction.

"Your words," he gently prompted again.

"Yes, I'm sure," I breathed softly.

I didn't know why I was whispering. No one else was in the house. But the moment felt intimate, and it was throwing me off a bit. I was used to quick and dirty one-night stands or afternoon quickies. But all my guys had been taking their time with me, and I didn't know what to do. I was in uncharted territory.

Luckily for me, it seemed Derek had a bit of a control kink, and the idea of relinquishing control, even if it was just for a little bit, had me squirming.

He dropped his hand from my cheek, and I stifled the whine in my throat. Who was I? Whining at the loss of an innocent touch? I was no blushing virgin, but the intensity in his eyes had me weak in the knees.

His warm hands covered mine, and he pried my fingers off

the straps of my backpack, sliding it gently off my shoulders and setting it on the floor. My coat was next, and even though I had another layer underneath, I felt bare beneath his gaze. His hands came back up to cup my cheeks, and finally, with aching slowness, he lowered his lips to mine.

I rose to my tiptoes, crushing my lips to his and trying to take back some of the control I could feel slipping away. He indulged me for a few seconds, letting me lead and control the kiss. Then his hands tightened on my jaw, and he tilted my head.

I was lost.

His tongue swept into my mouth and curled along mine. When he pulled back, drawing my bottom lip in between his teeth, the zing of sensation traveled straight down to my clit. I arched, pressing my body against him in a sweet friction that wasn't nearly going to be enough. He deepened the kiss again. I was breathless by the time he pulled away.

"Wow," I breathed, eyes closed. "That was some kiss."

He chuckled. The sound was low and dark and did not have any business making me squirm the way it did.

"I know you probably have this idea of me as the same nerdy, shy kid I was when we met, but I think you'll find my tastes run a little bit darker now that I've grown up a bit."

My eyes widened as possibilities flashed through my mind. He grinned, as if reading my thoughts.

"Are you okay with that?" he asked softly, lowering his head to brush his lips across my jaw, ending with a nip at my ear that had my toes curling.

Fuck yes, I was okay with that. The curiosity nearly had me spilling *all* the questions, but the anticipation was probably worth the wait. Besides, I trusted Derek. I trusted all of them. Maybe not with all my secrets, but I knew I could trust him with this.

"Show me," I said, leaning forward and pressing a kiss to his throat.

He let out a soft groan, then swept me off my feet with a quickness that had me letting out a very girly yelp.

I narrowed my eyes at his soft chuckle, but let him carry me up the stairs.

He brought me to his room and set me down in the middle of his dark gray rug. The guys always teased Derek about being a closet clean freak because his room was always immaculate. With the events of the last few minutes, though, I had a feeling it was less about being clean and neat and more to do with control and order.

He cupped my chin, bringing my attention back to him. "What do you want to be shown?"

I shrugged. I wasn't totally sure what I was asking for, but I was curious about what he liked.

"I need your words," he said. "Consent and communication are at the core of my kinks. What do you want me to show you?"

Those might be the sexiest words a guy could utter. I bit my lip, feeling suddenly shy. "Show me what you like. I'll let you know if I don't like it."

He studied me, nodding slowly. "You'll need a word to stop if it gets too much. For now, stop or no will work."

"What if I want to choose a different word?" I asked, heat spearing through me at the thought of being pinned beneath him, at his mercy. It wasn't anything I thought I would like with anyone else.

He grinned, the dark smile spreading across his face. "Yeah? You like the idea of being at my mercy?" he asked, pulling me into him roughly.

My breath caught as I landed against his hard body. I nodded, and he arched an eyebrow.

"Yes," I said, remembering that he wanted my words.

"Okay then," he said. "Pick your word. Nothing football related," he teased. "You talk about football too much that it might actually slip out."

I pursed my lips. I didn't talk about football that much, even if the guys teased me that I did. Okay, maybe I did talk about it a lot. But wouldn't you talk about your greatest escape? I thought of a word that I would remember but would never say. Cloves. That was what *he* always stunk of. I was pretty sure it was his cologne. The smell clung to him and lingered like a toxic cloud around him. It was a scent I had adamantly avoided since.

A year or so ago, Noah had brought home a candle in that smelled like it. I'd panicked and thrown it away. When he'd asked, I'd said that I had knocked it off the counter accidentally, and I'd bought him a new one to make up for it.

"Cloves," I said decisively.

For a moment, I was worried that Derek would ask me about the word, and I braced myself for his question. If he was curious, or felt my body stiffen against him, he didn't ask; he just nodded.

"Cloves. Got it. You say that and everything stops."

I tried to find some humor to break the seriousness. "Are you going to show me what you got, or are we just going to stand here all afternoon?"

He smirked, and the wickedness in his eyes had my toes curling. "Is that sass I hear?" he purred.

"Maybe." I smirked back. "What are you going to do about it?"

"I would tell you, but I think it'll be more fun to show you instead."

He pressed his lips against mine in a hard, dirty kiss before his hands went to the hem of my shirt, tugging it up and over my head. My pants were next. He undressed me with a methodical precision that would have been clinical if it weren't for the soft touches he brushed across my skin.

I wanted to ask him if he was going to do anything except undress me, but I figured I should save my sass for the right moment. I had a feeling he would draw it out even longer if I said anything now. The knowing glint in his eye said he had an inkling of where my thoughts had gone. I arched an eyebrow at him, and he let out a throaty chuckle as his hands skimmed up my back up to unhook my bra.

Finally, I was left standing in only my underwear, immensely grateful I had put on a nicer pair after training this morning. Derek, on the other hand, was still fully dressed. There was something uniquely vulnerable about being practically naked with him still in his clothes. Especially when he circled me to stand behind me, my back pressed against his chest. The rasp of the t-shirt against my bare skin had goosebumps breaking out across my skin. The warmth of his breath danced along the back of my neck, and I swayed towards him.

"Steady," he whispered, catching my elbows. "Hands behind your back," he instructed, gently taking my forearms and crossing them behind my back until I grabbed an elbow with each hand. "Keep them there," he said. "If you move them, I stop."

"Stop what?" I breathed shakily. I gripped my elbows tighter. This was almost worse than being tied down.

"Taking you apart," he said, dropping his lips to my shoulder.

He trailed soft kisses from my shoulder up my neck. When he reached the base of my neck, he caught the skin there between his lips, then sucked hard in a bruising kiss that had me gasping. I nearly forgot to keep my hands where they were, and I suddenly realized his plan. Fuck, this was going to be torture. He laved the spot he'd bitten with his tongue and continued his passage up my neck, alternating gentle kisses and sharp nips.

It was a struggle to stand still and not move, especially when his hands started wandering. He moved them from my hips and ran them up and down my sides, coming just shy of cupping my breasts before running them back down to my hips. On his next pass up, he cupped my breasts in each hand. His thumbs traced around my nipples before he dropped his hands to tease my stomach, one finger swirling in my belly button before he came just shy of the top of my panties.

I wanted to groan with frustration, but neither of us had made a sound since he started, and I refused to break first. I bit my lip as he repeated the same movement. I arched my chest slightly into his hands, trying to get some friction, and his chest rumbled with soft laughter.

"Do you need something?" he asked quietly, his thumbs finally brushing over my nipples in soft, feather-like strokes.

My breasts had never been much of an erogenous zone for me, but his touch unlocked something that had each slight touch sending an ache straight to my core.

I bit my lip to stifle my moan as he rolled my nipples between his thumb and forefinger. One of his hands left my breast, and he cupped my jaw from behind, rubbing his thumb across my bottom lip.

"The only one of us allowed to bite that lip is me," he said in my ear. "I want to hear every sound you make."

"Sounds of impatience?" I sassed him. "You've barely touched me."

He chuckled. "Someone is impatient. Hasn't anyone ever taken their time with you?"

"Not this long," I grumbled. And it was true.

"If a man isn't taking his time with you, then you've been with the wrong men."

"So the alternative is someone who likes torturing me?"

Derek laughed. "Torture? I'm just getting started."

I groaned and fell back into his chest. He chuckled but took my weight, his hands starting their slow journey again. This time, when they reached my breasts, his fingers starting plucking my nipples. Softly at first and then with a bite of pain.

A whine escaped my lips as the sensation shot straight to my clit. He gently rolled my nipples between his fingers before cupping my breasts and squeezing them in an erotic massage.

I squirmed against him, pressing my thighs together to get some friction against the part of me that ached the most. Reading my thoughts, or maybe just reading my body, one of his hands left my breasts and slid down my front. He pressed his palm against my stomach, fitting me against him so there was no air between us.

I fully expected him to keep up the torture and skim his hands along my panty line, like he did before. Slipping his hand underneath the hem, he traced it to my hip. A sharp jerk, and the sound of fabric tearing had me gasping. Had he just torn my panties off? Fuck, that was hot.

"Did you just tear my panties off?"

"I thought you were getting impatient?"

He slid his hand down until his palm cupped my wet heat. He ground the heel of his palm into my clit, and I moaned at the friction, spreading my legs wider. As quick as he started, he stopped, spreading two fingers and tracing my folds but never putting pressure where I wanted him to.

"Derek," I groaned.

He laughed and nipped at my neck before grinding his palm against my clit again. This time, he let me ride his hand longer before he pulled away, and I groaned in frustration.

"Your mind might be telling you this is torture, but your body is sure enjoying it," he said, running his fingers through the wetness that was seeping out of me.

He circled my clit with wet fingers, and I arched against him. He dropped his other hand, which had been teasing my breast, to around my stomach, pinning my body against his and forcing me to take what he was doing.

His fingers left my clit, but before I could protest again, he was spearing two of them into me. The sharp stretch had me gasping even as I clamped down on him. He pumped his fingers a few times, and the pleasure built inside me. He had barely touched me, and I was already ready to come. His chin rested on my shoulder so he could see what he was doing. He twisted those clever fingers inside of me, and I moaned. Fuck, he was too good at this.

He pulled his fingers out, and I groaned. I could feel his smile against my ear as he brought his fingers up to his mouth to taste.

He groaned. "Okay, on the bed. I need to taste you."

With his hands on my hips, he guided me to the bed. "You can move your hands," he said. "Climb up, then lie on your back and grab the headboard when you're settled in."

My legs were shaky as I crawled onto the bed and flipped onto my back. His headboard was slatted, and I wondered if he had bought it with this in mind. Unexpectedly, jealousy bubbled up inside of me. I arched an eyebrow at him and looked up at the headboard.

He smiled. "You're the only one I've had in this bed, Alexa."

I fought to keep the blush off my face as I processed his words. This was supposed to be friends-with-benefits only. No feelings. Yet a smug sense of satisfaction filled me about being the only one in his bed. This was dangerous territory.

Luckily, Derek provided the perfect distraction by pulling his shirt over his head. He had a lean swimmer's body, and his muscles were carved in sleek lines. He dropped his pants but kept his boxers.

He crawled up onto the bed, his black hair falling across his forehead. He wrapped his hands under my thighs and pulled me down the bed until my arms were stretched above my head. He kneeled between my thighs, forcing them apart as he studied my body.

There was an intimacy about this moment that had me squirming. This is why I stuck to one-night stands or afternoon quickies. They would already be all over me, and we would be well on our way to a happy ending. But not with Derek.

He dragged his eyes back up to meet my gaze. "You're beautiful."

"You already have me in bed." I huffed, fighting a tendril of panic that threatened to claw at my throat. "There's no need for flattery. I know what my body looks like."

I knew I had more of an athlete's body than a woman's body. Hard muscles where soft curves should be. But that wasn't what caused the tendril of panic to rise. *He* used to call me beautiful. Call my athletic body beautiful and tell me that only he would want my body like this, hard muscles and no curves. He would call it beautiful. Right before he violated me. Hearing the words now, even years later, caused me to flash-back to those times.

There was a crease in Derek's forehead as he studied me. "What do you mean?" he asked, his thumbs tracing circles on my hips.

I shrugged my shoulders the best I could with my hands above my head. "You know... I have an athlete's body."

Derek narrowed his eyes. "I know you're an athlete," he said slowly. "But I don't see how that conflicts with what I said about you being beautiful."

I shifted, uncomfortable with this conversation, and his gaze softened. He placed a hand on the bed next to my stomach and leaned up to brush my lips with his. "I'll drop it for now," he whispered against my lips. "But you should know another rule in this room is you can't put yourself down."

I smiled up at him, grateful. "I'm beginning to figure out you like rules."

He smirked down at me, his face inches from mine, allowing me to see the flecks of silver in his gray eyes. "I do like rules, yes."

"What happens if someone breaks them?" I teased, arching

my back to press my hips up against his, trying to shift us even further away from the *you're beautiful* conversation.

I brushed against his hard cock, and his breath hitched softly before he could hide it. "Did you want to find out?" he asked hoarsely.

I hummed and pretended to think about it. "Maybe later." I did want to find out, but I also didn't want to be teased for another few hours. I was getting impatient.

"Good choice," he purred. "Coz I'm dying to taste you, and I would hate to have to deny you that."

"Confident in your abilities, aren't you?" I teased.

"Why don't I show you and you tell me what you think?"

He pressed a suckling kiss to the base of my throat before inching down on the bed, tracing the lines of my abs with wet kisses that had me squirming. Finally, he reached my entrance.

I fully expected him to tease me, but he licked me so thoroughly my head fell back against the pillow. His hands came to my hips as he ate me out, holding me in place even when his mouth made me want to thrash on the bed. I was torn between wanting more and unable to take the sensations. It was a brutal pleasure, the kind that crashed over you and took you out at the knees. Yet every time I approached the edge, he backed off, building the wave even higher. The added mental restraint of keeping my hands where he told me added another layer of heat that threatened to drown me.

The noises spilling out of me with every talented movement of his tongue were practically illegible. A combination of his name and the need for more. I didn't even realize I had let go of the headboard to run my hands through his hair and hold him to me until a sharp nip to my hip bone had me looking down.

"Hands back on the headboard, Alexa," Derek said huskily, his lips glistening with my arousal. "Or this all stops.

Reluctantly, I lifted my hands off his head and threaded my

fingers back on the headboard. "Fuck," I panted. "I can't take much more of this."

"Do you want something?" Derek grinned wickedly.

"You know what I want. Do you want me to beg or something?"

"No need to beg. You can have whatever you want if you only ask." His eyes were serious even as he grinned at me, and I had a feeling he was talking about something else outside the bedroom, but my brain was too scrambled with pleasure to think of what.

But I wanted to come, desperately so...

"Please make me come."

He pressed a soft kiss to the place where he'd nipped my hip and smiled. "As you wish."

Two fingers slid into me as his tongue traced circles around my clit, building me back up to the level of pleasure I had been at. His fingers thrust lazily inside me, stoking the flames but not sending me over the edge just yet. He moved them faster, twisting them until they hooked over my G-spot every time. His lips closed over my clit, and he sucked *hard*.

The wave of pleasure that had been building slammed into me, and I shattered into a million pieces, muscles spasming as my whole body shook. I gasped for air as the pleasure coursed through my body. When my vision finally cleared, Derek was kneeling in between my legs, eyes on my shaking body.

He leaned down and kissed me, and I tasted my arousal on his tongue. He drew back. "Worth the wait?"

I rolled my eyes at him, and he chuckled. He leaned over and plucked a condom out of his nightstand. I went to move my hands, and he arched an eyebrow at me. All right. I guess I was still not moving. I didn't mind necessarily. I had just come harder than I had in a while. Well, with other guys, not my guys. Well, not *my guys*. You know what I mean.

While I was distracted, he had taken off his boxers and rolled the condom on. "How are you doing?" he asked, leaning over me and pressing his cock to my entrance. "Want more?"

"If you don't get in me right now, Anderson, I might hurt you."

He laughed and kissed my jaw. "Are you making demands now?"

"Maybe. Will it get me what I want?"

"I told you. All you need to do is ask."

My words were stolen by his smooth thrust into me, pushing all the air from my lungs. I gasped as he pulled out and thrust in again. His thrusts were slow and steady, sliding into me so I could feel every inch of him. My hands gripped the headboard and then relaxed. I desperately wanted to touch him.

"You can move your hands," he said.

"Thank fuck," I said, dropping them to his shoulders and grabbing onto the smooth muscle there.

I took a few moments to run my hands down the smooth muscles of his back and up his chest, exploring his body in a way he had denied me earlier. He groaned as my fingers brushed over his nipples. I smirked and did it again. He grabbed my hands, interlacing our fingers together and pressing them into the mattress next to my head.

"Hey," I protested.

He smirked down at me. "Just coz I said you could move them doesn't mean you get to try to take charge."

"I was just trying to make you feel good," I protested innocently.

"That's my job," he said, thrusting into me hard and deep. I moaned. "Besides, I've got you in my bed, and I'm deep inside this pretty pussy."

My muscles clenched at his dirty talk, and he grinned, thrusting his hips deep again, stoking the fire that hadn't quite gone out from earlier. He thrust deep again, and I moaned, pleasure overriding my brain and stealing my ability to speak. He kept up the irregular rhythm of slow and steady thrusts punctuated by hard and deep, keeping me on the edge of pleasure. I bore down on him the next time he went hard and deep, and he groaned.

"Please, Derek," I gasped. "Enough teasing."

He buried his face in my neck. "As you wish," he said into my ear.

If I thought he was thrusting deep before, I was sorely mistaken as his hips began moving faster. Each deep thrust raked across my G-spot, and when he slipped his hand between our bodies to rub circles around my clit, I was gone.

I shattered around him, muscles spasming. He groaned into my ear as his thrusts stuttered and he buried himself deep inside me, cock jerking as he came. He lay pressed on top of me as we both caught our breath. I panted as I stared, unseeing, up at the ceiling. Fuck, I think he might have ruined me. They all were ruining me for other guys.

He caught his breath first, pushing up on his hands, then slowly eased out of me. "I'll be right back," he said, pressing a quick kiss to my lips.

He stepped out of the room, and I tried to get my body to move, to get out of bed and start getting dressed, but he had wrecked me.

He stepped back into the room, boxers back on and a washcloth in his hand.

"What are you doing?" I asked as he approached the bed.

"Taking care of you," he said simply.

"You don't need to." I suddenly felt shy beneath his gaze.

I didn't hang around after sex. That was one of the things Brandon, the lacrosse player from last year, had liked about me. There was never any cuddling afterwards. Not like there had been these last few times. Jamison had been a fluke, and with Noah and Asher, I was tired from the game. Or, at least, that's what I was telling myself.

"Aftercare is one of my favorite parts," Derek said softly. "But if you're uncomfortable, I don't have to."

I bit my lip. I didn't want to say no but couldn't find the words to say yes either. I settled for a nod. His jaw clenched like he wanted to ask me to say the words, but he must have read my face. Sometimes it was scary how well Derek could read me. How well they all could read me.

He cleaned between my legs gently and then tossed the washcloth into his hamper. He pulled the sheet over us and pulled me back against his chest, twining our legs together. Tears pricked the corner of my eyes unexpectedly, and I swallowed against the lump in my throat.

This was why I didn't hang around after sex. Pesky things like feelings arose afterwards. If they kept doing this, treating me like this fragile thing, I was going to start catching feelings, and that couldn't happen. They had been clear at the beginning. This was a temporary friends-with-benefits situation that had an end date. This wasn't forever.

Now, if only I could tell my heart that.

LEXI

J was a hundred percent sure that I did not know the guy who'd just slid into the seat across from me at Ramsey's. Which was the first red flag about him. The second red flag was the cocky smirk on his face that indicated he knew something I didn't.

The hairs on the back of my neck immediately stood up, but I forced myself to keep my face neutral as I lowered my fork to my plate and set my phone down. I had been texting Inez, keeping her updated on the events of the last few days. She would much rather get her updates in person where she could blow out my eardrums with her squeals, but since she was working on one of her final projects, she was making do with texting me in all caps..

"Do I know you?" I wasn't really inclined to be polite to a random cocky stranger.

"You're Alexa Simmons, right? The girl quarterback? I'm Matt."

The girl quarterback? Who was this guy? Grandview was a small university, and he was definitely not giving off freshman vibes.

"I'm the quarterback," I said, leaving off the *girl*. "Again, do I know you?"

"Not very friendly, are you?" His smile was more of a jeer. "I'm a recent transfer student, so our paths haven't crossed, but the rumor around campus is you've got a harem of guys you fuck around with. Some of them you even live with, and I was wondering where I put in an application. Do you fuck as good as you play?"

The audacity of mediocre white men never failed to astound me.

I just blinked at him, completely dumbfounded. The rumor around campus? I mean, there were always rumors, but was this one new? Did someone catch the guys and me? Logically, I knew that couldn't have happened. We had been so careful. But what if we hadn't? Did I fuck as good as I played? Was that a compliment? *What the actual fuck was happening?*

"No words?" he asked when I blinked at him again. "I mean, I thought you had some intelligence. I know you fu—"

I held up a hand. "I heard you the first time. I was just trying to process the complete bullshit that just came out of your mouth. Well done. I haven't heard that level of bullshit in quite some time, especially from someone whose dick is probably about the size of this carrot." I kept eye contact as I lifted one of the baby carrots on my plate to my mouth and bit into it with a satisfying crunch.

His nostrils flared with anger and then he rolled his eyes like I was being the unreasonable one. "Oh, so now you're going to be a bitch? Did I strike a nerve? Is fucking around how you got onto the team? Are you fucking the coach too?"

That last sentence struck a nerve, although not in the way he probably thought. The last thing I needed was those rumors spreading around. In high school, rumors flew about everything. From what someone had for lunch to someone's nail color. It was insane. Before *he* left, rumors were always flying around about someone on the football team (usually me, but a few of the guys got targeted too) sleeping with the coach. The administration thought they were bullshit—as they thought most of the rumors were—and they never got any traction.

But from the glint in this asshole's eyes, he had something to prove here. Especially now that I'd insulted his dick size. If there was anything that men were sensitive about, it was the size of their dicks. I had to shut him down before this got too much out of control.

My leg desperately wanted to bounce under the table, and my fingers itched to pinch the skin on the back of my hands, but I took a measured breath, determined not to show him any reaction. I opened my mouth to find some rebuttal to shut this dick down.

"Cap, you okay?"

I had never been so grateful to see Finn Collins in my life. He stood next to the table with some guys from the soccer team. I didn't know their names, but I recognized them from the athletes' dorm. He eyed Matt, who still sat across from me, with a look of suspicion I wasn't used to seeing on the good-natured defenseman.

"I'm good," I said with a tight smile.

While I was grateful for the interruption, I didn't necessarily want anyone else hearing Matt's bullshit. It was bad enough that there were apparent rumors going around. I didn't need to add fuel to the fire.

"Are you fucking him too?"

I looked up at the ceiling and sighed. I guess it was too much to hope that Matt would keep his mouth shut.

One of the guys with Finn laughed. "Nah, Cap's got a strict no-fucking-the-football-team policy. Finn's not her type."

"Which means you're not hers either," Finn said slowly. "I recognize you. You're the new transfer kid. From Western. They kicked you out of school and off the football team, so you came begging for a spot over here."

Matt shifted, looking uncomfortable for the first time since he sat down. "I don't know what you're talking about."

Finn smirked. "No. I recognize you. I was getting taped up earlier and saw you coming out of Mac's office begging him to play. But you rode the bench at Western all year. Mac told you to fuck off and didn't even give you the time of day, but I heard him talking to Lyle afterwards."

Finn leaned forward, placing a hand in the middle of the table and leaning into Matt's face. "I know why Western kicked you out. My advice? Keep your head down here and forget about joining the football team, or any sports team, for that matter. We don't take kindly to guys like you."

I was stunned by the ferocity in Finn's tone. Finn Always-Smiling Collins making threats? Whatever Matt got kicked out of school for must have been bad. When Matt slid a dark look over my way, a chill went down my spine. Fuck. I had an idea, and it wasn't good.

Matt shoved out of his chair and stormed off. Finn straightened and watched him leave. "I'll see you guys at the table," he told his friends. They gave me the bro head nod that all guys did and then headed into Ramsey's.

"Whatever crap he was spouting, shake it off," Finn said. "He's just trying to start shit. Rattle you before the game."

I gave him a tight smile. "It's okay. I don't rattle easily."

Finn nodded. He rubbed the back of his neck, looking like he wanted to say something but didn't know how to bring it up.

"What is it, Collins?" I asked, trying to get him to say what he wanted to say.

My leg was bouncing under the table now, and I just wanted to get out of here. I knew what Matt said was bullshit, but despite my words to Finn, I was a bit rattled. I just wanted to finish my lunch and shut myself in my room for a while.

He hesitated before blurting it out quickly. "If you did want to have a relationship with anyone on the team, it wouldn't be anyone's business but yours."

My eyes widened. That was not what I thought he was going to say. I gave him a tight smile, thoughts swirling.

"I'm not in a relationship with anyone on the team."

That was technically true. It wasn't a relationship. It was just a friends-with-benefits arrangement. Did he think I wasn't committed to the team? Was he going to tell Mac about this? The other guys on the team?

"I wouldn't risk the championship like that," I said, wincing internally when I heard the defensiveness in my voice.

Finn held his hands up. "I'm not accusing you of anything. And no one is questioning your commitment to the team. I've never played with anyone more dedicated. We're not going to know what to do without you next year. But..." He hesitates. "You deserve a life, too. Find happiness, find love."

No, I don't. The thought flashed through my mind before I could stop it. I was tainted. Maybe even irreparably broken. There was no love for me. Maybe fleeting moments of happiness but not love. There was a time when I didn't even want to live anymore.

Tiny pricks of sensation crawled over my skin like ants were climbing over my body, and I just desperately wanted Finn gone so I could get out of here without causing a scene. I didn't need anyone seeing me lose it. I didn't need any more rumors spreading.

"I'm just rambling," Finn said when I was silent. "I just... think about it. The guys all respect you. It's just... Anyways, I'll let you get back to your lunch."

Except I was no longer hungry. I waited until Finn sat down at the table with his friends. I pushed the food around on my plate for a few more moments, trying to keep my body from visibly shaking as the feeling of a thousand eyes traced over my skin. I had to get out of here. I pushed my chair back and grabbed my bag. Depositing my tray, I fled out of Ramsey's into the chilly fall air.

Even outside, it still felt like thousands of pairs of eyes crawled over my skin. Logically, I knew there was no threat, but fear wasn't logical, and this fear was deeply ingrained in me. My brain broke up the present with flashbacks of the past.

I pinched the skin on the inside of my elbow hard to bring me back to the present. A couple passed me, chatting quietly. The girl flashed me a smile, but I wondered what she was really saying. Did she believe the rumors going around? I pinched my skin again, digging my fingernails in this time, but the bite of pain couldn't keep the memories away.

After the first time it happened, he said no one would believe me. That everyone would believe I did it willingly to get onto the team. All of my accomplishments would be cheapened if I came forward, so I stayed silent. Always silent. Until the unsaid words threatened to suffocate me, and I lost the desire to fight to keep them in.

One particular dark night, I wanted to just end it all. To allow the unsaid words to actually suffocate me. For some reason, Jamison called, with Lewis on the other line. They were arguing about something stupid and wanted me to weigh in. They kept me on the phone until I fell asleep and then did the same thing the next night. They never knew what happened. Maybe they'd guessed?

No. *He* was still breathing.

Lewis wouldn't have allowed *him* to keep breathing if he knew. Which was another reason I kept quiet. I didn't want them to have their futures ruined because of me. Especially not after they saved my life that night. So I kept quiet and gradually buried it so deep inside that it rarely surfaced.

Except when assholes like Matt tried cheap digs.

My brain kept spinning, and it felt like every step was

pushing through viscose gel. My eyes blurred. Sounds muffled. Darkness edged my vision. My lungs felt tight. A fine tremor started in my hands.

The guys. I needed to get home to the guys. They could distract me from all these thoughts. Even if I was trying to keep the lines separate in our arrangement. They were my best friends first.

After what felt like eternity, but was only a few minutes, I hit our street. My surroundings blurred, and my breath was uneven and choppy as I made my way to the porch. I paused before opening the door. I needed to get myself together. If they saw me now, they would definitely know something was wrong. More than being bothered by Matt. They would know something was really wrong. And I didn't want that. Not yet. Not ever.

I forced myself to take deep breaths. *I was fine.* I clenched my shaking fists. *Everything was fine.* I shook my head, clearing my vision. *I was safe.* I bounced on my toes a few times and loosened my neck. *He wasn't here.* I unclenched my fists and wiggled my fingers to get my circulation going again. *It was all fine.*

Feeling slightly less shaky, I turned the doorknob, desperation still making my hands tremor a little. Feminine laughter filled the foyer. It was coming from the kitchen. I froze in place.

They'd brought girls home? They didn't usually do that. The sharp bite of betrayal took a chunk out of my heart, and my chest physically ached so badly that I rubbed it. I must have done something in my interactions with them. Tipped them off that I was getting feelings, and they were reminding me that ours was a strictly physical relationship.

Hands clenching my backpack straps, I dropped it with a heavy thump in the foyer, then stiffly walked into the kitchen to see who'd invaded my space. Irrational tendrils of anger rose in me. Home was supposed to be safe. I was supposed to have this space to relax, and someone had invaded it.

Four members of the dance and cheer teams stood in my kitchen. Asher and Noah were laughing at something one of them had said, and even Lewis had cracked a grin. Jamison's back was to me, but I knew he would be grinning too. Baskets decorated in blue and gold littered our table, and there was glitter everywhere.

That's right, it was spirit week, and it was a tradition that the dance and cheer teams delivered goodie baskets to all the players. I knew this, but when one of the girls placed her hand on Lewis's arm, I saw red.

The knife of betrayal twisted as Noah laughed at something one of the girls said and smiled down at her. I wanted to wipe that smile off his face. She didn't deserve it. The force of my anger shocked me. What was happening to me? Betrayal? Jealousy? These guys weren't mine. They were making that extremely clear, and I needed to get on board.

I knew it wasn't the girls' fault, but I couldn't seem to get the anger rising in me to settle. The guys could have just said something. Given me a verbal reminder that our arrangement was purely physical and temporary. They didn't need to bring girls home and rub it in my face. I was a rational human being.

You're not being very rational now. A voice whispered inside me, but I ignored it, moving farther into the kitchen, not announcing my presence as I began opening cabinets, searching for a glass. The cabinets were empty, and the sink was full. Did no one do the fucking dishes?

I grabbed a glass and started scrubbing it.

"I can do that." Derek's voice had me jumping. He stood next to me, eyes on my stiff movements. "I forgot to load them this morning."

"It's fine. I've got it," I said shortly. He frowned, but I turned back to scrubbing the dish. I saw him flash a look at the others, but I ignored it.

"Hey, Lexi! Check out these new compression sleeves Tiffany brought over."

Oh, did she now? I tried to keep the seething ball of emotions down as I looked over my shoulder. Jamison flashed me a wide grin as he held up the navy sleeves with little golden rams on them. His grin dimmed slightly at the look on my face, and I forced a grin.

"Looks great," I said, turning back to the dishes.

I winced as the girls chattered with my guys about the upcoming game. I just wanted them gone. I started scrubbing a plate, taking out my rage on the surface until it was glistening. I could feel Derek's eyes on me, and my skin crawled as it reminded me of all the other eyes on mine.

"Thanks so much, ladies, for bringing this stuff over," Asher said smoothly behind me. "We've all got some homework to finish before the game."

"Are y'all coming out tomorrow night?" one of the girls, I think her name was Kara, asked.

"Not on game weeks," Jamison told her.

"How about after the game, then? When you win?" Tiffany all but purred, and my grip on the glass tightened.

"We'll have to win first," Noah said.

"Of course you'll win!" Tiffany's voice faded as my—the—guys escorted the girls out.

I listened as the door closed, then the house became blissfully silent again. I could hear the guys file back into the kitchen behind me, but no one spoke as I finished the dishes in the sink.

I had no desire to break the silence, but Asher asked, "Lexi? Everything okay?"

Then it all exploded out of me.

"I know we're just in a physical arrangement, but I would appreciate it if you didn't bring y'all's hookups into our house. I thought we talked about that."

"We weren't hooking up with them," Lewis said quietly, his voice level.

I wiped my hands on the towel and spun around. "Whatever. Potential hookups, then."

"We're not hooking up with anyone else." The *just you* part was left off Noah's sentence. Probably because they couldn't promise me that. I was the one who had let myself have feelings for them all because they were good at sex. Well, not the whole reason, but still...

"I don't care if you do," I said, grabbing a glass I'd just washed and drying it with the towel wrung in my hands.

"We're only seeing you," Derek said, speaking to me like a wild animal that needed to be soothed, which just pissed me off more.

"Well, maybe we should see other people," I said, going to the fridge and grabbing the pitcher of water we kept in there.

I barely held in my frustration as the pitcher was empty. Asher winced as I shot them all a look and slammed the pitcher in the sink. I flicked the faucet on, letting it fill.

"Maybe we should see other people. Then I won't get ambushed in the fucking dining hall trying to have lunch."

"Ambushed?" Lewis growled. "Who the fuck ambushed you?"

Oh, now they wanted to know what was going on. The small voice in the back of my mind was screaming that I was being irrational, but I shut it down.

"Doesn't matter," I bit out. "But there are rumors going around. New ones. Maybe we should just stop this all together." I jerked my hand between them and me.

"I thought we talked this out," Derek said slowly, glancing at the guys with an unreadable expression on his face. "Talked about our concerns."

"We also talked about how if things changed, we would reevaluate," I shot back. "What if someone actually believes the rumors and starts investigating? What if Mac hears about it? Do you want us to get kicked off the team and ruin our chances of the championships?"

"No one is getting kicked off the team," Asher said, his hands out.

"You don't know that!" I slammed the glass down on the counter and flinched when it shattered.

Frustration had me growling as I spun to get the broom. A hand landed on my elbow. I jerked.

"Hey," Derek said softly. "Let's all just take a breath. I'll clean this up. I think we all just need to take a breather."

I bit my lip, my blood itching for a fight, but the guys were all watching me warily. I spun on my heel and headed for the stairs, snatching my bag up on the way up. Derek said we all needed a breather, but I knew he meant me. Even as I climbed the stairs, I knew he was right. Shame filled me as I thought about my reaction downstairs. Even though it was true, and we were only in a physical arrangement, I had acted like a jealous bitch and a completely irrational human being. I was a mess. Maybe the guys were better off without me.

LEXI

he house was quiet over the next few days. We had fought before. We were best friends and roommates. But the other day hadn't been a normal fight. I had overreacted and blown up badly. The guys were all giving me space, but I didn't want that. Or I did? I didn't know. My thoughts were swirling and chaotic and not even practice could get me focused.

I skipped out on family night, hanging out at the library until midnight. I avoided Inez as well. I wasn't ready to sort out the emotions swirling in my head. I needed to apologize to the guys, but I didn't know how.

Hey, sorry, I was completely irrational the other day. I have this big trauma I've never told you about, and I let some asshole spin me up. Then I took it out on you because I was jealous, even though we said this arrangement would be feeling-free.

Yeah, that would go over well.

Groaning, I threw myself backward on my bed. My psychology textbook thudded to the floor, but I couldn't muster the energy to care about retrieving it right now.

A knock on my door had me raising my head from the navy-blue comforter. I bit my lip, hesitating. The pause sparked anger inside me. I needed to get over myself. I wasn't this weak, broken being who shied away from conflict. I was a strong, confident captain of the football team and a straight-A student. And these were my best friends. And I was the one who was risking blowing up our friendship, which was the exact opposite of what I wanted to do. I needed to put my big girl pants on and figure out how to apologize and get over it.

"Come in," I called.

My door cracked open, and I wasn't that surprised to see it was Lewis on the other side. I was a little surprised he had given me as much space as he had. He was usually the type to face everything head on and force others around him to do the same. He had mediated many a fight between Jamison and me in the early days by forcing us to sit down across from each other and talk it out.

Part of me wished I had told him about everything in the beginning, but I was confident he would have confronted *him* and likely ended up in jail for assault, and I didn't want to ruin his career before it started. Of all of us, he was the most interested in a career in football, even though his major was criminal justice. He would be an excellent coach and telling him back then would have risked his career.

And it had been so long now that if I told him, he would be angry. Maybe partly at me for not telling him for so long, but mostly at *him*, and not only would he be angry, but the guilt that he couldn't have stopped it would eat him alive. I couldn't bear to see pity and guilt on his face every time he looked at me. Like I was broken. I worked too hard to never be seen as broken. Besides, it had been years, I should be over it by now. Every time I let it have control over me, I gave *him* control. I just needed to get over it. Bury it so deep it never came out.

"Lexi." Lewis's voice cut through my thoughts.

I focused back on him, and it was clear it wasn't the first time he had said my name.

"Sorry." I gave a half shrug the best I could while lying on the bed. "Trying to study."

"I heard the death of the textbook from the hallway," Lewis said with a wry grin.

I laughed. "Yeah, it was frustrating me."

He opened the door more fully and stepped into the room. Pausing by my bed, he leaned down and rescued the discarded textbook, setting it on my desk before taking a seat on the edge of the bed. I rolled up and swung my legs around to sit next to him. The bed dipped as he settled his weight, and my side pressed against his, but I didn't shift away.

My psychology textbooks would call it 'touch starved,' and before this arrangement with the guys, I would never have thought that term would apply to me, but after these last few weeks, I found my body craving more touch even as my brain screamed protests. I was feeling out of control, and I desperately wanted it back.

"Are you ready to talk about it?" Lewis asked, blunt as always.

I let out a huff of laughter. "Talk about how much of a raging bitch I was?"

He bumped my shoulder with his. "You weren't a bitch."

I shot him a look, and he laughed. "Fine, a little bit of one. But we aren't mad, just worried."

I winced. That sounded like 'we aren't mad, just disappointed,' which was worse than being mad.

"I'm sorry," I offered. "It's just been a long semester, and with classes and the championships coming up, I'm a little stressed trying to balance it all. And I took it out on all of you."

"I get that," Lewis said. "I think we're all feeling the pressure a bit. But you don't have to balance it alone. We made this arrangement to take stress off your plate, not add to it. If it's stressing you out, you can call it off with no hard feelings."

I stared at my wall as I thought about his words. I knew I could call it off at any time, but the deepest parts of me didn't want to. I liked sex, but more than that, I liked sex with them. It was just my own pesky feelings getting in the way. But I could smother those. God only knows I was used to doing that.

"No," I said slowly. "I don't want to call it off. I'm just... I don't want anything to go wrong for the championships. So much is riding on it, ya know? I don't want to let anyone down."

"You're not going to let anyone down," Lewis said. "It's a team effort, anyways. The team feels good. We've got a real shot at this. But even if we don't win, it's not the end of the world."

"It might be the end of mine," I said half-jokingly.

He rolled his eyes, and I grinned at him. My eyes traced over his face. With his strong jaw hidden by his neatly trimmed beard, his dark hair and broad shoulders, he was an intimidating force on the field, but I knew he was just a teddy bear. My fierce protector on and off the field.

I'd always thought my guys were attractive, but I'd never let myself follow that train of thought before. Now, in the quiet privacy of my bedroom, I let my eyes trace over his features. Tendrils of desire curled in my gut.

He noticed my slow appraisal of him, and his green eyes went molten as the air between us thickened.

"Lexi." His voice was thick with a growl, and my thighs clenched.

"Lewis," I replied breathlessly, teasing him lightly.

"I didn't come in here for this. I just wanted to check in on you," Lewis said, but his eyes dropped to my lips.

I bit my lip, a slow smile spreading across my face as his gaze tracked the movement. "We talked," I pointed out.

"Why do you think the world will end if we don't win the championship?" he asked, ignoring the charged air between us.

I could appreciate his checking in on me, but I was after a different type of distraction. However, I also knew he wouldn't let it go until I answered him satisfactorily. That was just Lewis. He wanted to know what was bothering us, so he could fix it. But he couldn't fix this, so I gave him half an answer.

"I know the world won't end if we don't win, but winning the championship just opens more possibilities for us, ya know? If y'all change your mind about playing professionally, it'll only help there."

"None of us really want to play football after college, so winning doesn't really affect our future."

"It'll still give you a head start in the real world with that accomplishment. And it's our senior year. It's a way to go out with a bang. To have this memory to reminisce about when we get together for a reunion in ten years from now."

"Who says we won't be together for the next ten years?" Lewis arched an eyebrow, and I fought not to roll my eyes at him. He was believing in a fairytale.

"We have to be realistic. We're all about to graduate and go in different directions; wherever graduate school or our jobs take us. I just want one more memory for us to hold on to."

Lewis frowned, and I was distracted by his full lips again. I really didn't want to keep having this conversation.

"Lexi," he warned, and I laughed.

"What? We've talked about the feelings and all the things. If you don't want this, then that's fine. I won't push."

Lewis looked like he was going to hold out and demand we still talk, but looking at me, he caved. He hauled me onto his lap in a movement that was almost too fast for me to track.

"I'll always want you." His rough confession tugged at me stronger than it had any business doing so.

I traced my hands up his arms, letting my fingers run over the corded muscles there. He stilled under my touch, letting me explore. I traced my fingers up the side of his neck, along his jawline, feeling the scratch of his stubble against the tips of my finger. His arms tightened around me. I leaned in, letting my lips barely touch his, so our breath intermingled.

"Distract me, Lewis," I said softly. "Make me forget for a while." He didn't need to know it was a distraction for more than just school and the championships.

His eyes searched mine, as if he could pull out my deepest secrets with just a look. I was too raw to admit that he might be able to if he pried hard enough. Instead, when I brushed my lips against his, he took my lips for a deep kiss.

My eyes fluttered shut as he explored my mouth. One of his hands came up to cup my neck, holding me in place as his lips explored mine. I tried to press against him harder, to deepen the kiss even more. I wasn't looking for gentle. I was looking for distraction, but his grip on the side of my neck kept the kiss soft and sweet. With every stroke of his tongue against mine, the heat in my gut grew stronger. I groaned as his tongue tangled with mine, and his lips quirked at my reaction.

Needing more skin on skin, I dropped my hands to his shirt, tugging it up and over his head so I could explore. It was his turn to groan when I ran my hands over his chest. His hands tugged at my shirt, and I leaned back so he could whip it over my head. I unclasped my bra and watched as Lewis's eyes darkened. He buried his face in my barely there cleavage and ran his lips up my sternum to kiss my neck.

I tipped my head back, letting him drag his lips up my neck. He sucked on a sensitive spot, and my hips jerked, grinding against him. We both cursed at the same time and then laughed together. Eyes twinkling, he lifted me to a standing position, allowing him to take off the yoga pants I was wearing.

Now only in my underwear, I climbed back on his lap, grinding against him. He groaned, hands going to my hips to hold me still.

"Patience, Pixie," he growled. I bit my lip to contain my

smile, but he caught it. He glared at me. "I want to take my time with you."

I leaned forward and nipped his jaw. "What if I don't want patience?"

He flipped me onto my back and loomed over me. "Well, you'll just have to lie there and take it while I take my time."

Except I was no longer in the bedroom with Lewis. Instead, I was sixteen years old again, lying on the athletic trainer's table with *him* looming over me. My breathing quickened, and my muscles jerked as my vision blurred.

The man that loomed over me immediately dropped next to me on the bed. "Easy, Lexi, just breathe. It's me, Lewis."

Over and over, the man repeated those words in a soft voice until the familiarity of the voice and the figure came back to me. This was Lewis. It wasn't *him*. I was in my bedroom at Grand-view University. I was safe. Broken but safe.

I blinked to clear the last of the fog from my head.

"Hey, Pixie," Lewis said softly from next to me. "Are you okay?"

My face burned so red I was sure the sheets were on fire. Oh god. Lewis just saw me completely freak out for no reason. Or, at least, no reason that he knew about. Fuck, this wasn't good. He was going to have all kinds of questions.

"I'm fine," I whispered hoarsely. "Sorry I killed the mood."

"I don't care about the mood. What the hell happened?"

"I'm fine. I don't want to talk about it. Distract me." Now that the panic was gone, my brain was trying desperately to dredge up all sorts of bad memories. I needed a distraction, and what better than the one in my bed? Especially if I could distract him from asking too many questions.

Lewis had a stubborn look on his face, so I decided to bring out the big guns. "Please, Lewis. Make me forget," I said softly.

His lips twisted, but he nodded. "Just answer one question for me. Is me on top a trigger?"

I avoided his eyes as I shrugged. "It's not usually. You just surprised me."

"Okay." He nodded. "And you're sure? I don't want..."

"That's two questions," I teased, cutting him off.

I just really wanted him to stop asking me about it. I knew already my slipup was going to stir up questions, but maybe I could play it off as a bad experience in college. It would kill Lewis if he knew the truth.

He studied my face for a moment longer before nodding. "Okay, but we go at my pace, and you have to tell me if it's too much."

"I will." I bit back the lump in my throat at his caring words.

If he saw even the slightest sign of tears, he would call a halt to it all, and I desperately needed to get out of my head right now. I shoved all thoughts away and leaned forward to brush my lips against his.

His hand came up slowly, still trying not to spook me, and cradled my cheek. We lay side by side and made out for a few minutes before I got impatient again, and my hands started wandering.

"I thought I said my pace, Pixie?" He broke the kiss to arch an eyebrow down at me.

"But your pace is so slow." I teased. I willed him with my eyes to speed it up. I wasn't made of glass, I wouldn't break. Not when I was already broken.

Eyes watching my face closely, he brought one hand up to cup my breast. When my eyes fluttered close as he strummed his thumb across my nipple, he scooted lower on the bed to take the other one in his mouth. The wet heat around my sensitive bud had me tossing my head back. All my thoughts slowly started to drain out of my head until all I could focus on was him. Yes, this is what I needed. This is why I sought out sex in the first place. It was ironic that the thing that had traumatized me was also the thing that made me forget for a while.

One hand left my breasts to smooth over my hips and brush across my stomach. I bent one knee and placed it on top of Lewis's hip so his hand would have more room. He took my invitation and ran three fingers over my entrance. I gasped and rocked my hips forward into his hands. I wasn't that wet yet, but I knew that would change if he kept that up.

He rolled onto his back, breaking away from me and scooted down the bed. "Come here," he ordered gruffly. "Ride my face."

"What?"

I had never done that before. Sure, I enjoyed receiving head —what girl didn't if it was done right?—but I had never ridden anyone's face. That was something you read in books not experienced in real life.

"You heard me. Ride my face. I want to taste you, and you want to be on top."

My brain was still processing as I started to move. He helped me settle in, knees up by his shoulders and one hand braced on the headboard. I hesitated, but he tugged my hips down.

"Lower, Pixie."

"I don't want to suffocate you," I protested.

He smirked. "That's how you know you're doing it right. Now lower, Pixie."

His hands tugged at my hips gently again, and I lowered onto his face. The first touch of his tongue to my clit nearly had me rocketing back off again, but his hands clamped down. His tongue circled my clit. Every rough rasp of it against the sensitive bud had me gasping and moaning as my hips twisted to get more friction.

His tongue traveled lower and burrowed into me, then he started fucking me with shallow thrusts. His nose bumped my clit, and my hips jerked, grinding down onto him before my brain caught up. I tried to lift my hips so I wouldn't suffocate him. I know he said he wasn't worried about it, but he still needed oxygen. He retaliated by jerking my hips down again and grinding them against his face, and my body got with the program.

I chased my orgasm as much as he was throwing it at me, and I knew the collision was going to wreck me. When one of his hands snuck down to sink two fingers in me while his mouth closed on my clit, I detonated.

I threw my head back with a cry as my body shook. Both hands grasped the headboard as I tried to find something to hold on to. His fingers fucked me through my orgasm until I begged for mercy.

"Enough," I panted. "I want you inside of me."

He wiped his face with the back of his hand, his green eyes glittering up at me as he sat up, holding me in his lap. "I don't have a condom," he said.

"Nightstand drawer," I panted out.

He reached over with me still in his arms and grabbed a condom. I took it from him, motioning at his boxers. He shimmied the fabric until his cock popped out, and I swallowed hard. He wasn't the longest cock that I had seen, but he was the thickest. Fuck, he was going to stretch me.

"Don't worry. It'll fit," he said with a cocky smirk. I raised a brow and he laughed. "Sorry, Pixie, but your face told on you."

He plucked the condom out of my fingers and tore it open. Rolling it on, he gave his cock a few strokes with his hand before hesitating. "Is doggie-style okay for you?" he asked.

I nodded. All sex positions were usually fine for me. What had happened earlier was an anomaly I was blaming on the chaos of the last few days. The memories had been closer to the surface instead of in the box I usually kept them in.

He helped me swing a leg over him, turning towards the end of the bed. His hands tugged my hips backwards as my back arched. I twisted my head to look at him. He smoothed his hands over my back and down my hips. Fingers trailed across my entrance, and I wiggled my hips back into him.

His low chuckle had no business being as sexy as it was, but he obliged my silent request, pushing two fingers into me. I groaned as he pushed them in and out before adding a third finger. I bit my lip at the stretch but welcomed the sting as it helped shove all other thoughts away until my world became just his fingers thrusting into me. He pulled his fingers out and notched the head of his cock at my entrance.

"Are you ready?" he asked.

To answer him, I shifted my hips backwards, and we both groaned when the head of his cock slid into me.

"Fuck, Lexi," he groaned as he slid in a few more inches.

I let out a gasp as the stretch hit me and he snaked one hand under my hips to rub at my sensitive clit. He kept up small, consistent circles as he slid the rest of the way in until I could feel his hips pressed against the back of my thighs.

I moaned as he pulled out and thrust back in, my body getting used to the stretch. His first few thrusts were careful, but when I started pushing my hips back to meet him, he dropped his hand from my clit to grab my hips. The force of his next thrust pushed the air right out of my lungs, and I gasped. I barely drew in a breath as he set a punishing pace until all thoughts fled from my head. My whole world centered around his cock sinking into me, rubbing against my oversensitive walls as he sent me hurtling towards the edge.

A string of nonsensical words spilled from my mouth as I raised myself onto my hands to brace myself. His arm snaked around my middle, pulling my back against his chest and sinking him impossibly deeper into me.

"Fuck," I groaned. "Lewis... Fuck... Please..."

He brought his free hand to my clit, and I keened as the sensations clashed together inside me. In this position, he couldn't do more than thrust shallowly into me, but God, it was still so deep. His finger pressed down on my clit, rubbing short, tight circles around it, and I detonated for the second time in his arms.

He groaned, burying his face in my neck and suckling the skin there as he thrust up three more times before he came. The warmth triggered another series of mini-explosions inside me.

I sagged back into his chest, and he held my shuddering body as I came down from the intense orgasm. His hands rubbed my skin softly, and the gentleness had tears pricking at the back of my eyes, but I shoved them down.

Feeling free, I reminded myself. *Focus on the semifinals. That's what's important here.*

But I struggled to keep those thoughts at the forefront of my mind as Lewis gently laid me down and cradled me in his arms.

LEXI

*A*fter Lewis and I had gotten cleaned up the other day, we'd headed downstairs. As the rest of the guys had trickled back into the house, I had apologized to each of them for losing my shit the other day. They all accepted my apology, but I could see in their eyes they were still worried. Apparently, Lewis wasn't the only one who could call me on my shit anymore.

Jamison had looked like he'd wanted to say more, but Lewis had cut him off, saying we were focusing on the game this weekend. We'd decided to order from our favorite takeout restaurant, and Asher had suggested we watch Tolston University's past games, then laughed at the look in my eyes.

"We know you," he had teased me. "You'll be stressing out unless we do this."

I had rolled my eyes and shoved him playfully, but I was grateful we had gotten back to normal. Or, at least, close to normal.

If I had been dealing with the aftermath of our fight as well as the pressure of the semifinals, I think I might have fractured. Even just stepping off the bus at Tolston University today, I could feel the pressure in the air like a palpable weight threatening to choke us. We played hard for the first half of the game, but Tolston was no pushover.

"Receiving team! You're up!" Mac's voice had me breaking out of my thoughts.

I looked out onto the field to see that our defense team had forced a punt from Tolston at their 60-yard line. I slid my helmet onto my head and jogged towards Mac as the receiving team took the field. We were up by one touchdown, and our defense had just given us the opportunity to make it two.

I clapped Noah and Asher on the shoulder as they jogged past me for the bench. "Nice job," I told them and the others gathered there. "Y'all gave us a real shot for another touchdown." With only ten minutes left in the last quarter, we needed all the advantage we could get.

"Go out there and crush it, Cap!" Collins shouted, still high on sacking Tolston's quarterback.

I grinned. "We'll do our best. Offense! Gather 'round."

Jamison, Lewis, and the others joined me around Mac.

"Listen up!" Mac barked. "Now's not the time to get cocky. Keep your eyes focused and aware of your surroundings. Simmons has the plays."

"Yes, Mac," we all chorused.

I turned back to the field and watched as our players got into position. The ref blew the whistle, and the Tolston kicker launched the ball into our end zone. Becker scooped it up and sprinted up the field. I yelled along with the others from the sidelines, encouraging him to run faster. A Tolston player took him out at the 40-yard line. It was an impressive return, and I clapped Becker on the back as we took the field.

"Great job," I yelled over my shoulder.

"Thanks, Cap! Give 'em hell!" he yelled back.

Becker was a sophomore and an overall good guy. He struggled in school sometimes, but the team always helped him out by quizzing him at practice on whatever class he was struggling with that week.

We got into position on the field, and I called the first play, a short passing one to Jamison that gained us just over ten yards, putting us just under fifty yards from our end zone. I called out the next play, a rushing play where I handed the ball to Crawford. He gained just five yards, and on the next play, we made the first down.

"Set! Hut!" I called out as Springer snapped the ball back into my hands.

I looked for Jamison, intending to throw a tight spiral into his hands only five yards away from me, but two Tolston players were guarding him, and I didn't have an opening. I looked for Kenting, my fullback, to send it to him, but his back was to me. Fuck. The pocket around me got tighter as the Tolston players closed in on me.

I looked downfield. Crawford was streaking towards the end zone looking back at me with his hand out. I quickly judged how far away he was from me. Twenty yards. Not terrible, not great either. I pulled my arm back and let the ball fly just as Lewis's back bumped into me as he kept the big Tolston player in front of him from flying into me. I tracked the ball with my heart in my throat as it spun towards Crawford.

"Yes!" I cheered as he caught it and sprinted towards the end zone. Jamison and Kenting flew after him, helping to keep the Tolston players off him.

Springer and Lewis whooped as Crawford neared the end zone. He looked behind him as he crossed over, tossing the ball away and throwing his arms in the air in his elaborate victory dance he did for every touchdown as the stands roared. My eyes narrowed. Did he get across the end zone before he tossed the ball away? I hoped so. Crawford wasn't a rookie. Surely, he wouldn't have made that mistake.

I groaned when Tolston's coach used his challenge to challenge the touchdown. In college football, coaches could use one challenge per game. Tolston must have been confident he let go of it early if he used his challenge here.

"What happened?" Springer asked. "Why is there a challenge?"

"I think he might have let go of the ball early," I said with a frown.

Springer frowned as well. "Fuck."

We waited anxiously to hear what the ref would say. I jogged over to Mac as the rest of the guys stayed on the field.

"What the fuck happened?" I wasn't offended by Mac's tone. It was just how he talked.

"I think he let it go early," I said, stopping in front of him. "Couldn't tell from back there."

"I saw it," Derek chimed in grimly. "He did."

"Fucking hell," Mac grunted. "Get back out there. They're about to call the play."

I nodded and jogged back to the team.

The ref came on over the speaker. "Upon further review, number Thirty-Seven lost control of the ball one yard before entering the end zone. Game will resume on the one-yard line."

Well, that was better than nothing, I guess. I caught the guys shoot dirty looks at Crawford, who stood tall and tried to pretend like it wasn't affecting him. I knew he was probably embarrassed, and he should be, but it wouldn't help us now for them all to lay into him, so I broke it up quickly. "We'll talk about it later," I snapped. "Get your heads in the game now. I need your absolute best here and now. Do you understand me?"

"Yes, Cap!" Most of the guys gave their agreement, and I gave long looks at the ones who didn't until they nodded agreement.

"Good. Let's win ourselves a football game."

This close to the end zone didn't leave us a lot of options. There wasn't a lot of room for a passing play. A rushing play was better, but it relied on brute force to get in. And Tolston was bolstered by their successful challenge. Their players yelled insults and condescending phrases at us, but I blocked it all out.

I called a rushing play, spinning on my heel to hand the ball to Kenting. A Tolston player tackled him a moment later, and I fought to keep in my groan. Tolston's defense was going to be all over my players. I needed a new tactic. I tapped Lewis on the arm before we got back into position.

"Make me a hole," I murmured to him.

His eyes flashed to mine, and I knew he hated when I did this, but he nodded, anyway.

I called a short passing play, and when Crawford and Jamison ran to the corners of the end zone, they drew some of the Tolston defense with them. Lewis barreled his way through the defense, leaving me just a sliver of a space to slip through. I darted forwards and pushed my way into the end zone. That one yard felt like one mile, but when my foot crossed the line, I dove forward, twisting to land on my back. I grunted as a Tolston player landed on me hard, but the ref's whistle had me smiling. Touchdown!

Someone pulled the Tolston player off me and yanked me to my feet.

"I hate it when you do that," Lewis grumbled as he dusted me off.

"I know. But it always works." I grinned at him, tossing the ball to the ref and jogging back to the sidelines.

"Nice job, Simmons," Mac barked. "Defense. Try not to fuck this up."

Derek appeared at my elbow, tugging me towards the trainer's table. "Let's get you checked out."

"I'm fine," I said. "I wasn't hit at all. I dove to the ground as soon as I knew I made it over."

"I would still feel better if you got checked out," he said. "You've taken quite a few hits over the last few weeks."

I managed to not roll my eyes and let him get me situated on the table. It was going to be faster and easier to let him do his thing than it would be to argue with him. As he ran his hands over my joints and limbs, I discovered a new problem. Since we'd fucked, my body's awareness of him was at an all-time high, and freaking goosebumps broke out on my skin as he moved my shoulder around.

He noticed them but wisely didn't say anything, and I was grateful for it. Jamison hopped up next to me, and together, we watched the rest of the game. I saw Crawford sitting a few benches down, laughing and joking like he hadn't just made a stupid, rookie mistake, and the frustration that I had buried on the field bubbled to the surface. We were in the semifinals, for crying out loud. And he had risked it all to do his elaborate victory dance for the crowd's attention?

He must have felt my eyes on him as he looked away from his conversation and met my gaze. He narrowed his eyes at me and then turned back to the conversation, jerking his thumb back in my direction. I could only imagine what he was telling those sophomores about me. Was he the source of the rumors that asshole Matt had heard around campus?

My muscles tightened under Derek's fingers, and he looked at me with concern in his eyes. Jamison followed the direction my gaze had gone and lightly bumped my shoulder with his.

"Don't let him get to you."

"I'm not," I said half-heartedly. "But it needs to be brought up. It was a stupid mistake we can't afford to be making."

I was going to have to address it during the debrief, anyway. With him running his mouth, it would make it that much harder as he sowed seeds of discontent before the championship just to assuage his bruised ego about making a stupid mistake. It was times like these that I really hated being team captain. Exhaustion weighed down on me, and I sagged on the table. All I wanted to do was go back to the hotel and sleep, but no, I had to be team captain and take care of this shit.

Tolston tried to rally in the last few remaining minutes of the game but just managed to score one more field goal. As the timer ticked down, the team's spirits on the sidelines lifted, and when the clock struck zero, the sidelines erupted. I found myself being swept along with the energy, even though exhaustion tugged at me. We had done it! We were advancing to the championship game!

The energy carried through to the locker room until Mac broke it up for the post game debrief. He rattled through the plays we had executed, making comments on the good and the bad until Lyle knocked on the door. Mac stepped out with a meaningful look at me. I had chimed in with my opinion on a few of the plays, but I'd mostly stayed quiet. Or at least quieter than Mac was used to in these debriefs. But now I knew he wanted me to address the elephant in the room.

I shoved the bone-deep exhaustion down deep inside me and got to my feet. I made a small lap around the room before pausing in the middle.

"Someone remind me of the team policy on victory dances?" I asked the silent room. Most guys cut their gaze to Crawford, who remained stonily quiet.

"Kenting," I called on the fullback. "What's the policy?"

"Victory dances are acceptable unless they are unsportsmanlike or risk our integrity on the field," Kenting recited for me, and I nodded at him.

I turned to face Ryan Crawford, well aware of all the eyes on me. "Crawford, do you agree you broke that policy and risked our win today?"

A big part of my philosophy as team captain was accountability. We helped each other out when we stumbled, but we started with accountability first. Crawford knew this. Whether he was going to agree to it was a totally different matter, especially when I called him out on it in front of the entire team.

"It worked itself out in the end," Ryan said, glaring at me.

"Not the point." I shook my head. "Do you agree you broke team policy today?" I threw him a lifeline when I added, "I know we all make mistakes, but it starts with us admitting to them. Then we can move forward."

"You know what, Simmons? Fuck you!" Ryan exploded. "You think you're all great and shit because you made that touchdown, but I made it first."

"But you didn't hold on to the ball." I kept my voice level, although the temptation to lay this dickhead out was strong. Mac and Lyle had entered the room behind him, but Ryan didn't notice as he cussed at me again.

"Enough," I cut Ryan off. "We all make mistakes. I get that. But you know damn well that accountability is a core tenet of this team. Do you agree you broke team policy today? Admit it, and we can move on. If you can't admit it for yourself, admit it for your teammates, who had to work harder today to make up for it."

"Fuck you, Simmons, just because you walk around here all high and mighty while you're probably fucking everyone on the team..." Ryan's rant was nothing I hadn't heard before, but the entire room stilled as Mac stepped up behind him.

"That's fucking enough, Crawford," he barked, anger lacing his tone. "I've told you this before, and I'll tell you again. If you cannot stop with the attacks and insults of another member of this team, then you are out. Simmons is right. We live and die by being a team, and that requires some goddamn accountability."

Ryan shut right up, and I envied Mac's ability to make him do so.

"You're running drills the next few days after practice," Mac barked at him.

"We'll all run drills," I corrected Mac. I heard a few guys groan, but they knew where I was going for this. "We live and die as a team. We fail together. We succeed together. And we learn together."

"Yes, Cap!" Lewis barked.

"Yes, Cap!" the rest of the team, minus Ryan, chorused.

"Now get out of here and shower off. This room stinks worse than my grandmother's feet, God rest her soul."

Mac dismissed us, and the room erupted into conversation and footsteps as they jostled towards the showers. I ducked out of the room, heading to the separate set of locker rooms they reserved for me. Footsteps behind me had me whirling around. I was still jumpy from the confrontation and didn't have the greatest memories of being alone in locker rooms.

Asher held up his hands. "Easy, Lex, it's just me. I'm going to wait outside while you shower and get dressed. We don't trust Crawford right now."

I didn't have to ask who 'we' was. He continued, "Noah is going to switch out with me, so we won't miss the bus back to the hotel."

I wanted to argue with him, but I didn't have the energy. The same deep exhaustion I had felt out on the field weighed down on me again. I nodded and turned away. I didn't have the energy to fight. I just wanted to sleep for a few years and then load up to go home tomorrow.

*** ASHER'S POV ***

"So we all agree something's up with Lexi, right?" I asked, staring around our group.

Noah nodded but stayed quiet. He was still looking at the elevators that Lexi had disappeared into an hour earlier like someone kicked his puppy. I hated to see my usually exuberant twin so down, and a quick glance around at our friends showed he wasn't the only one. Lexi had us all tied up in knots.

We were sitting in the lobby of the hotel near Tolston University. A lot of the guys on the team went out tonight, eager to celebrate our win, but we hadn't felt like celebrating. Something was wrong with Lexi. From being on edge over the last few weeks to the weary look in her eyes as she called it a night, something was off with our best friend, and we needed to figure out what it was.

Derek looked around the lobby, making sure no one was within earshot. The last thing we needed was someone over-hearing us and adding more stress to Lexi's plate.

"Whatever it is, she's not talking." Lewis took a sip of the sodas we had snagged from the hotel vending machine. A deep frown covered his face. I knew it killed him that she had clammed up on him. Lexi, Lewis, and Jamison were usually thick as thieves, brought closer by their extended history.

In the beginning, I was jealous of their connection, but Lexi moved between all of us so seamlessly without seeming to notice. We each had our own special thing we did with her, but lately it seemed like she was pulling back from all of us.

"Maybe it's senioritis?" Jamison suggested.

Lewis tilted his head. "Maybe. She kept talking about us going our separate ways after graduation." He looked at Derek. "I know we agreed to wait to tell her how we feel, but I think we're running out of time."

Derek held up his hands. "Don't look at me. It was a group decision."

"Derek's right," I said. "We all agreed to be patient with her. But I think it's worth revisiting the conversation. Maybe she would feel more secure knowing how we felt?"

Noah finally spoke up. "I don't think whatever is going on has to do with us. Or, at least, not totally. She's always been at ease with us."

Lewis looked like he wanted to say something, but the doors

to the hotel opened, and a family walked past us, chattering away at the game.

Before he could speak, Jamison said, "Did you all see how exhausted she looked tonight after dealing with that dipshit Crawford? Like, where does he get off disrespecting her like that?" Jamison's voice was heated, which wasn't uncommon for our hothead.

"Easy there, tiger," I said as the front desk clerk raised her head to look at us. "I get it, but let's not get ourselves kicked out of the hotel."

Lewis still looked like something was on his mind, so I prodded him gently. "Lewis, what are you thinking?"

He startled, and I frowned. "What if..." he began hesitantly. "What if whatever it is has been going on longer than a few weeks?"

He looked pained when he said that, and I felt for him. Lewis was Lexi's confidante. If she had been hiding something from him, it would wreck him.

"What makes you say that?" Derek said, leaning forward so his elbows were on his knees.

Lewis hesitated. The doors to the hotel slid open, admitting a group of our loud, drunk teammates. I let out a soft groan as they spotted us and headed our way.

"We'll talk when we get home," Derek said as our drunk teammates got closer.

We nodded, and I pasted a smile on my face as Collins launched into a story of what had just happened at the bar they were at, but my thoughts were miles away. What was wrong with Lexi? What was she hiding?

LEXI

J tugged the thermal long sleeve shirt over my head in the Grandview locker rooms. Shaking out my muscles, a small grin played on my face. I felt great.

After the game on Sunday, I had actually slept in, shocking my guys when I stumbled downstairs at 11 a.m. Derek had asked if I wanted to go for a run, but the urge to do something just wasn't there. Instead, I'd cuddled on the couch between Noah and Jamison as we did a movie marathon. Halfway through the first movie, I'd fallen asleep on Jamison's chest, missing the rest of the movie marathon, but I had woken up yesterday morning feeling like a brand new woman.

Shutting my locker, I snapped the latch shut and grabbed my water bottle. Exiting the locker room, I ran into Finn and Asher as they were exiting the guys' locker room.

"You look bright-eyed and bushy-tailed, Cap." Finn smiled at me.

"Thanks. Got some damn sleep for once, and it's amazing what it can do."

"We've only been telling you that for years," Asher griped half-heartedly.

I rolled my eyes at him, and Finn laughed.

"Did you all hear Mac's conducting interviews today to replace Reeder?" Finn asked us as we headed out of the tunnel into the indoor training center.

"I didn't know that was happening today," I said. I was happy for Reeder but sad to see him go. The new coach would have big shoes to fill.

"Yeah, he wanted to do it while we were still in season to see how they jibe with the current team. I mean, half of our all-stars are leaving next year." Finn looked at Asher and me.

"Sorry, buddy, I can't do any more years of school," Asher joked. "Besides, you get to be the big dog next year." Finn was staying for one more year to be a 'super senior,' and he was thrilled to be the top dog.

"It's not going to be the same, though. This is the best team I've ever played on," Finn griped.

"You can make a better one next year," I said, pushing open the door before Asher could.

I hadn't told Finn this, but I had already recommended to Mac that he be the team captain next year. He was a good guy, funny but solid, and he would be an excellent team captain.

We joined our teammates in the small training field. Grandview definitely invested in its athletics. It wasn't a full football field size, but the fifty yards of turf helped us run drills all winter long without being stuck in the snow that was starting to come down.

I chatted with Jamison and Springer about classes while we waited for Mac to arrive. We were towards the back of the group, so when Mac came out of the side door, I didn't immediately see the new coach.

"All right, gather 'round!" Mac's familiar bark had the room quieting down, and I turned with the rest of my teammates to face him.

Broad backs moved in front of me as the group shuffled

around Mac and the four men standing around him. Springer shuffled to the right, and time froze.

Standing to the right of Mac was my living nightmare.

The sound of rushing water filled my head as my vision blurred. Every muscle in my body froze, and my breaths started coming more rapidly.

Fuck, fuck, fuck. No, no, no.

My heart threatened to beat out of my chest as I went dizzy from lack of oxygen. I felt someone shifting next to me, Jamison perhaps, but I couldn't look his way. My world narrowed down to one point of focus even as black dots flashed across my vision.

"Lexi, Lexi." My name was being whispered, but it was faint, like it was coming through a tunnel.

I wanted to run, but that would draw attention to myself. Why was *he* here? How could *he* be here?

Someone moved in front of me, blocking me from seeing *him*. *He* hadn't noticed me, thank God, and I struggled to get my breathing under control. Someone touched my shoulder, and I jerked before strong fingers caught my elbow. I looked up. Lewis.

"Eyes on me," he mouthed, and I nodded mutely.

Oh God, I was making a scene. I looked around me to see Jamison, Noah, and Asher had subtly moved to block me from everyone's view. I was never so grateful to be shorter than them before.

Lewis rubbed my elbow with his thumb, silently drawing my attention back to him. "What's wrong?" he whispered.

I jerked my head from side to side. There was no way I could speak right now with the ball of emotions clawing at my throat. He moved his hand down to grab my wrist, placing my hand on his chest.

"Breath with me," he whispered softly.

The first few breaths were a struggle, but gradually I got my breathing under control. Fuck. I had to make it through practice. Leaving now would cause a scene, and we had the championship game coming up in two weeks. I couldn't afford to let the team down.

Fuck, fuck, fuck.

Lewis squeezed my wrist as my breathing quickened again, and I forced myself to take big, shuddering breaths. Behind Lewis, I could hear Mac introducing the four potential candidates and *his* name, but I blocked it out. I had to get it together. I closed my eyes.

Okay, I could do this. I hadn't been prepared to see him. Now that the shock was wearing off, I could keep it together to get through practice. It would be fine. Everything was fine. I gathered every paralyzing feeling that was coursing through my body and imagined squishing them into a ball. Then I shoved that ball into a box and buried it so deep in my mind that there was no chance it could escape. This would work. It *had* to work.

I opened my eyes to see Lewis still looking at me with concern. I managed a shaky smile at him and dropped my hand from his chest. He reluctantly let go of my wrist as Mac barked at everyone to spread out and start stretching. I kept my eyes on the turf and headed for the back of the room. Usually, we stuck up near the front, but I needed to put some distance between me and *him*.

God, I needed to get it together. What were the guys thinking? I didn't dare look at them, even though I knew they'd followed me to the back of the room. They would ask questions. Questions I didn't want to answer.

Sure enough, as we sat down to start stretching, Jamison hissed, "What the hell was that?"

I shrugged, keeping my eyes down as I stretched one leg out and reached for my toes. "I must not have eaten enough this morning. I just got a little light-headed."

"Bullshit," Jamison snapped, but a thud followed, and he

blissfully went silent. I looked up to see Lewis shaking his head at him and motioning with his chin behind me.

"It's good to see all of you again." Blood drained from my face at the sound of *his* voice, and I ducked my head to hide my reaction.

He had a smooth voice. Most people called him charismatic because of it. But it grated at me, rubbing me raw. I barely held in a shudder as I felt his oily gaze on my back.

"Coach," Lewis said gruffly, looking up at him. "It's been a long time."

"Yes, it has. It's good to see my star players doing so well for a university I hope to coach at."

Jamison grinned, but it was his fake grin. "Best of luck to you on the application."

"Thank you."

Someone called his name, and I felt his gaze slide away from me. I watched out of the corner of my eye as he approached another group, and once he was gone, it felt like I could breathe again.

"Who was that?" Asher asked quietly.

"He was our high school coach for a few years. He left... what was it, junior year, Lexi?" Jamison asked me.

I nodded, still not trusting my voice just yet. I switched legs and stretched out my other side before moving through our stretching sequence.

It's fine. Everything's fine, I chanted to myself in time with my breaths. By the time Mac started breaking us up into drills, I was feeling more stable.

Or I was at least until Mac called *him* and another potential candidate over to help me and Rory, my backup QB, with our passing warm-up.

"Sorry, I didn't catch your name earlier." I smiled tightly at the candidate.

"Freddie MacIntire." The guy held his hand out for me to

shake. He was about my height at 5'10" and had pale skin and fire-red hair. "Nice to meet you. I've been following Grandview's season closely. You've got a great record."

"That would be thanks to me," *his* voice joked. "I developed her in high school."

Freddie shot *him* a look out of the corner of his eye, and I bit my lip. At least someone else saw through *him* as well. Freddie turned back to me and clapped his hands together. "Okay, I understand you're taking it kind of easy for this week, so let's start with three-yard passes and then back up every third pass. I'll move around a bit, but we'll keep it fairly simple to start."

I nodded, and he picked up a ball out of the cart on the side-lines and tossed it to me. His throw was actually pretty decent, and he laughed at the look on my face.

"I was a kicker, but I always dreamed of being a quarterback."

Beside me, Rory was starting his own drills with *him*, and I fought to block him out. The three-yard throws started out easily enough. I could do those in my sleep, and it helped focus my mind and get my head in the game. We backed up a step each time until we were at ten-yard throws. Then *he* walked behind Freddie as I was launching a pass, and my arm wobbled, sending the ball flying to Freddie's left. Noah caught it as he went by and raised his eyebrows at me.

"Sorry," I called at him. "Slipped out of my grip."

"Do you need some chalk?" Freddie asked.

"Here," *he* said. He walked over and handed me the chalk bag. I kept my eyes on his shoulder.

"Thanks," I muttered, taking it and moving past him to set it back down. I could hear my heartbeat in my ears as I dusted my fingers with chalk and rubbed my hands together. *Get it together,* I chided myself as I returned to my position.

Freddie tossed me the ball again, and we stepped back to twelve-yard throws. I tried to focus on the game, but my throws were wobbly and all over the place. I couldn't shake the feeling of his eyes on me, even when I would glance at him and see him focusing on Rory. It was like his very presence was throwing me off. Thankfully, Mac called for a new set of drills, and I jogged over to Freddie.

"Sorry," I apologized. "I had a rough night and am not on my game today." I felt bad for disappointing him when he seemed like such a fan of Grandview's football team.

"It's no sweat, kid," he said. "You can't be perfect every day. Better here at practice than at the game."

I winced. "Yeah, I should work out of it."

"Seriously, don't worry about it. But if I can offer a piece of advice? Find whatever centers you and focus on that. That'll help when your days feel out of control."

I smiled tightly at Freddie and nodded. I liked him. He seemed like a good guy, but I didn't know what centered me other than football, and I wasn't doing so hot at that right now. My eyes found my guys as they finished up their sets of drills. Lewis was joking with Asher as they teamed up against each other. Noah was chatting with Derek by the water cooler, and Jamison was showing off his victory dance to another potential candidate. A real smile spread across my face this time. Maybe the guys were my center?

Mac called for us to gather around, and *he* moved closer to me under the guise of listening. My body locked up, like a stone statue. I barely breathed, only relaxing when Mac separated us out for drills. Thankfully, he paired me with Jamison today. Lord only knows how it would have gone if he'd tried to pair Crawford and me together to run passing drills instead. Instead, Rory got stuck with Crawford.

Even with *him* at a safe distance away, I could not seem to get it together. My body was wired, and my brain struggled to focus as Jamison and I ran drills together. My passes were either too short or too long, too far left or too far right. It was only due to our many years of playing together that he was able to read my body language and dive for the ball or jump up to get it. After the next pass went soaring over his fingertips, Mac called me over.

"What the hell is going on, Simmons?" he asked as he stood in the center of the room, keeping an eye on everything around him while he talked to me. "I've never seen you like this. Even in freshman year. Is it championship nerves?"

"No, sir," I said, trying to keep my voice even as *he* moved behind Mac into my line of sight. "I didn't get a lot of sleep last night," I repeated the lie I'd told Freddie. "And I didn't eat enough this morning. I'm just a bit off today, but I'll be better, I promise."

He moved his gaze from the room to give me a once over. He took in my pale skin and frowned. "Are you sure you're not coming down with something? Lyle can check you out."

"No, sir, I'll be fine. Just an off day. I promise I'll get it together. I won't jeopardize our championship run."

"I care about the championships, sure, but your health comes first. If I don't see some improvement, I'll have to bench you," Mac said.

"I understand, sir. I won't let you down," I said.

My stomach dropped at his words. I had come too far to be benched at the final hour. The team would likely do okay with Rory as QB, but I knew they were relying on me to lead them. Fuck, I had to get it together. I couldn't let them all down and risk the championship win because of my issues.

"Go," Mac said. "Practice is almost over, anyway. Go eat something and get some damn sleep. I'll see you in the weight room tomorrow."

I nodded and headed towards the side door, keeping my gaze averted from anyone else's. Guilt filled me that I hadn't been able to keep it together for the team. The championship was too important. I had to get my head on straight.

I tried to keep my breathing even as I showered, struggling to shove all the emotions down into that box deep inside me while trying to scrub his gaze from my skin. I dressed quickly, hoping to avoid everyone else while they finished practice. I knew the guys would have questions, but I couldn't answer them. Not without that box full of emotions exploding. And we didn't have time for me to deal with all that.

Finally, I pushed open the door to the training center, welcoming the bitter fall air as it sank into my lungs and nipped at every inch of exposed skin.

"Alexa."

I froze, my body becoming like ice at the sound of *his* voice.

He waited for me, hands in his down coat pockets, looking like just a regular person out for a stroll in the cold weather, not my living nightmare.

"How is my special star doing?"

Bile rose in the back of my throat at that nickname. Immediately I was a sixteen-year-old girl again, desperate to prove herself on a competitive high school team, soaking up the special attention of the head coach, never seeing him for the monster he was until it was too late.

He walked closer to me, and it felt like a million bugs crawled over my skin. I tried to force my feet to move, to get away, but they remained frozen to the ground.

"Did you forget about me with your new school? Forget that I made you who you are?"

I wanted to vomit, but even those muscles wouldn't work, frozen in his gaze.

"Won't you look at me, my special star?"

I lifted my gaze to his shoulder.

"Look at me," he barked and my eyes flew to his.

The pleasure in his eyes made me want to die. To fall into an endless black hole and cease to exist. I wanted to set myself on fire, if only to get away from his gaze.

"Have you been keeping our special training a secret?" *He* arched an eyebrow at me, and I forced my head to nod.

"Good." A smile spread across his face. On anyone else, I would call him handsome, but I just saw evil standing before me. "You wouldn't want to risk my chances at getting that assistant coach title, now, would you? Not this close to the championships? If certain... things got out, well... people might question your accomplishments as a quarterback and wonder about your integrity off the field. A female quarterback... people will always wonder if that's why you've accomplished so much."

I knew he wanted a reply to his twisted words, but if I opened my mouth right now, I was going to either vomit or cry. My throat was frozen, so I had a feeling it was the latter, and I didn't want to show him any more weakness. Not when he already looked so pleased at my fear. He was repeating my deepest fears back to me. And he was right. If anyone found out, my career would always be overshadowed by that. And worse? So would my guys. Anyone I played with would be put under scrutiny. Their careers would be tarnished, and I would be responsible.

The door opened behind me. "Trying to cozy up to the new coaches already, Simmons?" Crawford's voice grated at my eardrums, but I was also incredibly grateful for the distraction, even if it was an insult.

I turned towards him, grateful for the excuse to look away from *his* gaze. "No," I managed to mutter through clenched teeth.

Crawford's eyes narrowed on me, taking in my pale skin. But he apparently couldn't bring himself to be a decent human being, and he brushed past me to introduce himself to *him*.

"I'm Ryan Crawford, our star running back."

If I were able to, I would have snorted at his introduction, but I felt like I was one wrong move away from shattering.

Ryan kept chatting with *him* while they walked towards the staff parking lot. I spun on my heel, trying to keep my steps steady and not sprinting away like I wanted to. When I was twenty yards away, I let my stride lengthen, practically speed-walking to get away. I thought I heard someone yell my name, probably one of my guys, but I didn't stop walking. If I didn't stop walking, I wouldn't shatter. If I didn't stop walking, no one would know I was broken.

DEREK

"*I*'m calling an emergency family meeting. We need to talk. Now," I said to Asher and Lewis as I watched Lexi speed walk away.

Noah and Jamison burst through the door behind us. We had all rushed to catch Lexi, but she was already gone by the time I hit the hallway. When I had run for the door, I just caught a glimpse of her back as she practically ran away.

"Where's Lexi?" Noah asked.

"She's gone," Asher said.

Movement at the corner of my eye caught my attention. My eyes narrowed. Fucking Crawford and was that... their old high school coach and one of the potential assistant coach candidates. My stomach sank. Too much was adding up in my head, and I hoped I was wrong.

The door opened behind us again, and Mac came out. He narrowed his eyes at us, assessing our group, and I had a feeling he was looking for Lexi as well. Most of the team likely hadn't noticed her odd behavior today, but Mac would have.

He approached us. "What's going on with Simmons, boys?"

I glanced at Lewis, who shook his head slightly, and I fought not to roll my eyes. I wasn't going to tell Mac anything. None of us were. Right now, we didn't know anything for certain, and Lexi would die if we risked her spot on the team.

"Just an off day." I shrugged.

Mac rubbed his face with a weathered hand. "Look, I know you all are thicker than thieves and you're not going to tell this old codger anything."

"You're definitely not old," Jamison spoke up with his usual humor, trying to distract Mac.

Mac shook his clipboard at him. "Stop with the distractions. I'm not out to get her. She was cagier than you all are when I asked her what was going on. I've been in this business for decades. I know the difference between not getting enough sleep and something else going on. Whatever it is, fix it. This close to the championship, we need to be protecting our star player. Can I count on you for that?"

Lewis folded his arms and nodded. "We'll take care of her, Mac."

Mac studied him for a long time before turning that stare on each of us. "See that you do. But don't add to her problems while you do it."

With that abrupt warning, he turned and walked back into the athletic center.

After he left, Noah asked, "What do we do now?"

"I'm calling an emergency family meeting," I said. "Let's get back to the house."

We walked quickly back to the house, and after dropping our bags off in our respective rooms, we gathered in the family room.

"I know we agreed not to talk about the specifics of our relationships with Lexi," I started. "But I think we all agree something's going on."

"We all agreed on that already," Asher snapped, although I knew his anger wasn't at me. "But what is going on?"

"She's exhausted, jumpy, had a damn near panic attack at practice." Jamison ticked things off on his fingers.

"You said she kept talking about going our separate ways after graduation, right?" Noah asked Lewis. "Could it be that?"

"Fear of change could be a factor," I agreed. I remembered how Lewis wanted to say something the other night, but we were interrupted. "What were you going to say the other night, Lewis? You said you thought it might have been going on longer than a few weeks?"

Lewis rubbed the back of his neck, hesitating. "I'm only telling you this because I think it's going to help us figure out what's going on. I feel like I'm breaking Lexi's trust even doing it, but something is going on, so…"

He paused, and we all waited with bated breath. He looked up at each of us. "Also, Lexi and I figured it out between us, and we're fine, but the other day, before the game, we… had sex. And there was a moment where she was on the bed and I was over her that triggered a panic attack."

Fuck.

Muffled swearing echoed around the room, but it felt like rushing water in my ears. Too many of the pieces added up.

"I think maybe it was a bad experience she had in college that maybe she's too embarrassed to talk about?" Lewis offered.

"But why is it happening now? And nothing's affected her playing before like it did today."

Noah looked over at me and read my face. "Derek," he said, cutting through the room. "What are you thinking?"

This time, I was the one who hesitated. I didn't want to share unless I was sure, but all signs pointed to it. The strive for perfection and accomplishments, the hypersexuality but also the trigger of being loomed over, the appearance of their old high school coach today… There was only one way to find out.

"Did anything ever happen in high school?" I asked, looking at Jamison and Lewis.

Jamison was sitting on the arm of the couch, legs outstretched in front of him and arms folded. He looked at Lewis, who was leaning forward, elbows on his knees. Jamison shook his head.

"No."

Lewis agreed with him. "No, nothing happened."

"We were thick as thieves in high school. We did everything together. Football, parties, studying. Everything," Jamison said.

"You guys couldn't have been with her all the time," Asher pointed out slowly. From the horrified look on his face, I think he knew where I was going with this. His sister's best friend had been through something similar, and I think he just put the pieces together.

"Do you think it had anything to do with your old high school football coach?" I asked softly.

Lewis looked like he was going to protest, then stopped. I saw Noah get up out of the corner of my eye but focused on Lewis, who was looking at Jamison.

Lewis and Jamison's faces were pale. "Those special trainings," Lewis murmured. "But you went to those."

Jamison shook his head. "I didn't go to all of them."

"Fuck!" Lewis got up from the couch and started pacing. He whirled around. "You don't think..."

I held up my hands. "I don't know. But the signs are all there. He was there at practice today. And he could barely keep his eyes off Lexi."

"And she had a panic attack on the field," Asher said. "She would never let anything affect her playing if she could help it."

Lewis and Jamison looked lost, like someone had ripped the floor out from under her feet. "She never said..." Jamison trailed off.

"She was likely threatened to keep quiet," I said grimly.

"Fuck, she probably was." Asher gripped his head in his

hands. "That's what happened to Skylar. She only confessed to Ainsley."

Noah came back into the room with his laptop in hand. "What are you doing?" Jamison asked him.

"I'm looking up that guy's information," Noah said.

I nodded, remembering he was minoring in computer science.

We all piled on the couch around him, minus Lewis, who was still pacing and muttering to himself, clenching and unclenching his fists.

"What was his name again?" Noah asked Jamison, who rattled it off quickly.

Noah typed it into an official-looking registry. His fingers flew across the computer as different screens popped up and flew away. I'd once asked him why he didn't pursue computer science as a major, and he'd said he liked the versatility of the business degree with the added benefit of the computer science degree.

He cussed softly under his breath.

"What is it?" Asher asked.

"He's on the sex offender registry."

The amount of swearing that echoed through the room would probably have a priest showering holy water on all of us.

"How the fuck did he become a coach?" Jamison snarled, getting up to join Lewis in his pacing.

"He used his mother's maiden name and asked to have his record sealed as he'd only just turned eighteen. Looks like he came from a small town, so his family probably knew the judge."

"Can you find anything else?"

"There's an article here from years ago that he was a suspect in an assault, but the girl ended up recanting her story."

"Fuck, so he's done it before." Asher looked like he was going to be physically ill.

I heard Jamison whisper to Lewis hotly. "You triggered her the other night?" he hissed, whirling to face Lewis.

"I already said that. And I calmed her down, and it was fine."

"I can't believe you would continue after..."

"She said she was fine with it, and you weren't there," Lewis said hotly. "I would never do anything to hurt her."

"You should have stopped."

"She asked to be distracted."

"Yeah! From abuse!"

"I didn't know that!" Lewis roared. "I thought it was just a bad experience in college."

"How could you not have known that?" Jamison got all up in Lewis's face.

I had a feeling we were seconds away from a fight breaking out. Neither of them was actually mad at each other, but both of them felt helpless. This had been going on right under their noses, and they'd had no idea. That had to hurt, and they had to get it out.

"How could you not have?" Lewis shoved Jamison away from him. "You attended the 'special' trainings with them!"

"Hey! Take it outside!" Asher shouted as they stumbled into the coffee table.

"Noah, referee them," I said grimly as they headed outside. "They're going to need to get this out, but don't let them break any bones."

Noah nodded and closed his laptop, setting it aside and following them out the front door.

Asher swore next to me. "What do we do? Do we ask Lexi about it?"

I chewed on my lip as I thought. "I don't know if we should. She could get defensive and deny it. It might send her spiraling even further. Trauma like this... it's got to be done at her own pace. All we can do is be there for her and keep her away from him."

"I just want to bash his face in," Asher growled.

"Join the club," I said wryly. Anger saturated my veins as well, but we couldn't all lose our shit at the same time.

"WHAT THE FUCK?"

I swore. Lexi was home.

LEXI

$\mathcal{B}$y the time I made it onto our street, I was feeling a lot more settled. Class had helped focus my mind, followed by a stop at Chocolate Chasings to see Meena and get some chocolate goodness. I brought the to-go cup to my lips and took a sip of the sweet, sugary drink. As the sugar hit my taste buds, I could feel my brain settling. I wasn't naïve enough to think I was over it completely, but at least I had gotten my shit together enough to go home and face whoever was there. There would be questions, for sure.

It was a rough night's sleep. I didn't eat enough this morning. I was stressed about classes, championships, senior year. I repeated the excuses in my head as I got closer to our house.

I squinted at our yard. Who was fighting in our front yard? Was that Jamison and Lewis? I watched in horror as Jamison reared back and clocked Lewis across the face.

"WHAT THE FUCK?"

Noah stood up from the steps at my shout. Why was he just sitting there watching them? Derek and Asher burst out onto the porch as I approached. Jamison and Lewis didn't give me so much as a glance, totally focused on beating each other up. They were rolling around on the ground now, and I debated pouring my drink over them for a half second, but that would be a waste of chocolate.

"Hey, Lexi." Asher descended the steps and put an arm around my shoulder, carefully guiding me past the fight and up the stairs.

"Don't *hey Lexi* me," I said. "What the fuck is going on? Why are they fighting?"

Derek held the door open for me. "They're just getting some things out. They'll be fine. Noah's watching them."

"What things?" I eyed Derek and Asher carefully. They were acting weird, treating me like I was glass as they bundled me into the kitchen and took my bag.

"Guy things," Asher said. "Don't worry about it."

"No one in the history of ever has anyone stopped worrying because someone told them not to worry about it," I snarked at Asher, who let out a strained chuckle. I frowned at him. "What's going on?"

"Nothing's going on." Asher wouldn't look me in the eye.

The dread and panic from earlier started curdling in my gut. Something was wrong. Were they fighting about me? Over me? What was going on?

Commotion came from the front entryway, and soon Jamison, Lewis, and Noah filed into the kitchen. Jamison and Lewis sported matching black eyes, and I stood up from my chair.

I got up and went to the freezer. I opened it up and grabbed two bags of frozen vegetables we kept for that purpose. I tossed them to Jamison and Lewis and then leaned against the counter and pinned them with a glare.

"What the fuck is going on? Why are you punching each other?"

For a minute, I didn't think they were going to answer me.

"Did our old high school coach rape you?" Jamison blurted.

I stumbled backwards a step, catching myself on the counter. I felt the color drain from my face as I swayed. "What?" I winced as my voice went up two octaves.

"You heard me." Jamison's face was unreadable. Was he angry? Disgusted? I couldn't tell. "Did he rape you?"

"Jamison." Derek's voice cut through the tension between us. "You can't just ask her that."

I spun away and tried to get myself together.

"Why the fuck not? Answer the question, Lexi."

For a second, I wanted to answer him honestly. I wanted to say yes. But then *his* words filtered in from earlier. If I opened my mouth and told them all the truth, they would go after him. They would ruin their shot at the championships. Or they would be so disgusted with me that it would cause tension on the team, and it would all come out. I took a shaky breath, still looking out the window over the sink.

"Do I seem like the type of person who would let that happen to herself?" My words tasted like ash on my tongue, but my voice was steady. "Would I stay in a sport I loved if I had that kind of trauma from it? Could I have accomplished all I have if I was broken like that?"

I slowly turned around and met their gazes. They were unreadable, and uncertainty had my breath catching in my throat.

"It would be okay if it happened." Asher paused. "Well, it wouldn't be okay; it would be so far from okay. But if it did happen, you can tell us. It's not your fault. You were a kid, and he has a history of doing this. Noah even found where he changed to his mother's maiden name to avoid detection."

I froze, my ears ringing at his words. *He has a history of doing this?* He had done this to other girls? Had he done this to others after me? Could I have stopped it?

Lewis broke the heavy silence, looking at me with guilt clear in his eyes. "I told them about the other day. What happened when we had sex. When you got triggered."

Anger sliced through me. I thought the unsaid rule was that we didn't talk about each other's relationships. What happened there was private. I didn't think he would go spreading that information around. My lips pinched tight as fury and betrayal warred in me. How dare he?

"Just because we're having sex now does not mean you get to jump all over me when I'm having a bad day or a bad few days. I didn't think friends did that to each other, but maybe as soon as sex entered the equation, I lost your friendship." I lashed out at them.

"Lexi, that's not what he meant" Noah reached for me, and I flinched back *hard*. They all stilled.

I squeezed my eyes shut. If I wanted to convince them that it wasn't true, I was doing a hell of a job at it. When I opened my eyes and saw the *knowing* on their faces, I panicked.

"I've got to go. I can't be here right now." I pushed past all of them, grabbing my bag from the door and fleeing out of the house. I had to get away.

* * *

THEY'D FOUND OUT. *How had they found out?*

Because you're an idiot, that's why. You couldn't have been more obvious at practice today.

The voice inside my head was nasty and cutting but no less true. I had blown up my deepest, darkest secret, violently exposing it to the light. And now that it was out there, I had no idea how they would react.

What were they thinking? Were they disgusted by me? Were they running to the athletic center now to tell Mac? Oh God. What if they were? No, they wouldn't do that. Would they?

Lewis might be hunting *him* down right now. Fuck, this was all such a mess.

He has a history of doing this.

Asher's words kept ringing in my ears. Was that true? Was I the first or the last? Shame flooded me. Because I wasn't strong enough to stop him, because I was too broken in the aftermath, had someone suffered like I had? My knees went weak, and I stumbled a step before righting myself.

I looked up. I was in the middle of campus. Luckily, most people were in class, so no one was watching my freakout, but I had to get out of the open. I veered right for the library. Scanning my student ID, I jogged up the stairs to the fourth floor. Up here, no talking was allowed. I didn't have to speak to anyone, and I could hide in the personal cubbies. But, more importantly, I could see for myself if Asher was right. If I had failed anyone else so badly.

Luckily, one of the cubbies was open. I ducked into the pod-like structure, dropping my bag on the floor next to me as I jiggled the mouse on the computer to get it to wake up. When the login screen finally appeared, I signed in as a guest and opened an incognito browser.

My hands shook as I typed his name into the search engine, then I forced myself to take a few unsteady breaths. I hesitated before I typed 'sexual assault' next to his name. I had never named what happened to me before in my head. It was always buried so deep inside me. But naming it, while it terrified me to see, also brought a weird sort of peace if just for a few moments.

The mouse hovered over the search bar. If I clicked search, I couldn't hide from the results. I would know either way. Did I want to know? Was I ready for everything that came with knowing? Probably not, but I was already broken, anyway. Why not cut myself a little deeper? I might have been a coward before by staying quiet, but I could be brave now and see if, by staying quiet, I had hurt other people.

I clicked the button before I could chicken out. *His* smiling face was the first thing that popped up, and I recoiled from the screen. My stomach churned, and I scrolled down the page quickly, hiding *his* face. Articles of his coaching career were listed on the first page, and I scrolled past them to the bottom. I clicked on the last page of the search results and started scanning the links. Noah had taught me a few things from his computer science classes. One of them being most people stayed to the first two pages of search results, but you could find some interesting finds on the last few pages.

Most of the articles here were old or didn't contain the words I was looking for, but I kept scrolling. There. Buried three pages from the end of the search results was a link to a travel blog. The headline was clear. "Local teen gets away with assault."

I swallowed back the bile that was gathering at the back of my throat as I clicked on the link. It was a travel blog run by a girl named Lindsey. Lindsey wrote in her article that the local papers weren't covering the story based on who *his* parents were, so she was writing it for the victim. She disclosed she was friends with the victim's sister and shared a photo of her with her consent. The photo was innocent enough: the three girls with their arms around each other in front of a lake. The girl in the middle, the victim of his assault, could have been my sister.

I squeezed my eyes shut, but when I opened them again, I couldn't deny the similarities. Wavy brown hair and blue eyes. I gagged softly with my hand on my throat. Did he search me out because I looked like her? Or did he just have a type that I fit?

The blog post didn't share many details, just that *he* assaulted her at a party, and his family covered it up.

"I just want someone to know what he's done," Lindsey wrote as the last line of the article.

With shaky hands, I copied down the web address onto a spare piece of notebook paper and backed out to the rest of the search results. Obsessively, I scrolled through page after page, hunting for more information, more proof that would either condemn me or assuage my guilt.

I couldn't find anything else. Noah mentioned *he* was going by *his* maiden name now, but I didn't know what *his* real last name was. *His* picture on the front page rolled my stomach dangerously. His last school, Knighton Private College, was listed underneath it. I bit my lip. This was a longshot, but most colleges had a student forum called CollegeChat. Students used it to find study groups, buy and sell things, and find out information.

I pulled up the CollegeChat site and found Knighton's forum. I typed in *his* name into the search bar and clicked enter.

Immediately posts started popping up. The first few posts were asking if anyone knew why *he* was leaving so suddenly mid-year. But as I scrolled through the comments, my heart sank. A few people in there called him a creep, but there was one comment that had my muscles tensing and my fist pressing to my mouth.

I heard that he came onto one of the cheerleaders, and she reported him.

A few comments down, someone replied to the original comment.

I heard he transferred from his last school for the same reason, except he actually raped a student.

Despite my hand covering my mouth, a sob tore out of me at the realization that he *had* hurt someone else. That there was someone else out there living with what I was living with. My silence had caused their pain. A second sob escaped before I could stop it and students across the way were looking around, wondering who was making noise on the library's quiet floor.

I quickly gave a muffled cough to make people think that's what they'd heard and then hissed out an apology. I couldn't stay here. I wasn't going to be able to hold it together, but I didn't want to go home. The sun was starting to lower on the horizon when I looked out the window. How long had I been in here? I bit my lip as I clasped my shaking hands together. My leg bounced as I tried to think about where I could go. In my pocket, my phone buzzed.

Hey, girlie, you good?

Inez. I could go to Inez.

LEXI

I knocked softly on the door to Inez and Meena's apartment. My hands still shook, and I knew that the paleness in my cheeks was still evident. Meena opened the door and took in my face.

"Hey, babe," she called over her shoulder, her worried eyes still on mine. "Lexi's here."

Inez appeared over her shoulder, stopping in her tracks when she saw me. "Thanks, babe, I think this might be a code chocolate."

Meena nodded. "You got it. I'll be back." She grabbed the keys hanging by the door and brushed by me, giving me a gentle squeeze on my shoulder.

Inez stopped in front of me. "What's wrong? Who do I need to kill?"

Her fierce protectiveness and open concern finally did me in, and I burst into tears. Her eyes widened comically at first, but she quickly bundled me up in her arms. Dropping my bag in the kitchen, she guided me back to their bedroom and onto the bed.

The whole story spilled out of me. Starting in high school and the first time it happened until the end, to college and reclaiming my sexuality, to the friends-with-benefits arrangement and my fears about them finding out, to him showing up at practice, to the friendships I was terrified I had fucked up irreparably.

Throughout it all, Inez just held me in her arms and let me blubber out the whole thing without interruption. Meena eventually returned looking like she had robbed the candy aisle at the local gas station, and she was cuddled against my back, both of them just holding me while I broke down.

When I finally stopped to take a hiccupping breath, Inez spoke. "So that asshole was here? On campus? Is he still here?"

Her tone of voice promised murder and death, and Meena lifted her head off my back. "Easy there, babe, you can hunt him down later."

I took a shuddering breath. "No? I don't know. I don't think so. It was just interviews."

Inez brushed back a strand of my hair that had escaped my ponytail. "Thank you for telling us," she said softly. "I can't imagine what it was like going through that, but you're so strong."

"I don't feel very strong. I feel broken." I choked out on a sob. I felt raw and broken, like I had been run over by a truck or sacked three times in a row. Every muscle ached, including my eyelids. I hadn't realized how much weight I had been carrying all this time until I finally set it down, even if for just a moment.

"You are. You are so strong." Inez hugged me tighter. "Trauma like this, it doesn't go away. And you've been running from it for a long time."

"The guys didn't know?" Meena asked.

I shook my head. "They didn't. I mean, they do now. I guess they do. I didn't tell them, but somehow, they figured it out. But they didn't know before today."

"I can't believe Lewis and Jamison didn't know," she said. "Those boys are constantly watching you."

I swallowed back a sob. "I didn't want them to know. He said that if anyone knew... You're the first people I've told. God, if this gets out, the school, Mac..."

"Will do nothing," Inez said firmly. "I know what he said. I know what he told you. And I know how he got you to believe him, but that's not the case here. He has a history of doing this. If he tried to come after you, we would bury him."

"Figuratively, right?" Meena arched an eyebrow at Inez, who rolled her eyes.

A watery chuckle escaped me, and Inez sighed. "Fine. Figuratively. Only so you have plausible deniability later. But I bet Lewis would help me."

I winced, and Inez gave me a look. "What was that look for? Do you not believe he would help?"

I bit my lip and looked down. "I don't know. You didn't see their faces earlier. What if they're disgusted by me now? What if they think I'm too broken? What if—"

Inez cut me off. "I'm going to stop you right there, sweet cheeks. I know that's your fear talking right now, and I know you know deep down that those thoughts wouldn't even cross their minds, but I'll remind you just in case. Those guys are *crazy* for you. They have loved you for years. I can guaran-fuck-ing-tee you that something like that never crossed their minds. They're probably going out of their mind with worry. In fact, I know they are." She held up her phone and shook it. "They have been blowing up my phone asking if I've seen you and if you are okay. Now I haven't answered them yet, because girl code, but they're crazy for you."

"It was just supposed to be sex," I said softly. "There weren't supposed to be feelings."

Inez laughed at me. "Girl, I told you at the very beginning it wasn't just sex to them, but you needed to put that boundary up to protect yourself, and I get that now. But those guys have been head-over-heels for you for years."

"But they were always sleeping around?" I protested half-heartedly. That didn't really bother me, but would they do that if they were head-over-heels for me?

Meena shook her head against my back. "No, they haven't. They haven't slept with other girls since sophomore year."

"What?"

Meena laughed. "It's the talk of the dance and cheer team. Has been for months. It's all just rumors spread by girls who want to say they caught one of them, but their focus has been solely on you."

And I had been the one sleeping around. Inez pinched me.

"Ow, what the fuck?"

She shook her finger at me. "You stop those thoughts right now. We make no apologies for enjoying sex. None. And besides, you were adorably oblivious; although I thought for sure that once you started having sex with them, you would finally realize your feelings. I even had a bet with Meena about it, and I, *your best friend*, lost!"

Meena smothered a chuckle behind me. "Sorry, babe."

My cheeks flushed, and Inez's eyes widened. "You bitch, you have realized your feelings!"

I shrugged, but she wasn't having it and pinned me with her death stare. "Fine, yes, I have feelings for them. They're my best friends."

"They would be more if you asked."

"What's the point of asking, though? We're about to head in different directions after graduation."

"Are you so sure about that?" Inez looked smug.

"What do you mean?"

"Nope, you have to ask them."

I rolled my eyes. "You're the worst."

"I believe you meant the best."

The three of us laughed, and my soul felt a little lighter. This is what I had needed.

"So what do you want to do now?" Inez asked me softly.

"I should..."

"Nope. What do you want to do now? Not what you think you should do, what do you want to do?"

I chewed on my lip while I thought about it. What did I want? While lying here with Meena and Inez was great, what I really wanted was to be at home. With them. And if they were actually disappointed by my brokenness, then I would rather rip off the Band-Aid sooner rather than later.

"I want to go home," I said finally. "I want to go home and tell them, I guess. Even if they think I'm broken."

Inez opened her mouth, but Meena reached across me and smacked her. She pursed her lips. "I know they aren't going to think that. But I also know you won't believe me until you know that as well."

"Why do you keep saying they'll view you as broken?" Meena asked softly behind me.

I swallowed against the jagged lump in my throat. "Coz I feel broken," I confessed softly.

"You're not." Inez's gaze was fierce. "Not in our eyes, and not in their eyes. You're not broken. You're so strong. Absolutely none of this was your fault either. All fault lies in that creepy... asshole. Urgh, I don't have enough words in the dictionary to describe that piece of shit."

I swallowed against the rising tears and nodded slowly. My brain was going to have a hard time accepting that, but maybe their belief in me could help.

"Come on, we'll drive you."

"I can walk," I protested.

Inez's eyes flashed dangerously. "Not while that psycho is out there. We're driving you. No arguments."

"Yes, ma'am," I said, secretly thankful she'd insisted. If she hadn't, I would probably find a way to chicken out before I got there, and from the look in her eyes, she knew that.

"Come on, let's get you to your men."

LEXI

*I*nez and Meena dropped me off with a promise to come back if the guys reacted badly. But as they drove away, Inez yelled out of the window, "See you tomorrow!" So she clearly was confident it would go well.

I wished I shared her confidence.

I hesitated on the front porch. Light streamed through the downstairs windows, and I could hear the TV playing through the door. The guys were still up. My hands were shaky as I dug my keys out of my pocket, and I blew out a heavy breath, frustration stiffening my spine. I was so damn tired of feeling weak and broken. If the guys reacted poorly, then they reacted poorly. I couldn't do anything about it. All I could do was tell them the truth and let them decide. I would rebuild my life either way.

The whole truth? a small voice whispered in my head, and my hand froze on the doorknob.

The whole truth didn't just include the abuse but also my cowardly reactions to it. My stomach churned, and I swallowed hard. The whole truth. If I was going to tell them, then I would tell them everything. Better to get all of my brokenness out now, so if they wanted to leave, then I would know up front and not sit in agony.

Resolve firm, I twisted the handle and pushed open the door. The house was quiet, other than the TV playing, but my entrance wasn't unnoticed. Footsteps came down the stairs, and Derek appeared on the small landing.

"Lexi," he breathed hesitantly, worry all over his face.

I bit my lip at the sudden onslaught of tears burning behind my eyes. I couldn't cry now, damnnit. But something deep in my gut unclenched at the sight of him. I was so fucked if they decided I was too broken to be around after this.

"Hi," I whispered hoarsely. "Can we talk? With everyone?"

He nodded, keeping his gaze locked with mine as he called up the stairs. "Lewis, Asher, get down here. Lexi's home."

Noah appeared in the doorway to the kitchen and family room. "Lexi girl?" He had a glass in one hand, and I smiled tightly at him.

"Why don't you go sit on the couch with Noah, sweetheart," Derek said. "I'll get the others."

I nodded and dropped my bag on the ground next to the door in case I needed to make a quick escape later. But, fuck, if I wasn't tired of running.

Noah extended a hand towards me and then dropped it again, remembering my reaction from earlier. They were being so careful with me, and it grated on me as much as it comforted me. I was tired of feeling fragile, but I couldn't deny how raw I felt.

Jamison was sitting on the couch, mindlessly staring at the action movie on the screen. He looked up as I entered, springing to his feet. I barely held in a wince at his black eye. Fuck, that fight was today. It felt like forever ago. Like the events of today had been spread over a week instead of being packed into twelve hours.

Thudding feet behind me had me looking over my shoulder.

Lewis and Asher hesitated in the kitchen door. Derek huffed and pushed past them. He held out a hand to me, and I took it gingerly. It felt like some of the tension bled out of the room when I took his hand. God, they must think I was insane after my reactions to everything today.

Derek guided me to the couch and took a seat next to me. Slowly, the guys all took their seats as well, but Jamison crouched before me.

"I'm so sorry, Lexi. I shouldn't have pushed you earlier. I was out of line."

I reached out my free hand to trace the bruise around his eyes gently. "It's fine. I..." I swallowed as the words caught in my throat. "You weren't wrong," I whispered softly.

His eyes flared in anger, but I kept going.

"I... I want to tell you. To tell all of you. But I've never told anyone about it before..." Besides Inez, and I hadn't given her the details, just skimmed over that part of the story.

"And you don't have to." Derek squeezed my hand gently. "None of us will push." He shot a glare at Jamison, Lewis, and Asher.

"I know." I swallowed again. "But I want to. I want you to know. Just..." I looked up at each of them. "Just don't interrupt. I don't know if I can start again."

Asher nodded. "Whatever you need," he said softly, hazel eyes intent on mine.

"Caleb Bradford was hired the summer after our sophomore year." I stopped and shuddered softly. I just realized I hadn't said his name out loud. Not even to Inez. "Sorry, I just realized I haven't said his name out loud in... in... I don't know. Anyways. He was hired to lead our high school football team."

I could feel the looks going around the room, but I didn't look up from my lap. If I looked up, I wouldn't be able to keep going. I knew that.

"He was the first coach to give me a starting position on the football team. I thought it was because I was a good player, but he had something different in mind. He put me on the starting team and said I would need to start doing special training with him to make sure I didn't let anyone on the team down." I swallowed hard. "At first, the special trainings started out innocently enough. We would watch plays together and discuss them. He would run me through different drills. I enjoyed the extra attention, and he kept it so professional that I got lulled into a sense of comfort."

"The first time it happened." I flinched, and a sour, bitter taste filled my mouth. "The first time it happened was a month into the season. Afterwards... well, he told me that if anyone found out, I would be kicked off the team and expelled from school. That no one would believe me. And it was right after Tracy..."

My eyes flew up to Lewis, and he cursed colorfully.

"What happened?" Asher asked him.

"Tracy was a senior when we were sophomores." Lewis rubbed his beard. "She accused a guy on the team of raping her at the party as payback for him breaking up with her best friend."

"So no one would believe anyone else who came forward with similar accusations," Noah put together slowly, devastation on his face as he turned to me.

I looked down at my lap again. I couldn't look at him and keep it together.

"We were on the fast track to championships," I continued softly. "The team was doing really well, and they were counting on me, is what he said. I didn't see a way out. So many of us on the team were counting on scholarships to college. I couldn't risk their futures, my future. I loved football, and I knew if I had come forward about it, I would never be able to play again. My time in the sport I loved would become forever tarnished by the shadow of the scandal. I felt trapped."

Jamison jumped up and started pacing. "But why couldn't you have told us? We could have helped you. Fuck, I attended some of those trainings with you."

I winced, but luckily, he didn't notice. Derek did, though, and his grip tightened on my hand before relaxing again. I would never tell Jamison that it was always worse after he attended the trainings. That was one secret I would carry with me to my grave. He didn't need to know that. No one did.

"We were best friends, Lexi." Jamison dropped to his knees in front of us, his eyes desperate. "You could have told us anything."

I shook my head. "I didn't want you going away for murder. You were hotheads back then."

Asher snorted. "What's changed?"

I looked at him, and he flashed me a small smile. His body was rigid with tension, even with his seemingly relaxed posture with one arm along the back of the couch.

"You would have killed him, and it would have done exactly what I was terrified of happening. It would have come out, and not only would your lives been ruined, everything I'd worked so hard for, the sport I threw myself into to escape, would have been ruined for me."

I swallowed hard. "From the moment he first touched me, he broke me. I was broken, and I didn't want to drag anyone else into my brokenness."

"But we could have stopped it." Jamison's voice cracked. "We could have saved you." He leapt up, his movements jerky as he gripped his hair with his hands.

"You did."

My quiet words had everyone freezing. I squeezed my eyes shut and took a shuddering breath. Derek rubbed his thumb on the back of my hand, and I held it tightly. Noah scooted in closer, slowly, as if judging my reaction, and I sank into the warmth at my side. This was it. The final piece of my brokenness.

"One weekend, my parents went out of town. They'd taken Taggert to a travel soccer game, and I... I was having a really bad night. I had just had another special training session earlier that afternoon, and I was sitting on my bed, in the house, all alone. And I remember... I remember staring down at my hands like I didn't know who they belonged to. I felt just so... broken and like my body wasn't my own, like it was a stranger to me. And I just desperately wanted it back. I desperately wanted some type of control back."

Noah wrapped his arm around my shoulders, and I nearly broke down. I stiffened, and he pulled his arm back. I glanced up at him out of the corner of my eye and gave him a weak smile. It wasn't that I didn't want his comfort; it was that if he gave it, I wouldn't be able to finish.

"My parents never locked anything up. They didn't have to, they thought. But my mom had a ton of prescription pills left over from one of her knee surgeries, and I knew she kept them in her bathroom, so I went looking."

I could feel the tension in the room skyrocket, but I kept speaking. "I remember staring at the pill bottles in her cabinet when Jamison called me. When you called me"—I looked up at him quickly—"it was about something stupid. You had Lewis on the other line and wanted me to mediate some stupid argument you two were having, but afterwards we stayed on the line and talked for hours, and I eventually fell asleep on the phone with you both. And then the next night, you did it again. Any night my parents weren't in town, you called me."

I took a breath, squeezing my eyes shut. "You did save me," I whispered softly, but my words might have been bullets for the impact they had on the guys.

I opened my eyes, finally daring to look up and meet their faces. They were all pale, staring at me with a mixture of anguish and horror, but as hard as I looked, I couldn't find any trace of disgust. Tension I didn't know was that deeply ingrained in my muscles seeped out of me, and this time when Noah put his arm around me, I let him.

They knew all my dirty secrets now, every piece of trauma that made me the broken woman I was today. If they left... well, it would gut me, but I would survive.

Derek squeezed my hand, drawing my attention to him. "Thank you for telling us," he murmured.

"I knew something was wrong," Lewis said, looking like he had just been hit by a bus. "But I just thought it was your parents traveling with Taggert more and the pressure leading up to the championships. I never thought... Fuck, Pixie." He stared down at his clenched fists, then he looked back up at me. "That's when you threw yourself into football. You always loved it, but that next season was when you ate and breathed it like it was your job and not your passion."

"It's my escape." I shrugged. "I..." I shrugged again. I didn't have the words for it. Now that I had gotten it all out, I felt exhausted. Like I had been carrying a thousand pounds on my shoulders for years.

Derek rubbed his thumb on the back of her hand as Asher leaned forward. "We're so sorry that happened to you," he said softly. "Fuck, Lexi, that never should have happened."

"He's right," Derek said. "The only issue I have is how you keep referring to yourself as broken. You're not broken, sweetheart, you're a survivor. You know that, right?"

I shrugged, sinking back into Noah further and hiding my face in his chest.

"So what the fuck do we do about that piece of shit?" Jamison asked heatedly.

"First, you calm down," Derek said, steel laced in his tone. "It's up to Lexi about what she wants to do."

"Lexi girl," Noah said softly in my ear. "What do you want to do about him?"

"I don't know." And truly, I didn't. I'd never even entertained the idea that he would ever pay for what he did. The courts didn't treat victims kindly, and it was my word against his. "I don't know. I don't want him to do it to someone else... I... I looked up his record."

"Oh, Lexi," Asher said, sympathy on his face. "That wasn't your fault."

"But I kept quiet." I choked on a sob, and Noah tucked me closer into his chest.

"You were sixteen, baby girl." Asher got up and sat next to Noah. "You were a kid and something horribly traumatic had just happened to you. It wasn't your fault. It's only his fault."

A finger brushed under my chin, and I opened my eyes to see Derek looking at me softly. "Do you trust us? To handle him?"

I chewed on my lip. "I do, but I don't want you to handle it with violence or jeopardize your futures."

"No violence," Derek said softly, shooting a warning look in Jamison's and Lewis's directions. "Just answer me one question. Do you want to testify or press charges?"

Bile rose in my throat, and my muscles stiffened. A soft hand rubbed my back, and I let out a shuddering breath. "Not really. The courts aren't... kind to the victims. I will if I have to, though. So he doesn't hurt anyone else."

I waited for the disappointment or disapproval in his eyes, but he just looked at me softly. "Okay, sweetheart, we'll take care of it."

I nodded, keeping my eyes locked with him as I took another shuddering breath. I felt... Well, not lighter, but I felt something. Maybe like I could finally take a deep breath. Even if they decided to leave later, I would be all right.

"So, now you know how broken I am." I tried to bring

humor back into the room. "I would understand if you wanted to cut and run. It's a lot to deal with."

"God, Lexi." Jamison stood up, drawing my attention as he ran his hands through his hair. "When are you going to realize we're crazy for you? We don't care about anything else, the game, the team, your past, any of it. We love you. All of you. You're all we care about. You're all we want."

LEXI

"You what?" I whispered hoarsely, stunned at his words.

"We love you," Jamison repeated. "We all do."

I scrambled to sit upright so I could see all of their faces. "All of you?"

"All of us," Asher confirmed, his gaze soft and warm.

"And not as friends either," Lewis said. "If that was the next excuse you were going to come up with."

I bit back my words, as that was the exact question that had popped up into my head.

"As lovers, as forever family. We love you." Lewis's eyes were fixed on me. He was serious.

"For how long?" My head spun. They loved me? When had this happened?

Noah shrugged. "For Jamison and Lewis, since high school, probably. For us, since our sophomore year here."

Jamison kneeled before me and put his hand on my knee softly. "Do you remember when I said a few weeks ago that we only wanted a physical relationship with you? I lied. I thought that was the only way we could keep you, if you thought it was just physical. But it was never about the physical side of that. Although that's been adequate." He wiggled his eyebrows at me, and I laughed as I remembered my words I'd described their reputation with that day. "But all we truly want is you. All of you. Every piece you think is broken or bent. Every part of you."

"But, but, but..." I stuttered as my brain tried to process. I had come into this conversation, expecting them to leave once they learned how broken I was, but now they not only wanted to stay, they loved me?

"But what about after graduation?" I stammered, "We're all going different directions?"

"Are we?" Lewis arched an eyebrow at me. "I distinctly remember only you talking about that. The rest of us, we want to go wherever you go."

"But... I don't want to hold you back. You're going to medical school." I turned to Derek, "And you're all getting jobs..."

"I applied to all the medical schools that were at or near schools you applied to," Derek said smugly.

"We'll make it work, Lexi girl," Noah said. "We want to make it work."

"But..." I closed my eyes as my brain spun. It was all just a little too much. The emotional roller coaster that this day had been... It was one for the record books. "You don't even know if you'll like being in a relationship with me," I said weakly.

"And what have we been doing for the last few years?" Asher said. "We've lived together, fought with each other, and supported each other. That sounds like a relationship, no?"

"Hey," Derek said softly, "This is a lot. I know." He squeezed my hand. "How about this? We'll table this discussion for now. Till after the championships, maybe. We know how important that is to you, and we won't get in the way of it."

I squeezed his hand back gratefully. Maybe that made me selfish for not giving them an answer now, but I didn't even know if I could put two thoughts together right now, much less make a decision on a relationship, even if Asher was right. We had kind of been in a relationship for years now.

"But," Derek said. "If you think time will change our minds, it won't. And we aren't going to stop courting you, either."

"Who even says courting anymore?" Jamison screwed up his nose playfully and laughed when Derek shot him a look.

"I agree," Asher said. "You can't change our minds. You're stuck with us now."

"And that's how every true crime podcast starts." Noah glared at his twin. "Way to sound stalkerish."

"It's not stalkerish if I'm saying facts," Asher pointed out.

Noah sighed, and Derek cut him off before he could speak. "So discussion tabled for now, then."

He looked at me expectantly, and I found myself nodding. That worked. If they were crazy enough to want me despite my broken pieces, I might just be crazy enough to let them. And I couldn't deny that knowing they weren't going to leave me after graduation settled a large part inside me that I hadn't realized had been restless.

"Good. It's late. We should all head to bed." Derek looked outside at the darkness that had settled in outside the windows.

One by one, they all stood, pressing a kiss to my forehead or cheek until Derek remained. I stared at him, too tired to process. and he smiled gently at me. "If you want space, I can give you space. But I thought after everything, I might take care of you."

I hesitated, and he continued. "No sex. Just let me take care of you tonight."

I rubbed a hand over my heart. I wanted that. I nodded, and he smiled gently. "Your words."

I gave him a tiny smile. "Yes, please, Derek."

He took my hand and guided me up the stairs and down the hall to my room. It felt like I was in a daze or like I was dreaming. Everything seemed soft around me. They not only believed me, but they weren't running away. *Not yet*, the little voice in me said, but I stuffed it down. That was a worry for tomorrow.

Derek hesitated once we were standing in the middle of the room.

"What is it?" I asked.

He turned to me and ran his hands up and down my arm. "I want to take care of you tonight."

I nodded. "That's what you said downstairs," I said teasingly. He smiled, but his eyes were still worried. "Just spit it out," I said softly.

"I want to help you shower and then maybe give you a massage, but it also occurred to me that you might not want to be touched after all of that."

My heart melted. Even when I reclaimed my sexuality, I'd never had a guy ask if it was okay to touch me. Not until them. I reached up and cupped his cheek, the soft stubble of his chin scratching against my palm. He had forgotten to shave today. I wondered if that was because of me.

"Physically," I started, "I got over what he did when I started reclaiming my body for my own. Mentally, I know I'm not there yet, but that comes from years of avoidance, I think. What you're suggesting sounds wonderful. I know you're not him."

His gray eyes softened, and he turned his head to press a kiss against my palm. A shiver rippled through my body. "You remember your safeword? Cloves?" he asked.

I nodded.

"Even when we aren't having sex, you can still use it."

I nodded again. "Take care of me," I requested softly, tears prickling at the back of my eyes. "I... I don't want to think tonight."

"I've got you," he murmured, drawing me close and wrapping his arms around me. "I've got you."

We swayed in a hug until I felt boneless. I sagged against

him, and he bent slightly, picking me up and carrying me to the bathroom.

I shut my eyes when he flicked the lights on, the bright fluorescent burning. "Keep them shut," he instructed softly.

I kept them shut, wrapping my arms around myself as he left the bathroom, flicking the lights off as he did. He was back just a few moments later. Or maybe it was a few minutes, I didn't know. I still felt like I was in a daze.

A soft click sounded as he got something set up and instead of the bright lights of the bathroom, a soft warm glow lit behind my eyelids. I opened my eyes to see my desk lamp sitting on the bathroom counter.

"Keep those eyes closed," Derek said, catching me peeping.

I smiled and closed my eyes again. I felt his warmth behind me and only jumped a little bit when he put his hands on my shoulders. He paused, and I leaned back into him. He kept one hand on my shoulder as he reached past me to flip my shower on and then came back behind me. Slowly, he undressed me, tracing his fingertips against my skin as he removed each article of clothing until I was standing naked in front of him. His hands left my body, and the soft thud of his own clothes hitting the floor came from behind me.

Hands on my hips, he guided us both into the shower, and I gasped as the warm water hit my body. A soft cloth touched my skin, and the click of my body wash cap echoed against the tile. He ran the cloth up one arm and across my shoulder, slowly washing every inch of me and scrubbing away the events of the day. With each pass of the cloth against my skin, I felt a little more weight fall off my shoulders. He gently maneuvered me around to lather shampoo in my hair. His care and tenderness undid me.

The first tear that trickled down my cheek was hidden by the water. But the second and third didn't go unseen. His lips brushed against my cheek over the tears, and I broke down all over again.

Derek cradled me to his chest while I sobbed into it. All these years of crying alone in the shower, trying to mask my sobs, and this man just held me to his chest and let me cry. He smoothed my hair back so the shampoo wouldn't run into my eyes, and I tried to get myself together.

"It's okay," he whispered. "We've got you now."

Fresh tears flooded my eyes, even as I tried to get myself under control.

The bathroom door creaked open behind me. "Lexi?" I could barely hear Lewis's voice over my tears.

"I've got her," Derek said. "Grab the towel, though? Throw it in the dryer for a few minutes? We'll be right out."

The door shut softly behind me, but I didn't open my eyes. Now that my breakdown was finished, red bloomed on my cheeks as embarrassment threatened to choke me.

"Hey," Derek said. "No guilt, okay? We've got you. All you need to do is keep those eyes closed and let us take care of you."

His words threatened a new wave of tears, but I kept my eyes shut and nodded weakly. I'd spent my entire life taking care of myself. But as foreign as it felt to be taken care of, I didn't want to be anywhere else right now.

Derek carefully rinsed the shampoo from my hair and then worked the conditioner through the long strands, his fingers gently untangling any knots. Once he was done, he guided me out of the shower into Lewis's waiting arms.

Lewis wrapped a towel around me, pressing a soft kiss to my temple. The shower shut off behind me. "Lewis is going to dry you off, okay? All you have to do is stand there. We'll take care of you."

I could feel Lewis and Derek exchanging a look over my head, but I just nodded. Lewis kept me cradled into his chest with one arm as he gently dried me off with the warm towel. I leaned back against him, my wet hair soaking his shirt, but I couldn't find it in me to move. The door opening had me jolting slightly. I had been falling asleep on his chest standing up, it seemed.

"Easy, Pixie," Lewis rumbled. "It's just Derek."

"I brought you some clothes to sleep in." Derek's cinnamon scent filled my nostrils as he stopped in front of me. "I think we'll skip the massage for tonight."

Both of them helped me into a shirt that was way too large to be one of mine and a pair of soft shorts. Lewis passed me into Derek's arms so he could dry my hair, and I leaned my cheek against Derek's chest. A few moments later, he was laying me on my bed. The sheets rustled around me as they got me comfortable.

"Stay," I whispered softly, halfway to dreamland. "Both of you."

"We've got you," Derek said softly as the bed dipped on my other side.

"Sleep, Pixie," Lewis urged, as he gathered me to his chest. "We're here."

I was asleep moments later, feeling the safest I had ever been in a long time.

LEXI

$\mathcal{T}$he next week was what heaven felt like, I was sure.

Well, besides Mac taking a look at Lewis and Jamison our first practice back and barking "That's not what I meant."

I had looked at them, confused, and they had just laughed and told me not to worry about it. It helped that we had been on fire for practice, and Mac was quickly distracted.

But the rest of it was amazing. There was no sex. The guys were serious about 'courting' me, but at least one of them was in my bed every night. I had never slept so well.

When family night rolled around, we invited Inez and Meena over. Inez leaned over at dinner to whisper *I told you so* in my ear, and I had just grinned at her. After dinner, Inez had disappeared with Asher, Noah, and Derek while the rest of us cleaned up.

When they reappeared, I shot Noah a questioning look, but he just grinned and kissed me sweetly. "We're taking care of it," he reminded me, and I leaned in to kiss him again. Inez wolf-whistled at us, and I shot her the middle finger without breaking the kiss. I was trusting them to handle it and trying not to worry about it. Key word there was trying, but hey, it was a work in progress.

We kept the PDA under wraps while we were out around campus, although they often wrapped an arm around my shoulders or let the backs of our hands brush together while we walked.

Every so often, thoughts of *you don't deserve this* or *this is temporary* or *you're too broken to love* would sneak in, but the guys would be right there to distract me. They were doing an excellent job of showing me how this could be, and I was so tempted to say yes to the relationship, but the championships loomed, and I knew they'd made the right call.

Yesterday, we had ridden the bus from Grandview to Maysville, where the championships were being held in the town's professional football stadium. Derek rode the bus with us, and the camaraderie with the team was at an all-time high. We laughed and teased each other and generally got ourselves so riled up that when Mac got on to tell us where to go, he got right back off and sent Lyle in instead.

And now we were in the tunnel of the stadium, waiting for our names to be called to run out onto the field. This was it. This was the culmination of years of dreams. Our senior year and everything I had been driving for. Although, now new dreams were starting to pop up all around me.

The noise in the tunnel was almost deafening as the energy of the team bounced off the stone walls. We had carved out our own little corner by the entrance to the tunnel. Derek stood next to us as Mac and Lyle chatted behind him. Jamison was next to me while Noah, Lewis, and Asher stood in front of us. Jamison fiddled with his arm guards next to me. They were the navy sleeves with little golden rams that Tiffany had brought. I smiled and held my helmet and gloves out to Lewis, who took it without questioning.

"Here," I said, turning to Jamison. "Let me help."

Jamison held his arm out to me gratefully, and I pulled on the fabric until it lay smoothly against his skin. I couldn't help myself, and I let my fingertips trace across the skin on the inside of his arm.

"Lexi," he warned gently, amusement coloring his voice.

"What?" I teased, taking my stuff back from Lewis.

"Behave," Derek warned both of us as the loudspeakers blared through the tunnels, announcing the other team and our rivals from last year, Hastings University. Around us, everyone started pulling their helmets on as we prepared for our run out onto the field.

"I always behave," I sniffed primly, even as I jammed my helmet on my head.

"Don't lie, Lexi girl," Noah teased.

Derek cut off my comeback by grabbing the side of my helmet and fiddling with the straps, making sure it fit snugly on my head. I stuck my tongue out at him, and his eyes darkened dangerously.

"Behave, Alexa," he warned softly.

I looked around to make sure no one was paying attention. "What are you going to do if I don't?"

Mac's gruff bark cut off his reply, but the way his eyes flashed at me had me biting my lip. He shook his head at me, and I just grinned at him. Maybe it was that I had finally taken a breath, but the teasing with the guys over the last week and their no sex rule had me on edge but in a good way.

Around me, the guys were putting their helmets on, and a wave of nostalgia and gratitude hit me. I wanted to say something that would tell them what they meant to me, what this moment meant to me, but the words caught in my throat.

"Thank you."

They seemed to understand what I was trying to say without all the words.

"Always," Lewis said gruffly, and they nodded with him.

Jamison looked like he wanted to lean in and kiss me, regardless of our surroundings, but Noah hauled him back by his jersey.

"Come on," Jamison said, "We've got a game to win."

"And now, let's welcome the Grandview Rams to the field!" The announcer's voice cut through the tunnel. Our cheerleading team lined the entrance of the tunnel, and I heard Inez scream, "Get em, bitch!" as I ran by.

Just like last year, Hastings was a fierce opponent, and we had our work cut out for us from the first snap. Grandview won the coin toss, and we elected to receive. Although we battled down the field, we couldn't seem to get the ball in the end zone, but we forced them to take it from our twenty-yard line. Noah and Asher took the field with the rest of our defense and forced a turnover. Back and forth and back and forth we went, but as hard as we fought, the first quarter went without any points on the board.

The atmosphere on the sidelines was tense as we started into the second quarter, and Hastings had the ball. Even though there were no points on the board yet, I was proud of the team. Our teamwork today was unmatched. Every play ran like clockwork. Even Crawford finally seemed to get his shit together for the game. The problem was that Hastings was equally good.

The team groaned collectively when Hastings drove down the field to score a touchdown. I pulled my helmet on and gathered with the rest of the offense around Mac.

"Get out there and drive hard. Harder than you've ever driven all season," Mac barked. "They're good, but we're better. Let's go!"

Several of the guys whooped as we ran out onto the field. I shook out my hands as I called the first play.

"Go Rams!" we all shouted as we broke from our huddle.

Springer snapped the ball back to me, and we were off. I threw a short five-yard pass to Johnson, who made it just a few yards before he was tackled. The next play, I handed the ball off to Crawford, who made it through a hole in the defense to score our first down.

Even though we crawled down the field, the team was on fire. The problem was that Hastings was just as evenly matched as us and met us play for play. We were about thirty yards from the end zone and on third down when the ref blew the whistle, calling for a timeout.

I looked over to see Mac waving us in. I jogged over. "I'm putting McKenzie in," he said, referencing our kicker. "We need points on the board, and we're still eight yards from a down."

I bit my lip. I wanted to protest, but I knew any points on the board, especially in a game like this, mattered. "Okay."

The field goal team went in, and I watched with Lewis and Jamison on the sidelines as McKenzie kicked a clean shot straight through the goalposts.

Our defense took the field as Derek came up next to me, offering me a water bottle. "How are you doing?"

I shrugged. "I mean, I could be better if we had more points on the board, but it's early yet." I looked up at the scoreboard. Hastings's 7 to Grandview's 3 was in bright red.

"It is early yet," Derek agreed with me. "But the team looks amazing."

I nodded. "We've been on it for sure. Problem is Hastings is as well."

He bumped my shoulder with his. "You know it doesn't matter to us if we win or lose, right? Like the win would be great, don't get me wrong—"

"I know." I gave him a small smile. "I know. I just…"

"I get it," Derek said. And I knew he did.

But I still wanted to win. Despite everything else, I still wanted to win.

He bumped my shoulder as we turned our attention back to the field. Hastings was pushing down the field, but Noah and

Asher and the rest of the defense team weren't letting them move far.

I watched as our defense forced Hastings to attempt a field goal, which they completed, making the score 10 to 3.

"All right, let's get some points on the board!" Mac barked at us as we huddled around him briefly. "We've got three minutes left in this quarter. Let's make them count!"

"Yes, Mac!" we all shouted.

I was buzzing with adrenaline when we began our drive down the field as the clock ran out on the first half. Like before, we crawled down the field, but our pace was consistent. Five yards here, three yards there. We were second down and seven yards to go at the forty-yard line when I called the next passing play. Except when Springer snapped the ball to me, Crawford wasn't where he was supposed to be. I pivoted on my feet, looking for Jamison, but he was covered by two Hastings players. Johnson was also not free. My pocket was rapidly closing in on me. I looked for an opening to see if I could make it a few yards.

A Hastings player slipped around Lewis though and launched towards me. I twisted to keep the ball in my arms and let my non-throwing shoulder take the brunt of the tackle. I still landed on the ground with a grunt as the wind was knocked out of me.

The whistle blew, then someone yanked the player off of me.

"I'm fine," I said, cutting off Lewis's worried look. I got to my feet and tossed the ball to the ref.

"You okay?" Jamison said, jogging over with Johnson.

"I'm good. I'm fine. I saw it coming," I said, shaking out my arms and legs. "See, nothing hurts."

Jamison looked skeptical, but Johnson nodded. I threw a thumbs up at Mac to signal I was okay and got ready to make another play. The clock was running out.

We made it just seven more yards before the refs blew the

whistle, indicating half time. Hastings still held the lead but by only four points. It was still anyone's game.

Inez and Meena waved to me from the sidelines as we jogged into the locker room. I broke off from the rest of the team to head to my area, but a set of footsteps echoed behind me. I turned around to see Noah had fallen into step with me. I narrowed my eyes at him, and he held up his hands.

"Everyone agreed you weren't to be left alone until we get this guy."

"You really think he followed us out to Maysville?" I asked him but didn't put up much of an argument as I kept walking towards the locker room.

"I don't think anyone is willing to take any chances."

I shrugged but accepted his answer. Truthfully, I felt better having one of them nearby.

"How are you feeling?" he asked.

"Fine. Seriously, fine. It was just a regular sack."

"Still not ever going to get used to watching you go down, though," he said.

"I feel the same about all of you," I shot back at him.

I pushed the door open to the locker room they set aside for me and set my helmet down on the bench. Strands of my hair had escaped the tight braid, so I yanked out the hair band and started the process of re-braiding it as Noah moved past me to probably use the bathrooms at the back of the locker room.

I had just finished wrapping the hair band back around the tip of the braid when the door opened behind me.

"How's my special star?"

LEXI

I froze. Familiar old terror flooded my veins and dropped lead weights on my feet. How did he get in here? Why was he here? Did he really follow us to the championships?

He chuckled at the look on my face. "Surprised to see me? Your star running back invited me."

Crawford had invited him? What the fuck? He had seen how uncomfortable I had been the other week and he'd invited him, anyway?

I forced myself to take a deep breath and relax my muscles. Even though it had only been a week since I had last seen him, and I had told the guys what he had done, somehow, in the harsh fluorescent lights of the locker room, he didn't quite look like the monster I had created him in my head to be.

Caleb Bradford stood before me in khaki pants and a red polo shirt. His hair was combed back from his face, and it was thinner than it used to be. Don't get me wrong, he still starred in my worst nightmares, but the fear that had originally frozen me in place was starting to thaw. Maybe it was knowing that Noah was somewhere in the room with me, maybe it was knowing that I didn't carry this terrible secret alone. I didn't know. But my shoulders relaxed all the same. All this time, I thought it was my fault, that I had done something, that I had enticed him, that the weight of this secret was carried on my shoulders and mine alone. But now? Now I knew differently.

"What do you want?" I was proud when my voice didn't shake.

"I just came to watch my special star play." His voice was oily, and I struggled not to shudder as it slipped over me.

He approached me slowly, and I held my ground. I wouldn't cower from him. Never again.

"I've made a lot of special stars like you," he started, lecturing me like he was the only one responsible for my success. Was he a driver? Yes. But I was the one who'd put the hours in on the field. Not him. "Carefully cultivating them into star athletes." He was still talking, but I was only half listening. "And now it's time you do something for me."

I lifted my chin at him defiantly, and he smirked. "You see, I have a lot of money riding on this game. But unfortunately, not on Grandview to win. I need you to throw the game, so I don't lose. Well..." He looked me up and down, and bile rose in my throat. "Well, that and so our little secret doesn't come out."

"No." The word tore out of my throat like a feral dog just released to chase its prey. I didn't even have to think about it. I was never doing anything for him. Ever.

"Ah, ah, ah." He wagged a finger at me. "You might want to think about that answer. I could even give you part of the winnings, maybe. But either way, you will help me out here or the whole world will know your little secret."

"You mean your little secret," I spat at him. "How you... how you raped me," I choked out the words, and he laughed. Noah had to be hearing all of this, right? He wouldn't abandon me.

"That's a big word," he said mockingly, like I was a little girl. "I made you. Gave you a chance to be the first female quarterback in Blue River High School's history and now in Grandview's. I just needed something in return."

"That's coercion and rape," I spat at him again. "You took advantage of me like you did to the others."

His laugh was chilling that time. "I see someone's been using the computer. But there was never any proof."

"Because you threatened them like you did me."

"Threaten is such a strong word. You could have come forward at any time. But it would have meant you lost everything."

"That's exactly what a threat is, asshole!" Even though panic was still coursing through my veins, something stronger had been added to it. Anger.

"My, my, someone's grown a backbone since I last saw her. Could it be because of those boys you liked to hang around? Your running back told me how you picked up more of them, it seems."

"You leave them alone!"

"Why? You don't want them to hear how you screamed for me?" he said, leaning towards me with a leer on his face. "How you begged me to stop, but you were never strong enough. You're broken. No one would ever want you. No one except me."

"You're wrong." Noah's steely voice was firm, and my knees almost buckled in relief.

He stepped up behind me, silently offering me support, and I took a shaky breath as I saw his phone in his hand. Had he recorded the whole thing?

From Caleb Bradford's pale face, I was guessing he had, but this monster wasn't dead yet. He straightened. "So you are fucking him. What would the university think?"

Noah chuckled, the sound dark and menacing and so unlike him that I looked behind me to make sure it actually was him. "I think they're about to become a lot more concerned with you. Come in!" he called out loudly, and the door opened.

Two police officers streamed into the room, along with the rest of my guys, and I sagged backwards into Noah, who caught me.

Lewis strode right towards me and cupped my face. "We've got you, Pixie. It's over now."

"Caleb Bradford, you are under arrest for embezzling funds from Lansing High School, illegal gambling, failure to appear in court, and three counts of suspected sexual assault," one of the police officers said while cuffing him.

Mac stepped into the room as the officer finished listing the charges, and my heart jumped into my throat. Fuck. He knew.

Mac's face was impossible to read as he skirted around the officers, giving one of them a nod and walking towards our group. Lewis stiffened in front of me, but I laid a hand on his back, and he reluctantly moved to the side. Whatever Mac had to say, if he was about to bench me or try to get me kicked out of school, I would face it. It was worth it to watch the monster who had haunted me for years be dragged out of the room yelling and struggling in his handcuffs.

Mac studied me for a few moments, and I held my breath. "Are you okay?"

That was the last thing I expected him to ask, and I blinked at him as my brain processed his question. I nodded slowly.

"Are you sure?" Mac asked again, his gruff voice uncharacteristically soft. "The guys filled me in on the basics."

I looked at Derek, who nodded grimly. "When Noah texted us from the bathroom that he was here, we had to tell him. No details. Just what we found out."

"What did you find out?" I remembered the police officer saying something about embezzling funds, but it all seemed like it was in a blur.

"We did a little investigating and discovered that he was

neck-deep in illegal gambling debt and was embezzling from Lansing to help cover his debts," Noah explained, rubbing his hands up and down my arms as I stood frozen in front of him.

I blinked at him, and he chuckled at my stunned expression. "It's over, Lexi girl," he said softly. "He's never going to hurt anyone again."

Mac nodded. "I'm going to make sure of it."

"But the assistant coach position..."

Mac waved his hand. "He was never seriously in the running. The dean of Knighton asked me as a favor, but now I'm going to call him and give him a piece of my mind. Between the two of us, we'll throw enough weight around that he'll never work again."

"But none of that matters right now." Mac paused. "Are you good to play the rest of the game? No one would fault you if you weren't."

I looked around at my guys, slowly taking in that it was really over. Elation filled me. It was finally over. It felt like I had become a hundred pounds lighter in just a few moments. I felt like I could conquer the world or win a championship game.

"I'm good, Mac."

"Are you sure?"

"I'm sure. Let's go win ourselves a championship." I grinned at him.

Noah squeezed my shoulders as Jamison returned my grin. All my guys were smiling, and I was sure I looked deranged, my grin was so wide. I was loved and supported, and the worst chapter of my life had just been brought to a close. Maybe I would still have to testify, but none of that mattered today. Today, I got to live a dream without the cloud of my past hanging over me.

"Get your asses out on the field, then," Mac barked, but he had a soft look in his eye.

Asher handed me my helmet, and Derek held the door for us

as we poured out into the hallway. My guys surrounded me on all sides, and I couldn't be happier.

We all filed back into the locker room, and even though we got some curious looks, no one said anything.

"All right, listen up!" Mac said. "We fought hard in the first half. This second half, though, we've got to fight harder. Be tighter on your plays, be more efficient in your footwork. Take everything we've worked on all year, and let's get out there and win us a championship! We're not giving Hastings the satisfaction of beating us twice!"

The team whooped and hollered and stomped their feet. I grinned and hollered along with them.

Mac whistled and cut through the noise. "Captain." He gestured with his clipboard at me. "Any words?"

The guys all looked at me expectantly, and I pushed off from the lockers I was leaning on. I walked to the center of the room and looked around.

"Like Mac said, we've worked hard all year. We're a great team, and I just want to remind us all of one thing." I took a deep breath.

"This is it. This is our shot. This is the moment we have worked all year to get to. Seniors—" I looked around the room at the third of the guys who would be graduating with us this year. "Seniors, this is the last time we will wear these jerseys. The last time we'll walk out of that tunnel out onto the field. The last time we'll play with this team is right here in this moment." I punctuated my words by pointing my finger at the floor. "Right here, right now. Win or lose, the only thing we can control is whether we walk off this field tonight knowing we left everything on the field."

This would be the first time in years I got to play the game I loved without the cloud of Bradford hanging over me. I would also be able to leave every piece of me on the field tonight.

The team was smiling and nodding along with my words. I

grinned. "What do you say? Let's we go out and win ourselves a championship game?"

"Let's go!" Jamison yelled.

Finn started whooping along with him, and the noise in the locker room reached deafening levels. I caught Mac's approving nod as we pushed out the doors to the tunnel and ran back onto the field.

LEXI

*C*heers erupted as we took the field, and I waved at Inez as the cheer team launched into one of their routines.

I jogged alongside with Jamison, Lewis, and the rest of the offense. Adrenaline was coursing through me, but I funneled it into focus versus distraction. We had to be on our game here. I called the play, and Springer snapped the ball back to me. I held it to my chest as I pivoted on my heel, pretending to throw it to Crawford before swinging around and whipping it into Jamison's arms. He took off down the field, dodging Hastings' players as he raced towards the end zone.

The Hastings safety knocked him down thirty yards from the end zone, but we had gained close to thirty yards on the play. The guys were practically vibrating with excitement.

"Alright, nice job, Towers, but let's focus now. It's not over yet."

I called a rushing play, and this time Johnson slipped through the defense line, ball clutched to his chest with one arm as he ran like the hounds of hell were chasing him. He eked out just over ten yards. It wasn't much, but it didn't matter. Our momentum was building. Crawford gained us another five on the next play. He popped up after being tackled, looking pissed, but didn't say anything in the huddle.

The next play was supposed to go to Crawford again, but Hastings' defense was all over him, and I had to pivot and throw to Johnson. The sophomore was wide open, and Springer, Lewis, and I yelled encouragements until my voice felt raw as he sprinted towards the end zone. Five yards, three yards, one yard, TOUCHDOWN!

Lewis wrapped me in a fierce bear hug as Springer smacked the back of my helmet. Jamison and Jennings were celebrating with Johnson down in the end zone as we all jogged towards the sidelines. I bit my lip as I looked up at the board. The score was 9-10 Grandview to Hastings. In a game like this, every point mattered. Would a two-point conversion be worth it?

I switched directions and jogged over to Mac. "What is it, Simmons?" he asked.

"I think you should send me onto the field like we're going for the two-point conversion," I said quickly. "But we shouldn't go for it now. Maybe next time. But we might need it later, and I want to keep Hastings guessing."

He looked thoughtful but nodded. "Baker, Towers, Collins, Springer," he barked. "Back out on the field with Simmons!"

Lewis and Jamison looked surprised, but they joined me back on the field as Mac switched out some people from our kicking team.

"What's happening? Are we going for the two points?" McKenzie asked as we jogged up to the huddle.

"Not this time, although we're going to look like we are," I said, checking the play card strapped to my arm. "Let's do play 15 and fake them out. McKenzie, your job is still to make that extra point."

"Got it, Cap!"

We broke up, and I called out the play. Hastings struggled to focus on both me and McKenzie at the same time, and the play went off smoothly as the ball sailed through the goalposts.

I passed Noah and Asher on their way out to the field, and Noah swung me around. "Great job, Lexi-girl!" he yelled in my ear.

I tossed my head back and laughed.

"Put me down and go do your job!" I playfully shoved him away.

He gave me a cheeky salute as Asher smacked the back of his helmet, shoving him towards the field.

"Nice job, Lexi," Derek greeted me as I grabbed my bottle of water.

"Team effort," I reminded him as Johnson jogged up. "Nice work, Johnson!" I congratulated him on his touchdown. It was going to be a career highlight for the sophomore for sure.

"All I had to do was run." Johnson grinned at me as he grabbed his own water. "You set up the pass."

"Team effort," I reminded him, and he laughed.

He tipped his water bottle towards me, and we clinked them like we were tapping glasses of beer together.

"Team effort," he agreed.

Despite the defense's best efforts, Hastings drove the ball down the field for another touchdown. I downed some more of my water before tossing the bottle on the bench. My muscles were starting to ache, and I knew the others were feeling it as well. This game was one of the most intense ones we had played in a long time. I knew we were all feeling it.

"All right, let's do this," I said in the huddle. "I know we're getting tired, but remember, leave everything on the field!"

"Yes, Cap!"

I called out our first play, and we were off. The clock was ticking down as Springer snapped the ball into my hands. I threw a short pass to Johnson, who only made it a few yards before a Hastings player tackled him. He popped back up as I called another play. This time, Jamison was going to cut behind me like I was handing off the ball to him, but really, I was going to spin and send it to Crawford.

Except when I went to spin, Crawford wasn't where he was supposed to be. Instead of being three yards away, he was fifteen yards away. I pulled the ball back and threw it in a tight spiral towards him. As he leapt to grab it, a Hastings player leapt at him, and he went down hard. When he didn't immediately leap up, I cursed and ran towards him.

Lyle was already jogging onto the field with Derek, and I barked at the guys to clear a hole for them. Crawford struggled to a sitting position, clutching at his knee, and I winced. Knee injuries were the worst. Lyle assessed him quickly for a concussion and then Springer and Lewis helped him to his feet. The crowd in the stadium cheered as he limped off the field, and I caught Jamison rolling his eyes. I elbowed him discreetly in the side.

"What?" Jamison protested softly so the others couldn't hear us. "He brought this on himself by deviating from the play."

"We don't know that. It could have happened anyway," I said.

Maybe it made me a bad person, but I wasn't feeling all too bad that Crawford was out of the game. Especially after he had invited Bradford here.

"All right, let's huddle up!" I gathered the remaining players around me as Jennings jogged onto the field to replace Crawford. "We've got forty yards to go, and four minutes left on the clock. Let's make it happen! Jennings, it's coming to you first. They won't be expecting that."

The guys nodded grimly. The pressure was getting to all of us, but I just hoped we could hold it together to get this done. "We've got this. This is what we've been training for!" I gave some last parting words as we broke the huddle and got into position.

Springer snapped the ball to me, and I sent it straight to

Jennings, who managed to take it ten yards down the field before being forced off onto the sidelines. The success of that play seemed to breathe new life into the team, and our next three plays were textbook executions that earned us another twenty yards to make it first and goal. There was a minute left on the clock. If we scored a touchdown, that would bring us to a tie with Hastings and send us into overtime. While that wasn't the worst option, the team was also getting tired, and I didn't know if we were going to be at our best. The best option was looking like a touchdown followed by a two-point conversion.

In a two-point conversion, the ball was placed on the three-yard line and we had just one attempt to get it into the end zone. It was a risky play, because if we didn't make it, Hastings would win by one point. But if we did make it, we would win by one point. I looked over at the sidelines and made our signal for a timeout. The ref blew the whistle as Mac called a timeout. I motioned for the guys to stay there as I jogged over to Mac. Reeder, our assistant coach, stood next to him.

"What do you think, Simmons? Should we go for the two?" Mac asked me when I reached him.

I bit my lip as I nodded. "I know it's risky, but I don't know how fresh the guys will be if we go into overtime."

Reeder frowned. "We'll only have one shot at this."

"Do you think you can make it count?" Mac asked me.

The weight of the decision pressed heavily on my shoulders. Should we go for it? What if we didn't make it? I glanced over at the sidelines. Noah, Asher, and Derek were standing together, watching us. Noah grinned at me, and Asher gave me a thumbs up while Derek just smiled and nodded. Without consulting Lewis or Jamison, I knew whatever I decided, whether we won or lost, my guys would have my back.

"Let's put McKenzie on the field when we go for it. If it all goes for shit, I'll hand it off to him to make the kick."

I chose the safest option, and Mac nodded. "McKenzie, be ready to go in."

The ref called out a warning, and I jogged back onto the field. "Let's get this ball in the end zone, boys!" I called out. "Play 17!"

When I called the play, Jamison ran out in front of me while Johnson and Jennings crisscrossed behind me. I faked a handoff to Jennings and then handed it off to Johnson. He ran around the defensive line while Collins cleared a path for him straight into the end zone. TOUCHDOWN!

While the guys celebrated, I waved McKenzie onto the field. "Are we going for the two points?" Johnson asked in the huddle.

I nodded. "Yes. We get one shot at this, so make it count!"

"Go Rams!" Lewis shouted.

"Go Rams!" we echoed.

The atmosphere in the stadium was electric. The fans for both teams were on their feet. I could hear the echo of the announcer's voice over the speakers, but I drowned it out. A calm settled over me as my entire world narrowed down to this moment.

"Ready! Go!"

I could hear my voice calling out the start of the play, but it was like I was hearing it from outside my body. Johnson and Jamison immediately ran into the end zone, running in a zigzag, trying to get free of the Hastings defense. Jennings was covered by another two players. Hastings was taking no chances. The ball clasped firmly in my arms, I assessed my options. It felt like the world moved in slow motion around me.

I could try to pass to Jamison and Johnson, but we only had one shot at this. I could spin and hand it to McKenzie for the extra point, but there was no guarantee we would win in overtime. I danced back and forth behind the offense line. My eyes connected with Jamison's, and like we had so many times before, I tilted my head left as I spun to the right to throw it to Johnson as Jamison dodged left.

In a movement that had become second nature to me, I kept hold of the ball and brought my arm in a full circle to throw a tight spiral straight into Jamison's arms. As the ball landed in his hands, the world went back into focus as a deafening cheer rose from the crowd. We had done it! We secured the two-point conversion! Lewis picked me up and swung me around as the guys jumped around and pounded each other on the back.

"Let me down!" I laughed at Lewis even though I was screaming internally on the inside. We had done it! I mean, there was a chance Hastings could come back, but we had done it!

"It's not over yet. Come on! Let's let the defense finish it out!" I hustled the offense off the field as the defense ran past us. With twenty seconds left on the clock, Hastings would be hard pressed to score any more points, but it wasn't over yet.

Mac patted me on the back as I passed him. "Nice call, Simmons! Towers, good catch!"

"All Simmons, Mac, all Simmons!" Jamison grinned as I rolled my eyes and smacked him on the arm.

"Great job, Lexi." Derek passed out water to Lewis, Jamison, and me as we watched our defense wind down the clock. I took a quick drink, knowing that the stadium was about to erupt. I watched the clock count down on the official play as Hastings valiantly tried to make a comeback.

Five, four, three, two, one.

Lewis picked me up and swung me around when the whistle sounded. That fuzzy, out-of-body feeling was back. We had just won the championship!!! After fighting for it for so long, I was having a hard time grounding myself in what had just happened.

"Did we just win?" I asked Derek breathlessly once Lewis had put me down.

"We did. You did it!" He squeezed my hand before giving me a gentle shove towards the field where the team was celebrating.

A grin spread out over my face as I joined the team in jumping up and down and yelling until our voices were hoarse. And when Asher and Noah hoisted me up on their shoulders, the championship trophy in my hands, I lifted it over my head. It felt like a dream. It was a dream. The realization of a dream, actually. I looked down at all the grinning faces but specifically the faces of my guys. Lewis, Jamison, Asher, Noah, and Derek. Winning this championship had been my dream for so long, but a new dream was unfurling in front of me. One with all of them in it.

LEXI

few months later: Graduation Day.

"Congratulations, Grandview University Class of 2024! It is now time to move your tassels from the right side to the left side to signify your graduation. Parents, friends, and family members, please give a warm round of applause for your graduates!"

President Daniels finished his speech to a thunderous round of applause as I reached up to move my tassel from the right side of my cap to the left. On one side, Noah and Asher copied my movements, with Jamison and Lewis standing on my other side. Derek was up front as he had graduated with distinguished honors and, thus, had to sit separately from the rest of us, but we had made it!

After the championship game, we'd had a long conversation about our relationship and the future. The guys were still all in, and to no one's surprise, I was still cautious about it all. But I had been willing to give it a try, and the guys had been more than willing to prove to me it was worth it, so we had come up with some new rules.

The first was improving our communication. On family

nights now, we didn't just eat together, we also set aside specific times to talk about different things that had happened during the week. That had been Derek's idea, but Asher had also pushed hard for it. If we didn't have something specific to talk about, we used a book of relationship questions as prompts. I was still gun-shy about a future together—I still thought the guys deserved better than me—but at Derek's urging, I had begun seeing a therapist, and I was slowly working through some things. I promised them that after graduation, I would give them a definitive answer.

We did take our relationship public a few weeks after the championship game, though. And told our families about it. I wasn't sure which one was more nerve-wracking. I worried that the school was going to do something at first, but Lewis pointed out that we had just won the championship, and our time was our own now. We had gotten some shit about it, and the guys had come home with bruised knuckles a time or two, but the fiercest defenders of our relationship to the rest of campus were the guys on the football team.

Okay, not all of them. Crawford was never going to change his mind. But Finn, Johnson, Springer, and Jennings had been loud voices of support, in addition to Inez and Meena. The dance and cheer team were disappointed that the guys were off the market but most respected our relationship. A few still tried their luck, but the guys turned them all down and after a few brutal workouts designed by Inez, they got the picture.

But still, the football team's support had surprised me. Apparently, I was the only one who hadn't seen the affection the guys had for me as anything more than friendship for years. There had been a lot of ribbing when we'd first gone public, but it was all in good fun and never anything disrespectful.

"You deserve to be happy," Finn had repeated his words from the cafeteria a few weeks ago.

I had punched him in the shoulder as my face flamed red

before giving him a hug. It was my turn to make him squirm when I informed him that I had nominated him for team captain and it had been a unanimous vote of approval. The team was in good hands with Finn.

Our families had taken it well, or as well as we expected. Obviously, Derek's family had been definitely on board and had spent a long afternoon with us going into embarrassing detail all the ways to make polyamory work. I didn't think I'd ever seen Derek that red before, but it was hysterical to watch his parents practically give us a presentation on how to make it work. I was pretty sure one of his dads had even prepared slides.

Jamison's moms also took the news well. Lewis's parents wanted to be supportive but weren't quite sure how. Asher and Noah's parents were about the same. My family had been the biggest holdup, but I think any parent would be surprised to learn their daughter was dating five men. With the guys' and therapist's support, I also told my parents about my sexual assault. There were a lot of tears that day and a good bit of guilt as well. I gave the guys permission to tell their families as well but asked that I not be there when they did. I was still feeling raw over it all, even if Bradford was in jail pending a trial.

But my guys were there to provide distractions when I needed them. In a way, it was like nothing had changed. Noah and I still listened to true crime podcasts together. Asher and I debated topics over our over-the-top chocolate drinks. Lewis was still my rock when I needed to sound something out. Jamison still challenged me, and Derek was our steady anchor through it all. When I would wake up with nightmares, one of them was there to hold me, and when I went through a particularly vulnerable therapy session, they would pick me up chocolate chip pancakes from Jimbo's and watch movies with me. They said I wasn't broken, and under their loving attention, I felt like I was being put back together again.

Derek and I had received acceptances from our respective graduate schools and decided on the University of Kingston. He would be studying medicine, and I had decided to pursue my master's in sports psychology with the option to pursue a doctoral track upon graduation. The guys had already found us a house with a short commute to both campus and their new offices. It was all falling together.

After what felt like a thousand pictures later, the moms were finally satisfied with their photos and were discussing our restaurant reservations when Jamison pulled us into a circle. Finn had walked by a few moments ago with an invitation to a party later this evening, and I thought we were going to discuss if we were going or not. Instead, I froze as Jamison pulled out a square jewelry box.

They laughed at my face, and Lewis wrapped an arm around my shoulders, pressing a kiss to my hair. "Relax there, Pixie, you're not getting proposed to right now."

"It's a fucking square jewelry box," I hissed at him, eyes wide. "It's not that far of a leap."

"We're not doing the cliche proposal on graduation day." Asher rolled his eyes, gesturing to around to at least three couples that had happened to today. "When we propose to you, it will be more special than this."

He said *when* and not *if* with so much certainty that I swallowed hard.

"You're going to make her run away." Noah shoved his twin playfully. "And then we'll have to run after her like creepy stalkers."

"You are a creepy stalker," I teased him. "All those true crime podcasts are changing you."

Noah sniffed. "I resent the word *creepy*."

"All right, children," Derek chided. "We're getting off track. Focus."

"Yes, Dad." I smirked at Derek.

His eyes flashed dangerously like molten steel, and he leaned down to whisper in my ear a different name he would like to be called. I flushed bright red, and Jamison and Noah howled with laughter.

"All right, come on now," Asher complained good-naturedly. "The 'rents are getting restless. We do not need the moms thinking we are actually proposing right now. We'll never be done with pictures then."

We closed the circle, so our shoulders were all touching as Jamison flipped open the box. A plain platinum band was nestled inside with vines etched into it. I narrowed my eyes at Jamison.

"It's a ring," I pointed out.

He rolled his eyes. "Still not an engagement ring. We'll do better for that one. No, this ring is a promise ring. Here, try it on."

Lewis plucked it out of the box and took my hand, sliding it on my finger. It fit perfectly, and I shook my head at how smug they looked about that. I slid it off, studying the ring. The vines weaved together until you couldn't tell where one started and one began. On the inside was etched:

Always yours, L J N A D

"So what'll it be?" Jamison asked. I lifted my eyes to him. He had a nervous grin on his face. "Willing to be on our team for the rest of our lives?"

The guys groaned at the pun, but I couldn't help the wide grin that spread across my face. I looked around at all their faces, small but nervous smiles on their lips.

"Yes. Absolutely yes."

AUTHOR NOTE

And that's a wrap on Lexi's story! This was such an important book to me as I was also a young athlete under a tremendous amount of pressure that I definitely carried with me for too long. But like Lexi, I get to put it down now. If you want more of Lexi and her guys, check out this sweet bonus scene about life happily ever after: https://BookHip.com/THQGXNS

If you loved this book, please consider leaving a review. They are so important to us indie authors. Word of mouth is also another way to help an author out. Telling all your friends, whether they are book friends or not, is a great way to help out authors. If you love my books, recommend them to friends so they can enjoy the worlds I create as well.

To stay up to date on updates and follow more of my work, visit my website at www.authorsunnyhart.com or join my reader's group Hart Book's Rays of Sunshine, https://www.face book.com/groups/2871054323110368 and let's talk about it. (though please try not to spoil anything for other readers)

Final note: The first time the abuser's name is spoken aloud in the book is by Lexi when she first tells the guys. To all of us who are too afraid to say their names outloud, I see you. And you're stronger than you could ever imagine.

ACKNOWLEDGMENTS

I feel like with every book I finish, the list of acknowledgements gets longer and longer. But first, starting with you, my darling readers! Thank you soooo much for reading Lexi's story! As always, thanks to my amazing friends and family! Without your continued support I would definitely not be able to stay grounded and on track. Huge thanks to my PA, Jennifer Webb, who is an iconic human being and without whom, none of this would have happened.

Big thanks to my editor, Kaye Kemp Book Polishing, and my cover designer Inessa at Cauldron Press Book Designs. Please consider using them for your next project.

And finally, in memory of Beverly and Cice. Two incredibly strong women who passed too early during the writing of this book. Your strength and courage will inspire me forever. Rest easy, dear friends.

OTHER BOOKS BY THE AUTHOR

Contemporary Standalone

Avoiding the Sack

Paranormal Fantasy

Unitam Realm Series

By Her Sight

With Her Sight

Beyond Her Sight

All Her Feelings

Make Me

ABOUT THE AUTHOR

Sunny Hart lives in the rolling hills of the Kentucky Bluegrass. She has spent her entire life expressing herself through writing and short stories until one NaNoWriMo, she challenged herself to write a book to share with the world. By Her Sight is the first book she has published but is one of many floating around in her head. When not writing, Sunny is spending time with her dogs and horse and working her 'day job' as a business strategy consultant.

For the latest news, updates, and giveaways, check out Sunny Facebook group, Sunny's Rays of Sunshine. (https://www.face book.com/groups/2871054323110368)

To be notified of new releases, follow Sunny on Amazon: https://amazon.com/author/sunnyhart

To sign up for her newsletter and more, check out her website at authorsunnyhart.com

Made in the USA
Columbia, SC
11 August 2024

39813044R00159